CAR
WASH

100 Lightnings

EDITED BY
STEPHEN STUDACH

And he said unto them,

" I beheld Satan as lightning fall from Heaven. "

Luke 10:18.

To Ray Bradbury.
For the thunder, the lightning, and the illuminated dark.

Paroxysm Press
PO Box 3107
Rundle Mall
Adelaide
5000
[Australia]

www.paroxysmpress.com

100 Lightnings
ISBN 978-1-876502-18-8

Cover art: Sean King.
Interior art: Greg Rich.
'100 Lightnings' concept © Stephen Studach 1999.
'Storm Warning' and 'Afterflash' © Stephen Studach.

CONTENTS

STORM WARNING

You saw the antique, canvas-covered horse-drawn wagon creak slowly into town late this night.

Almost the only thing moving in this world, your provincial little world.

The oddity of the mobile relic, the old grey wood of the square-backed carriage, the anonymous seasoned brown canvas; its leathery tautness resembling the piebald flanks of the two, past-their-prime horses in the traces, the ill-defined, tall hatted, upright driver... drew you after it.

Could such a throwback be the outrider for some time-lost caravan? Could it signal the approach of a carnival or circus?

Through the outer edges of the town you followed it on foot.

In time, to your surprise, it slowed then bumped and clatter-rocked over the kerb into a weed and masonry littered vacant piece of ground between two faded brown and grey, tall buildings, empty and condemned to some future execution.

Now, only those eyes on high, shattered and empty with neglect, and your own, see, by moon and sparse street lighting, the wagon come to a stop in that bare allotment between the grimy walls of the two long empty buildings. A space occupied only by ill and overgrown grass, dirt, weeds and scattered old bricks.

Only those eyes see an oddly garbed man, the driver, leap down to the ground and quickly move to the wagon's rear. There he unhooks and lowers the tailgate then agilely jumps up and enters the wagon proper. Moments later he emerges, drags out a long black bundle from the interior, drops it upon the ground.

The shadowy stranger then slowly walks about the abandoned allotment. Gaze roving, as if searching. . . He strides one particular spot, a flat, clear area, lightly grassed. Nods his head and returns to the bundle, drags it to his chosen area.

Still at a distance you see the man appear to unfold shadows. He goes to the wagon again, returns with a long handled mallet of some sort and a hessian wrapped bundle that comments in a clanking voice when he sets it down.

With brisk efficiency the man-figure sets up a black tent. He screws together lengths of tubular steel, with the sledgehammer he pounds stakes into the ground, he hauls on ropes and ties them off and slowly the old fashioned sideshow tent is raised. Not a large tent by circus standards. Black with branching, phosphorescent white lightning markings spidering here and there upon its surface.

Like some spectral, landlocked ship's sail the tent inflates and rises.

Finally, the man, who seemed in his practiced movements to have done all this many, many times before, lights a fuel lantern and hangs it on a hook above the tent's entrance. He then disappears inside.

Away in the distance you hear a subtle grumble of thunder.

You look around; the town itself is dead quiet.

You walk into the allotment, towards the tent.

The horses calmly regard you. An eerie silence seems to have been dropped upon the area. Your feet crunching upon the ground seem excessively loud.

You pause. Examining the small, sable structure in the lamplight. Its sides breathing in – out – as it squats there, like some tethered night creature, waiting. . .

Its iron stakes look scorched. And is that sharpened, central javelin emerging from the tent's peak not . . . a lightning rod?

Despite your concerns about safety you move closer to this ozone smelling structure, the walls of which are now a veritable lantern show of flickering shapes and images where once, from a distance, you saw but painted lightnings. Did you glimpse a kangaroo shape composed entirely of flaring white? A glowing phosphorous disc that could have been a flying saucer? A flashing feather or is it an eye? A fish? A foetus? A sea horse, seeming to rock in its inherent glare upon canvas? A floating brain – that was also a sea dragon or a tree composed from plasmatic burst?

Your eyes are fixed, roving over the lightning-prints.

The tent walls seem all white and gauze thin for a time and shadows from within flicker and play across the surface, a host of tantalising, fearsome, enigmatic shapes and sounds. Thunderings, squeals and squeakings, the sea, human voices, the laughter of children, the cawing of a bird, howling, screaming, the pulsing of great engines, the sawing and chopping of wood, rumblings, roarings, whisperings . . .

Then, the canvas, as it were, is painted mostly black once more. The tent no longer aquiver with sounds as if woven of echoes and thunder.

A not unpleasant radiance emerges from underneath the tent, soft, clean and white, sifts through patches in its well used hide that camouflages stains and scorchings, and peeks from a slight gap in the breeze caressed entrance flap.

You move to the entrance.

You pause, you call an unanswered enquiry.

You make a decision.

Upon entering you note that the tent interior is softly lit by a light blue and white, shifting illumination.

It is emanating from dozens, perhaps a hundred, mostly glass containers; mason jars and bottles and other receptacles that are set upon old wooden shelves on timber frames and ancient bookcases that line the tent's four, unmoving, canvas walls.

It occurs to you to wonder at how the other man in the tent could have set up this display so quickly. You had seen no shelves nor cases in the assembling of the tent. But then the fluctuating soft-sharp light glowing from those glass repositories shunts your thoughts onto another rail.

In spite of all that earlier external shadow play there is only one man standing in here when you enter, and that is me.

Standing and watching and smiling, as if I had expected you.

An elderly gent in black top hat and lightning striped forked-tailed coat and trousers and vest all of midnight blue. Black rubber gumboots (it pays to be insulated in my line of work) mark the perigee of my ensemble. A white goatee and generous mo all harpoon sharp. I remove my hat with black gloved hands white zigzag marked, and make a little bow, and I have long hair the colour of singed fur sporting a lightning bolt of white that strikes back through it from fringe to crown. Feel free to stare, for I am a curious sight. That's right, I have no eyebrows at present; stolen in a flash by my obsessional occupation. I keep losing them because I get too close to creation's flarings.

"Greetings, and welcome.

"Downstryk's the name. Trapping and tapping sky cracks is the game."

I shake your hand and my grip is dry, firm, hot to your touch.

"I am a professor of plasmatic plethoration and profundity, and this – is my lightning exhibit.

"And here you are, I've tempted you inside our little exhibition, no artificial lighting required as you can see. . .

"No, it is not brightly lit in here, in fact outside the soft glow of glassed nature and the occasional lumious flare, it's. . . well, mostly shadows. Moving shadows. . ."

Gazing all about you at the odd display, and the smiling showman who stands at its centre, you think at first perhaps that the containers hold clusters of glow-worms or fireflies, but the energy within them, you soon realise, is more like electricity, but no less living.

The hairs on your neck and arms are standing up to inform you about the charged atmosphere. The hair on your head is stirring and slowly dancing upright to the power's siren song.

The man named Downstryk pre-empts further supposition upon your behalf. "No, my young friend, not fireflies or cheap conjury," chin tilting up in pride, his smile grows wider, his eyes glint brighter, "not mirror tricks nor lightning bugs, but *lightning* itself!"

As you turn all about, so does he, with arms held wide. "Welcome to my modest little travelling display, or 'anthology', as it were. But a sampling from my museum, which contains thousands of examples from my more than half a century of collecting and preserving."

All about the 'walls' you see jars and glasses and clear vases and cubes. . . of coloured captured lightnings — a spectrum crossing radiance. "Yes, that's a corked beer bottle, dark glass with a different amber fluid in it now though. Yes – a cut glass flower vase with glass lid attached, fused on. Here, a brandy decanter, and there – Old Stoney ginger beer – that is clay clinging to it. Here – a necklace of cat's-eye glass beads, with something alive and moving through it, there – yes a pair of cracked lensed spectacles, winking with light shimmer, look close, they give a view onto. . . somewhere else. This? This is a poor old teddy bear's eye. . .

"Yes, I heard that distant rumble too.

"Fear not, this 'canvas' is fire retardant.

"But, now, to our specimens.

"You are our first customer here. I'll soon leave you to take your own tour.

"More thunder. Yes.

"It looks like there's a storm a brewing."

———————

———

' A Flash on the Horizon '

To me the flash fiction piece, when it is done well, is the literary equivalent of bottling lightning.

Short-short, microfiction, flash, flash spec, 1 minute fiction, postcard, sudden, nano, shotgun... the aesthetically challenged 'cigarette' or carcinogenic 'smoke-long' stories lacks a certain romance but is, nonetheless, effective... love it or hate it or show indifference to it very short form fiction is now rife in the field, burning across it like wildfire (or countless small grassfires) and it looks as if it's here to stay.

It is a form that I specialised in once upon a time. One that I still, regularly return to and gain enjoyment from.

Examples? Let's get the classics out of the way shall we?

> For sale: baby shoes, never worn.

> The last man on Earth sat alone in a room. There was a knock on the door...

Those two are often dusted off and trotted out as demonstration models. And rightly so, for they are classics. The first is credited to Ernest Hemmingway. Purportedly his personal favourite of his own writings. The second piece, many times exampled and attributed incorrectly (and no wonder), is by Fredric Brown, a past master of the short form, utilised cleverly in his 1948 story 'Knock'. But let's go back further with that concept...

> A woman is sitting alone in a house. She knows she is alone in the

whole world; every other living thing is dead. The doorbell rings.

That's from Thomas Bailey Aldrich, writing in 1870. Some very shallow digging will show that, whoever came up with the idea first, quite a few names have been attached to what has long become a standard. In 1957 editor and writer Ron Smith put his own take on it. His simple, one-word tweak, as with the other versions, opens up a world of possibilities. . .

> The last man on Earth sat alone in a room. There was a lock on the door. . .

I am sure that the basic premise has travelled further than a century or so to us, and will continue onwards. Will it continue to grow shorter in the telling? If it was conveyed prehistory, by firelight in a cave, how short was that example?

An old favourite of mine is Ray Bradbury's 'The Dragon'. At just a handful of words over one thousand it reminds you that though all writers are free to use the same words, in their own unique orders, dipping, more or less, from the same word well, a story full of Bradbury's word choices is worth so much more than so many other writers. Yet, back in the days when Ray Bradbury was producing works like 'The Gift', 'The Highway', 'The Last Night of The World', 'Perhaps We Are Going Away', 'The Pedestrian', 'Embroidery' and so many others, he was getting paid the same measly few cents a word, or fractions of a cent per word, as everyone else. Though 'The Dragon' is one of those stories that you really only read once – and get the full impact from – every other time you do it is with warm reassurance and admiration at his ability.

There is no lack of good flash and short-short fiction pieces out there. Though they are a-swim in an ocean of mediocrity and schools of bad examples. This particular species we are interested in comes in at between zero and one thousand words. Though there is no set regulation size in regards to maximum wordage, you are scraping the ceiling with flash at one thousand and generally two thousand five hundred words is the sky limit for short-shorts. They mostly swim in the shallow areas and you will throw back a lot of your catch before you keep one.

Truth be told – there is no concretely set length for any writing format unless strictly specified. As with the drabble, which is one hundred words, generally, the cheeky 69er or the more buttoned up 55 worder. Maybe I'll create one called the frisk – for crime shorts. Now what limit would suit there. . .?

Six worders were popular for a while. I've always liked this one by the word wizard Mr Alan Moore:

Machine. Unexpectedly, I'd invented a time

Now that's a keeper.

One of the best I've caught of late I discovered some years back on the net one day. It is by the American writer M.K. Hobson. Its name is 'Hippocampus' and it is another keeper.

To me it is a near perfect and inspiring example.

As far as Australian content goes, a number of writers like Martin Livings, Rick Kennett, and David Witteveen are creating consistently good flash fictions. One only has to read pieces like Joanne Anderton's 'Dredging', Witteveen's 'The River, Black with Night' and 'Dirty Laundry' by Eugene Gramelis to see that Australian writers, with craft and imagination, are forging lightning bolts of their own.

———————

————

' Framing Nothing '

Hung upon a wall in a gallery is a picture frame containing a blank sheet. You stare at this display. After a while you realise that the true artwork lies in the frame itself.

Did that amuse you? Did it cause you to chuckle, or even just briefly smile a little smile, or twitch the dimples in your mind?

That's primarily all a zero word story can be really. A joke, a title above an empty frame – the frame on nothing either tangible, physical in 2-D or in your head. The story fully encompassed in and by the title. Or the trick, the punchline as it were.

That's the paradox of the zero word story of course – it isn't really.

That's not to say that poignancy and impact and craft, not to mention art, cannot be encompassed in a zero worder. You just don't see many like that.

Some people don't get them, and that includes writers. I received hundreds of submissions for this anthology. Although the advertised guidelines clearly indicated 0 to 1000 words, not one of the submitted pieces was a zero worder.

As someone who has written zero word pieces, one worders, six worders and so on, the lack of nothing, as it were, was a little disappointing.

They can be a bit of fun, and I would have liked you to have found just a few in here, at the start. Like very light aperitifs, or an aromatic hint in the air.

Easy entrées. Lightning soup. One sip – they're gone. They were barely there anyway.

____

____

' The Short of it '

Maybe the short-short did originate as filler for inconvenient spaces in magazines from a past era.

Perhaps microfiction is the result of a cunning plan by publishers and editors to pay writers even less than the piddling amounts they are accustomed to.

Could be that it is all the inevitable result of our attention deficit society and the sound and sight bite media that feeds it. Like hyperactive brat children loaded up on vacuous, shallow sugar content and with low attention spa— Oh look — something shiny, something! Candy!

There is also the rather pathetic reason that people are giving these days for not reading very much. No time. Some say the problem is the short attention span that the human race has evolved, or devolved, to. I shrug my shoulders at that, see me shrug my shoulders? And make that face with the mouth and – you know? The danger is that if enough people keep saying it then it could become absolutely true, not only as the prime reason for the popularity of flash fiction but also why people no longer read.

Yet, some flash can make the reader work for its hidden-in-plain-sight reward.

Also, while statistics can be untrustworthy things, some show that people are *still* reading.

So, let us regard flash not as a marker of the decline of reading and writing, not as a limiter upon the creative imagination, but as a popular and successful form of the writing craft, as an exercise and a test and a proof of the triumph of the imagination.

Sure it dates back to Aesop's fables and Ovid's 'Metamorphoses', perhaps even beyond those tomes, to cave walls and campfires. You'll find many pieces that qualify as flash in the volumes of the fairy tales of the Brothers Grimm; the macabre 'The Stubborn Child' being one good example. Practitioners of the very short tale have included Guy de Maupassant, Chekov, O. Henry, Kafka, Jorge Luis Borges and Joyce Carol Oates. Even Poe, Bierce and Lovecraft had a crack at the form.

Popular word limits have been 1000, 500, 300, 100, 55, 6. . . These days however, with editorial wordage caps, it's basically pick a number.

You can get accidental flash too. As exampled by this flash stumble demonstrated in Tom Sant's 'Persuasive Business Proposals'.

After rotting in the cellar for weeks, my brother brought up some oranges.

I'd call that one 'Decomposing Participle'.

Or, as with any flash fiction, unconventional forms can be used, even adding a third dimension – a story in the twisted shape of a Möbius strip, or even a circle (for a flat display), proclaiming itself thus:

The lightning flashed and the wind whipped at the paper which seemed to whisper, *"This story never ends,"* as it was passed to the next in line who read: It was a dark and stormy night.

That piece courtesy of Blanket Barrowclough.

Flash is the cousin, or bastard love child, of prose poetry.

It's a grope on a packed train or bus, a quick slung whisky shot – at times 100 proof and brain burning, a stolen kiss on a speeding train in the brief blackness of a railway tunnel.

Flash fiction could mark the evolution of the short story.

Or its decline.

It may be a quick route to publication for fledgling writers. Hell, some writers have built an entire career on the short-short.

It *is* ideally suited to the Net.

There has certainly been a proliferation of e-zines that specialise in low wordage fiction – fanciful arrays designed for catching lightning.

Whichever, whatever, the form is a good whetstone tool upon which creatives can hone their abilities.

In a writing craft sense flash can be a fine warm up technique and a strop to sharpen one's storytelling skills.

Such exercise can, purportedly, assist with escaping the dreaded writer's block. Benzedrine, Dexedrine and Lisdexamfetamine can't, according to Frederik Pohl, Cyril Kornbluth and others, but writing flash fiction can.

It is furious, fast, quick and skinny.

It *can* be poetry in prose.

It *can* be brutally assaultive.

It *can* make you think.

And it *can* entertain *and* be *meaningful* work.

Once in a while it can be nigh incomprehensible. At such times, don't try to comprehend. Don't look for sense, just stick your nose out at the waft of its perfume, just. . . taste.

Our aim here is to showcase some of the best examples of the form that we could find.

So – a metaphoric presentation – an array of shot glasses. Each with a different blend of mind elixir, essence of story. Go ahead, toss 'em back. Though they be small doses, I'll wager many of their flavours will still be with you, long after you close the cover, press the reading device off, and leave this distillery.

‗‗‗‗‗‗‗‗

‗‗‗‗‗‗

' Ninety Seconds to the Minute '

Or

' Metaphorically Speaking '

A picture can paint a thousand words, but a thousand words can paint a heck of a lot of pictures too.

You have entered a place here where we have assembled for display one hundred, mostly glass, receptacles of flashing contents. The containers range from simple rusty lidded old honey jars, with remnants of scraped off labels still attached, through pickle and large mason jars to a gypsy witch's scrying ball and a skull carved perfectly in crystal. From stoppered, otherwise empty bottles of every description – one with a long drowned, longer beached, ship within, pale electric charge phantoms crawling and playing about the masts – to a marble and a glass eye and a stained glass window fragment. (We soon found that we could not use plastic items to hold 'em – they melted and our catches escaped.) Vials and amphora, ampoule, plugged test tube and warped mirror.

You'll see the name of each collector who has contributed each lightning beneath the name they've given it.

Look here, on one plank shelf black canvas backed, is a child's red metal sand bucket full of a spade's depth from a long forgotten beach – step closer. . . see within, the blue electric writhings caught in that silica, like ether worms. . .

The energies within those containments sizzle and arc and spread in blue white, lime, purple forkings, mandrakes of pale plasma, testing the glass surfaces, feeling with plasmatic ghost hands, laying their brightly glowing fingertips against the inner surfaces of their vitreous pens. Feeling, for a way out.

And you, dear patron, are going to release each one. By knowing its story. By allowing it to pass through you.

So, sample our wares, whataya got ta lose? Five minutes, one minute, twenty seconds, five? Heck, you could take in the whole showcase in less than a couple of hours.

Here, come along, unbottle these examples with your eyes and mind. Examine this assemblage of flares and thunder eggs.

It won't take long.

That storm is almost here. . .

' Lightning Unbound '

"Electric Epyllions!" the showman enthuses. "Some are small cracks of energy, others full scale light shows orchestrated by thunder, still others are lightning sprites, springing up like liquid plasma eruptions from the rooves of thunderhead clouds, sky volcanoes, burning their way into the void's further ebon reaches."

Settling, just a little, he glow gleams a bright white smile at you.

"Please, enjoy the offerings. Don't touch, and take your time." Downstryk sets his arms high, reaching to either side. "Time has a way of stretching, contracting and bending, in here."

And then, he is gone, or beyond your attention, because you walk forward and stare at the stored brightness in one jar . . .

And the light seems to spread, and consume you, to speak to you . . . And then you *see* what it has to tell and to show you. . .

Within a few minutes the flare seems to dim, the images dull and fade, the words whisper away . . .

And you move on to the next captured lightning . . .

AUTOBIOGRAPHY

Donated by
Fred Zackel

"Something fell out of the mirror," I said.
"Did you hold it upside down?"
"Yes."
"Did you shake it?"
"Yes."
"After I told you not to?"
"I got curious."
"What spilled out?"
"A lifetime of failure and blind ambition. Vanity."
"What spilled out wasn't worth—"
"Don't say it. Please don't say it."
"Now it's boring people to death."
"I'm sorry."
"Sorry isn't good enough."
"I should have listened to you."
"Do you know where it is right this minute?"
"Behind you. Creeping up on us all."
"Were you nuts?"

A BLANK PAGE

Donated by
Shona Snowden

She sat in class, words drifting over her head like butterflies. All around, more studious minds caught them and pinned them to the page.

Her page alone remained blank.

Under her shirt, her back felt as smooth as the page. So when ridges started to grow from her spine, pushing up like dragon teeth, she felt them immediately.

Her skin changed next, drying, thickening. The tiny lines on the back of her hands grew and deepened, pushing patches of skin apart. The patches turned from pink, to grey, to greenish.

Still the butterfly words fluttered past, lazy yet uncatchable.

Her fingers shrank and her nails sharpened into claws. Her swept-up hair hardened into a tiny crest. Behind her, a tail pushed out between the seat of the chair and the back, sliding down to loop around one of the chair legs.

She couldn't see the students around her any more. Their sighs, the squeaking of their pens, the stirring of their paperwork, had dissolved into nothing. Only the butterfly words remained, tantalising her. She felt their wings stir the murky air; smelt the trails they left behind. Inside her, something stirred. Uncoiled.

She flicked out her tongue. And caught one.

A SQUEAL, AND THEN A SQUEAK

Donated by
Sam Cooney

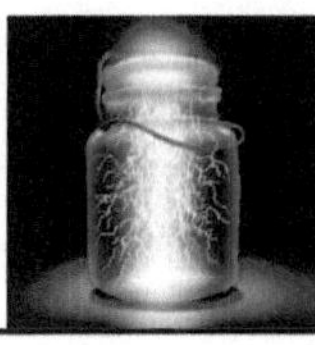

Lying still in his bottom bunk, Max is awake. It's the middle of the week that bridges Christmas and New Year. The bedroom he shares with his three brothers is hushed, muted. The sighs of sleep from Pete, Tom and Luke do not travel far. Two bunk beds, two cupboards, a wooden toy chest, scrunched clothes, hanging towels, plastic action figures and sporting gear leave little room for sound. Max wakes earlier than his brothers most mornings. A part of him blames the vertical crack of sunlight between the battered venetian blind and the window frame, but he also knows that he likes being awake first. He enjoys the power, the secret knowing that exists in the bedroom in the earliest yawn of day.

Max eavesdrops on his brothers' dreams – a half-moan here, a whispered sentence there. He isn't a good older brother. The mantle of wise protector refuses to fit his freckled shoulders. He hopes that if it came down to it, he would put himself in the way of anything that threatened them, but a part of him despairs, sometimes, quietly, that maybe he wouldn't.

Max can hear his mum moving around the other end of their weatherboard house. She is always up before he wakes. He can track her movements about the far rooms. The gentle morning clatter of clean dishes and the crunch of wicker washing basket gives hints to her position. If he stays utterly still and holds his breath and closes his eyes, and there are no cars passing and the wind is light and his brothers are quiet, he can hear every tread of her bare feet. He would recognise that trudging rhythm anywhere.

Crying. Like a waterbomb the familiar tempo of the morning splits and bursts. A string of strange sounds rush down the hall and into Max's warm ear. A squeal, and then a squeak. A hurried, irregular shuffling and muffled sobbing. Without thinking Max is up and out of the bedroom. He heads for the noises, stepping on the bottoms of his green and white striped pyjamas. They make him slide on the polished floorboards.

He rounds the last corner into the kitchen, his face babyish with trepidation. No one is there. The kitchen stands silent. The sobbing blubs out again, and Max knows it is coming from the laundry. Suddenly cautious after his earlier abandon, he treads in silence toward the not-quite-closed door. He stands there, still, and the world seems full of noise. He pushes the heavy white-painted door open like an animal that finds its cage unlocked. His mum is standing over the sink. Her shoulders are shaking with the failed effort of trying to cry noiselessly. She doesn't notice Max, but he catches a glimpse of her face. He's seen his mum cry lots of times, but this is different. The parts are familiar: running nose, flushed cheeks, rolling pins of flesh on her forehead squeezed white. But the overall impression frightens him, and he doesn't know why.

Her arms are in the low-slung laundry sink, yellow and green rubber washing gloves on her hands. The tendons of her forearms are straining as if connected to her clenching jaw. In the rubber straightjacket of her grip, under a foot of water, is a guinea pig. It is thrashing, kicking out with all four legs in holy panic. The water bubbles like a pot of spaghetti. There are fine brown and white hairs all over the surface, with some of them sticking to the metal sides. Her tears drip from her chin into the pitching sink, each drop trapping the early morning light that roars through the window.

Later, of course, everything is explained and re-explained. The guinea pig had to die. The eldest one, Martha, had given birth a few weeks earlier to a handful of sopping, slimy nuggets. No one had even known she was pregnant, although it wasn't a huge surprise. The guinea pigs had arrived two years ago. Shortly after, they were banished to the back fence with the other exiles, like the plastic clamshell kiddie pool and the compost bin.

So Martha had plopped out half a dozen miniature versions of herself, their innate abilities of eating and shitting and making a racket evidently well rooted. But something was wrong, and that morning Max's mum had realised: the father of Martha's babies must have also been her brother or cousin or son. Like royalty of old, the guinea pigs' inbreeding had affected the new offspring, so that some of them were physically or mentally disabled. Gammy legs or misshapen skulls or lacking the capacity to take in food; the mangled creatures would have to be killed.

For the longest time thereafter Max keeps hold of that feeling of awfulness. He holds it just under his skin. Like a landscape changed by the felling of a tree, Max is different. That morning, when he'd run down the hallway, feet sliding, hands bouncing off walls, when he'd reached the open-plan kitchen, breathless and not breathing, and when he'd leaned on the inevitably-white door of the laundry, especially then, Max had done so with the leaden anticipation of a world gone wrong. He'd expected to come upon something dreadful, had actually looked forward to it.

Much, much later, he'd realise that this was what being an adult always felt like: driving a car willing for an accident; travelling overseas in the hope of danger; reading books and watching films and getting married in the hope of fighting and mayhem and hate. Max had learned something that morning, or maybe unlearned it. Whatever the case, the knowledge took him even further away from his family. That kicking and crying and dying guinea pig signposted a juncture in Max's life that people would eventually look back to and say "Was that it?" And it wasn't remarkable. That was the thing – the whole incident reeked of everyday, ordinary, commonplace horror. That was the thing.

HOLE IN THE GARDEN

Donated by
yt sumner

I found the hole by accident.

In my backyard, just after a storm with my bed sheets flapping around me in big soggy slaps as I tried to pull them down. That's when I saw it. It wasn't very wide but it looked deep and when I leaned over I couldn't see the bottom. I nibbled my lip. It would not do having a hole in my garden like this. Someone could fall in.

I knocked next door and after apologising about the hour, asked my neighbour if I could borrow a shovel. He nodded and went to the shed smirking.

He smiled like that because he'd seen me naked once.

Late at night, dashing out in the rain to take my sheets off the line, there he was with his hands pressed against his window. It always seemed to rain when I washed my linen but it was the last time I forgot to put anything on before I rescued it.

Whenever he smiled like that, I knew he was seeing me naked again, the rain bouncing off my arse. It made me feel queasy but I couldn't do anything about it, and anyway I needed a shovel.

I seized it from him when he returned, careful not to let our fingers touch and hurried back to my yard. It was getting late but I didn't start right away. First I leaned on the edge of the shovel, balancing on my foot in a corner of my garden. Not until lightning cracked and illuminated the yard did I give it a good stamp and wedge up a dark clump. I liked the sound of the grass and roots tearing apart as I lifted it free and I was smiling as I carried the earth to the edge of the hole. It smelled pretty good. Not many things smelled as good as rain, but the smell of fresh earth always smelled like a brand new start.

I was about to toss the first heap down, like that bit they throw on a coffin at a funeral, when I heard the voice.

"Don't you dare."

I paused, the heap of dirt hovering over the hole. I paused because I do have an active imagination. My mother calls it overactive, but it's not like I see fairies at the bottom of the garden. I giggled at the thought, considering my current situation, and had to admit sometimes I did giggle at thoughts I probably shouldn't have.

"Throwing dirt is not a nice thing to do, you know."

This was definitely a voice. Coming from the bottom of the hole.

"Are you okay?"

I probably should have asked something else but that's what came out.

"Not as bad as you'd think. It's a bit muddy down here but comfortable enough I suppose."

His tone was conversational and I wasn't sure what else to say. I was getting uncomfortable in this awkward position and a little dirt trembled off the side of the shovel.

"All right then,"

I said down the hole.

"All right what?"

I frowned. I didn't know. It was just something I said when I wanted to wrap things up, like when my mother wouldn't stop talking on the phone.

"Aren't you going to ask me up?"

I blushed. I hadn't even thought of it. He was probably cold and would like a cup of tea. It was rude of me to not ask. My mouth opened with the invitation but I stopped it with a new thought.

"What are you doing down there?"

"Nothing."

I frowned at how quickly he replied. It reminded me of babysitting my nephews and how they answered when I asked what they held behind their backs. Whenever they answered that fast it was usually something like a bloated toad or fossilised dog poo.

I raised my voice as thunder rolled overhead and it began to rain again.

"I mean, what are you doing in a hole in my garden?"

There was a moment of silence.

"Er…can't I just come up? It's difficult to explain down here in the mud."

At his embarrassment I blushed again and pushed my wet fringe out of my eyes.

"I'm sorry, of course."

I heard scrabbling and then a new tone emerged from the hole, closer this time.

"Well, thank god for that…"

His voice didn't sound that civil any more.

"Because I was getting damn lonely down there…"

His voice definitely had lost its conversational tone. It sounded deeper, in fact it sounded almost like a growl.

"And to tell the truth, I'm absolutely *starving*."

The top of his head emerged, but all I saw before I brought the shovel down hard, was that there was an awful lot of hair.

His yell turned to a yelp as he thudded and cried out that he had mud all through his hair and instead of blushing I'm sure I grinned. I was still grinning when I heard the cough behind me and I swung around with the shovel raised to see my neighbour standing in the rain smirking at my clinging wet T-shirt.

"What do you want?"

I was as surprised at my tone as he looked. It didn't sound like my usual one, in fact it sounded more like the one down the hole than my normal voice.

"I was wondering if you needed a hand."

We both turned towards the hole as the thunder clapped above and underneath it I could just make out the hollering deep in the ground.

I looked at my neighbour and showed my teeth, I believe I even raised the shovel and waggled it at him a little.

"I think I'll be fine from now on, don't you?"

His smile faded and he muttered something about keeping the shovel as he hurried back next door. As he disappeared behind the fence I lifted my shovel in the rain and kept filling the now silent hole in my garden. And it smelled pretty good.

A LITTLE KNOWLEDGE

Donated by
Allen Ashley

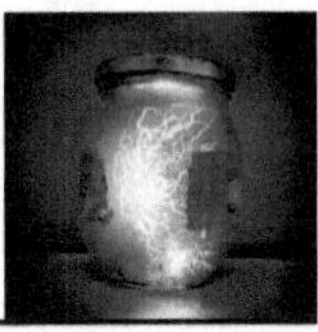

One -
What is this world I have awoken to?

Two -
The life-force imperative tells me to take another gulp. And another.

Three -
These others with their bright sheen must be like me, I believe. I catch my reflection in their shiny eyes and I have self-awareness.

Four -
What lies in that direction? There, beyond the rocks? And that way past the plants?

Five -
This cannot be all there is. The world/universe must consist of more. I await a sign.

Six -
Food from the heavens! And by whose godly fins? God? A god of goldfish?

Seven -
I recognise my predicament now. My world is merely a bowl.

Eight -
I refuse to swim in endless circles. I am devising a golden escape plan. First -

One -
What is this world I have awoken to?

THE FISH MARKET

Donated by
Ella Joseph

The fish are almost camouflaged in their glass cabinet,
missing only the quick flick, mass movement,
of their ocean schools. Eyes stare, alert -
Dead. Their sequinned skins are one with a surface world of chrome;
tonality extends to shades of white, silver, grey.
Their mattress of crushed ice mimics the scrabbly froth of a breaking wave,
or air-bubbled clouds, net ripping through the resisting current.

Linh's words slice as sharply and efficiently as the silver knife she wields:
"You want this one? This? Fresh – caught today. Something else?"
Her blade whips cleanly, deftly. The slivered carcass
flaps onto the glistening scales;
"Little bit over, OK?"

Around the market, sounds ebb and flow, the stream of shoppers
eddy around trolleys, pallets, polystyrene tubs like icebergs.
Scuttle-hunting like crabs, or floating
with the prevailing current, wafting gentle as kelp
until a bargain flickers in the periphery of vision
and they dart, with unexpected focus – a survival of the fittest.

Linh knows the fish, slaps them, rejected, back on to their trays
with the casual unthinkingness of a mother slapping at
her errant child; neatens the row of curled-up crays;
and at the end of the day, blasts the cabinets with a jet of biting water,
rubs hard at the naked shelves, sluices the walls and floors. The shop
is a wet, seeping, dripping beach at low tide.

Then Linh locks up, and emerges from behind the counter,
exposing marshmallow pink gumboots that hint at
softness.

EVOLUTION

Donated by
Jen White

He had always been drawn to water. Ponds, creeks, even the ocean, but rivers were best. He liked lying half in, half out of a river like some ancestral creature caught midway between water and land.

He made his first fish suit from an old dress of his mother's. Thick, gold material embossed with abstract swirls. Green and gold sequins at the throat. He remembered her in the dress, on her way to a party, bending down and kissing him goodnight, the sequins flashing in the dark as if she were some magical being from his book of fairy tales.

He cut out a basic oval shape, front and back, with a large hole at one end for his face to show through. At either side, a triangle of material signified flippers, with another at the bottom for a tail. Of course, he knew nothing about using a needle and thread. His sewing was awkward, every stitch an experiment, the material bunching in some places, gaping in others. And yet, standing some metres from the mirror, in the watery green air of his darkened bedroom, with eyes narrowed, the costume was effective.

It was several weeks before he ventured out with the suit. He knew a place along the river that was silent and lonely. He knew many places like that, but this was the best. He stuffed the suit inside a plastic supermarket bag and walked over the paddocks to the river. When he arrived, he stripped and climbed into the suit, completing his own modest form of species reassignment. Then he eased down onto the damp edge of the river and slid into the water, resting his head on the bank. It felt strange to him at first, until he realised that that strange feeling was happiness. He lay there for hours, drowsing gently in the water. Every so often he lowered his head under the water to glimpse other smaller fish gently nibbling at him, pond scum forming upon him, and tadpoles darting about his fins. For the first time in his life he felt as if he fit properly inside his skin.

He began to spend each day at the river. It was the happiest time of his life, but the material from which he had made the suit was old, and it soon grew frayed and torn.

His second suit was a mistake. A cheap stretch polyester, it grew heavy and sodden in the water, weighing him down. He discarded this suit within a week.

For the third suit, he selected a solid, green material scavenged from an old waterbed. He chose it for its strength, and because it was appropriate for a watery environment. The suit zipped up the back with a large, single zipper. In the suit, he could only move from front to back in a dolphin-like manner. He tried some kicks, some wiggles before the mirror. The movements felt satisfyingly fishy, not human at all. In this suit he was a mature river fish, a trout perhaps, which had grown huge and wily and could live by its wits.

He took his suit to the river, worked his way into it, and wriggled into the water. The suit was magnificent. All the pressures of human life and expectation dropped away from him. Inside the suit, he no longer possessed the agile, darting mind of a mammal. His mental processes became slow, considered, the swaying ruminations of a large, dark trout. Several times he actually forgot he was human.

When it began to grow dark and cold, he rolled himself onto the bank, realising then, with something near terror, that the material had tightened slightly. He could no longer reach the zipper. In his drive for authenticity, he had made the suit as close-fitting as possible, failing to consider the need for its eventual removal. Perhaps his ichthyic metamorphosis had transformed him inside as well as out. He truly had begun to see the world as a fish would, and fish do not need to consider the removal of their skin. With a growing, sweaty panic he managed, during the following hours, to hump his way over the land, forcing the process of evolution forward again by sheer will. He did not call for help. He could not bear the thought of the ensuing ridicule. Eventually, he came to a stop in a small, fallow paddock, too exhausted to cry out even if he had wanted to. But, even then, one small part of him was glad that no one had come. After all, how could he have explained?

Months later his rotten, gaseous body, encased like a sausage in the swollen fish suit, was found some distance from the lake. He must have crawled for days.

SEXY BRUTE

Donated by
Adam Walter

I guess it's since late spring that I've been working on this pond and mud pit in our backyard, preparing it for one of the offspring of the creature SuddenDeath. The creature belongs to my neighbour, a large appliances repairman named Ozzie Fenridge, a big guy with a gut like a zoo bear. The man has one hell of a setup, I'm telling you. And sure, I'm starting out with a pit only half the size of his, but I can always expand.

The creature SuddenDeath is magnificent. A wonder and a terror, believe me. It is eleven feet long and low to the ground. It has a tail as solid as a fence post and jaws that you just don't ever want to see aimed at you.

A few months ago Ozzie brought in a mate, a stud, and I was sure the poor guy was set to embarrass himself. I thought: how sad that Ozzie has lived so many years with the creature and all along he's taken it for a female! But then the mating began a little after midnight, and it woke up my entire house. The noise was like something I'd never heard, like a howler monkey going at it with a 400-pound sow. It went on for hours. And for three nights after that my wife and sons stayed with her parents while I toughed it out at home, alone. Several weeks later, the stud long gone, I watched as the creature packed a couple dozen large stony eggs into the wall of the mud pit behind Ozzie's house. That was when I decided to buy one of the hatchlings.

More than ever now, me and the boys spend hours looking over the fence and watching the creature. Me most of all. The way that some afternoons Ozzie will get down in the mud and wrestle with the creature, arm to arm, leg to leg – it takes my breath away and scares me shitless at the same time. Once he puts that trick hold of his on it he'll flip the thing and then roll it like it was a puppy dog.

So. I'm expecting pretty much *everything* to change around here when I've got my own – when a mini version of the creature comes to live in this fine new mud pit. Yes, things'll get a mite lively. TV and poker and table tennis be damned. We've got *entertainment* on the way.

I know how crazy it sounds, but sometimes I'll be watching Ozzie wrestle the creature SuddenDeath there in the mud, and I can't help wondering what it'd be like to actually make love to one of those things. Not as a man of course. Just as a fellow creature, a stud.

MINDING MATTHEW

Donated by
Martin Davey

Brian left the basement for the first time in three days. Jane made him bacon and eggs.

She watched him eat, his hair wavering grey to brown and then back to grey again, like a flickering image on one of those old black and white movies. "You need to eat more, Brian."

"Nonsense. I eat plenty." He sawed at the egg with his knife, yellow yolk spilling about his plate.

Jane turned the hot water tap. It coughed, emitted a violent torrent of cold water before grudgingly allowing a tepid trickle. "The boiler needs looking at."

Brian dropped his knife and fork onto the plate and pushed his chair back, the legs scraping loudly. "And when do I get the chance to do that?" His hair was brown, grey, then brown again. Clean shaven, grey-flecked stubble, clean shaven. Jane felt nauseous looking at him. He sighed, reached out to her. Sometimes he wore a watch, sometimes not. Jane didn't move away from the sink, she hated the feel of his skin. It was insubstantial, like a barely remembered dream. "My work is important. Think what it could mean for us. For Matthew."

At least his voice was unchanging. Jane closed her eyes and pictured Brian as he had once been. There was a silence. She could feel Brian looking at her. When she opened her eyes he was gone.

The banging and hammering in the basement started soon after.

When he finally did emerge from the basement it was 2 a.m. and Jane was lying fully clothed on the bed.

He didn't turn on the light before he laid next to her, his face a black hole of emptiness in the darkness. "I'm so close."

Jane stared at the ceiling and blinked back the tears. His was a multitude of voices, all speaking in the same voice, all speaking the same words, but overlapping and distorting one another. He was getting close, as he said. But the closer he got to Matthew, the more he was lost to her. She wanted to hold his hand but feared her hand would pass right through it, like trying to grasp a beam of sunlight.

"I tidied the house today," she said.

A long silence. "Did you go in Matthew's room?" Her skin felt cold listening to those voices. She was glad she couldn't see his flickering face.

"No. I still can't."

He said nothing. She could hear his face moving, shifting, changing. It sounded like the hum of a dragonfly's wings. "I heard his voice yesterday. I ran as fast as I could, but the machine pulled me back." The voices shimmered in the darkness, wavering in and wavering out like a bad reception on an old television set.

"I'm glad. I still need you," she said.

Brian's side of the bed was already cold. Perhaps he had never truly been there and she was speaking to nothing more than an echo of his self.

Jane had thought her eyesight was failing her when the changes had begun. She would catch sight of Brian from the corner of her eye, and she would see his face…*shift*, alter somehow – a fleshy cheek become tighter for a fraction of a second, the heavy purple under his eyes fading and then returning a moment later. She had ignored it. There was no ignoring it now. He was lost to her, lost in the unbounded strands of time. Lost to his machine.

Jane didn't hear any sounds from the basement for the next three days. She walked slowly down the stairs, a cricket bat clasped in her hand.

She had never seen the time machine before; a sleek black contraption crouched in the centre of the basement.

Jane hefted the cricket bat. Matthew's bat. How had she got it? She hadn't been in his room since that night thirty years before. Tears wet her cheeks. She lifted the bat again.

I heard his voice yesterday, Brian had said.

What would it be like, to hear that voice just once after so many years? A memory of laughter, shining bright blue eyes and the smell of freshly cut grass; of Brian showing Matthew how to keep the cricket bat straight, to keep his elbow up. The bat fell from her fingers as though it burned to touch.

Jane sat in the chair of the machine, pulled the lever back. It felt like jumping backward off a diving board, her stomach left far above her.

She climbed the stairs and walked slowly through the house. How little things changed in thirty years. And then she arrived at the door. Matthew's door. Brian had made a plaque in the shape of a racing car: *Matthew's Room*, it said on it. When Brian had taken that down, she had fallen to her knees on the landing. She had never been in the room since.

The plaque was there once more. She could hear Brian's voice. He was reading a story; she couldn't hear the words, only a deep, comforting murmur. Every few moments, a smaller voice would interrupt, asking questions.

Matthew was always asking questions.

Jane leaned back against the door, her eyes closed. Just to hear that voice one last time. But it wasn't enough. It could never be enough. She could hear a hum like the wings of a dragonfly. She wiped at a tear on her cheek; her hand seemed to pass right through it. The hum was louder, a constant drone in her ear.

She lifted her hand and pushed the door open. Sunlight streamed onto the landing and Jane fixed a smile to her shimmering face.

A FRIGHTFUL MISUNDERSTANDING

Donated by
Stephanie Gianopoulos

The great black bird gazed disconsolately into his untouched cup. From the surface of the cold tea, his own watery eye glared back at him, a round, beady accuser.

"I didn't mean to frighten him so!" he moaned for what, by the cat's count, was the twenty-sixth time. The bear's estimation hovered closer to three. Then again, when the bear let numbers go too much higher than three, they 'would' insist on getting rather fuzzy.

"There, there." The bear put out a gentle paw and patted his friend's feathered back. "Don't you feel well? I couldn't help noticing that you haven't touched your biscuits."

The bird gave a slow, mournful shake of his head. "I couldn't eat a thing. I feel just terrible. I didn't mean to frighten him so!"

"Then, um, then … that is, you wouldn't mind if I …" The bear glanced furtively from his plate, empty but for a scattering of crumbs, to the bird's, still piled neatly with biscuits.

With one claw, the bird pushed his plate in the bear's direction. "You enjoy them," he sighed. "I didn't mean to frighten him so!"

The bear beamed in gratitude, but quickly dropped his snout, rearranging his kind features into a more suitable expression of compassion. He continued patting the bird's back with one paw while every so often sneaking small bits of biscuit with the other, nibbling them with as much subtlety as he could manage.

The cat, on the other hand, watched his dining companions with an air of amusement that he made no effort to conceal.

"I merely meant …" began the bird, choking a bit on his words. The bear paused mid-bite, and the cat twitched his tail enigmatically. "I merely meant to offer …" the bird paused again.

"Go on," said the bear, though what came out around the moist mouthful of biscuit sounded more like "Mwr-awn." The cat, still seeming far more cheerful than the situation warranted, nodded his encouragement as well.

The bird took a heaving, broken, breath and wailed "I merely meant to offer a bit of helpful decorating advice!"

The bear looked thoroughly puzzled, and the cat cocked his head inquisitively.

So quietly that the bear and the cat had to lean in to hear him properly, the bird continued. "Above the door is no place for a bust. Someone is going to close that door too quickly one day and …" Solemnly he finished, "Somebody could get hurt."

The bear shook his head sympathetically. The cat rose from his seat, gave himself a long, lazy stretch and looked straight at the bird. "Dreadfully sorry," the cat said with a crazy smile. "And sorrily dreadful. But I must be off. There's a little girl who's got herself into a jam …"

"Jam?" echoed the bear hopefully.

The cat rolled his wide eyes and disappeared. His grin hung in the air a moment longer, a toothy salute to the hungry bear and the morose bird, then wandered off, presumably in search of its owner.

HOWLER

Donated by
Chuck McKenzie

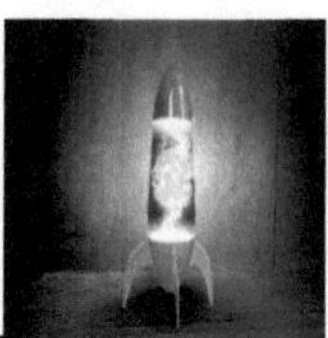

Bastards had it comin', messin' with us all these years. Finally abducted the wrong guy, sucking Ted up into their flying saucer and scooting off with him, out into space, where the moon's *always* full.

Lycanthropy's a bitch, ain't it?

Ted tells me they tasted a bit like chicken.

GARY SUMP'S HIDDEN CITY

Donated by
Aaron Polson

That guy over there, the skinny one with the big glasses and pinched nose, sitting alone at Java Stop having a tall regular, his name is Gary. He has a miniature city in his backyard. I live next door, and I've watched him from my second storey window. Gary is dull – plain yoghurt without sweetener – except for the secret city.

It started simply, just buildings made of spare wood, a couple of bricks he had lying around next to his house. Maybe he's lonely, I don't know. I never see the guy on the phone; he never goes out except for a tall regular at Java Stop. I've watched him since before his wife bailed about six months ago.

Anyway, he made roads, parks, and a lake – just like The Sims in his backyard. You remember The Sims, right? Scott used to play for hours back in the dorm, probably why he dropped out. Well, the people came later. Little critters – they look just like you and me, wearing clothing, everything. No, they aren't dolls or action figures. They move around. They live in the little buildings. They're alive.

After a while, I started watching them instead of Gary. I hooked up a camera looking out over their city so I could watch what happened when I'm at work. Eight hours of video zipped by in about twenty minutes on high speed. They work, too. The little people cook, create art, worship. They rearranged some of Gary's buildings, made one of them into a kind of church. I don't know if he ever noticed.

Gary goes to work at eight in the morning, returns at five-thirty, and turns off his television at ten. He's an accountant or something. Dullsville. On Saturdays he comes down here, has a cup of coffee and reads the paper. Not a lot of variation.

I've seen him in his bedroom, sobbing like a baby. One time I saw him look at the label on this bottle of pills – an orange one, like for prescriptions. Maybe Gary was pondering the undiscovered country.

Sometimes, in the middle of the night, he goes outside, tilts a house on its side, snatches a few of the people, and squeezes their heads until they swell and burst. Poof – little red cloud. After killing two or three this way, he slumps onto his porch steps and sobs, kind of like he did that night in his bedroom with the pills. He tosses the stained little bodies into the city. After a while, he goes inside slams the door.

They have funerals. They dig holes and plant the headless ones in a section of dirt over by Gary's begonias. Kind of creepy, really – they have this whole funeral procession thing and play sappy music. I've watched those people do everything; work, play, swim in the lake, even have sex in their little fenced-in backyards, but I only feel like a sleazebag when I watch one of the funerals.

Mostly, I feel sorry for Gary. The guy made a whole city and he still isn't happy.

ERSATZ VICTORIAN,
WITH REPRODUCTION GHOST

Donated by
Jason Colavito

Dr Reynolds Peck loved nineteenth century Victorian houses, especially the rambling Second Empire style wrecks that featured towers, mansard roofs, and rounded windows. He wished he could restore one back the way it once was, with gaslight and William Morris interiors, and special knee socks to cover the piano's legs. Unfortunately, Dr Peck lived in a rather modern town whose oldest structures were put up in the Depression. He had once hoped to move somewhere different, somewhere older, but his life's work left few options other than his continued presence in his present place. So Dr Peck did the next best thing.

Dr Peck collected old books and architectural plans, everything from nineteenth century copies of the Sears & Roebuck catalog to manuals on home decoration and design. From these sources and from measurements taken from historic homes in other, older areas of the country, Dr Peck had a slightly confused architect draw up plans for a reproduction Victorian that owed perhaps somewhat more to Charles Addams and *Psycho* than it did to the mansions of antique gentry, complete with a large and deep root cellar—for storage, Dr Peck said. The plans pleased Dr Peck inordinately, and he immediately purchased a plot in what had heretofore been a nice neighbourhood to erect his dream house.

It took almost a year to build his neo-Gothic "cottage," as he called it, and when it was done, it looked like nothing else in town. There, amidst the white-sided rows of neat postwar colonials, Dr Peck's red-brick monster squatted awkwardly. In form it was Victorian, with a central tower and two wings, arched windows beneath a sloping roof. In details, it was slightly wrong and betrayed its ersatz construction. The bricks, for one, were much too smooth and fit together too perfectly, much more so than any old-fashioned brick would. The windows, as well, were somehow wrong, perhaps fractionally shorter and wider than their nineteenth century counterparts would have been, and their plastic frames caught the light in a way older wood-framed windows never would. Even the angle of the roof seemed off somehow, as though the attic were hiding something outsiders were not meant to see.

The strangest features were within, though no one saw them until the day

Dr Peck hosted a housewarming party for family, friends, and colleagues. They came in their multitudes to view the interior of Dr Peck's folly, and their mouths gaped when they saw what he had done with the place. The hardwood floors were standard enough, but the walls and the furnishings! Dr Peck had collected antiques where he could and reproductions where he must. Horsehair sofas nestled beside Pottery Barn tables and imported Persian carpets. Stencilled wall painting imitated the look of William Morris wallpapers and chintzes, and every surface was covered with gaudy bric-a-brac of an old fashioned style, reproductions in metal, wood, plastic, and glass. But as with the outside, the details were wrong. The balustrade featured store-bought wood fittings, and the doorframes bore plastic pilasters and were crowned with plastic pressings of angels and foliage, all cunningly but not convincingly painted to resemble wood.

Quality workmanship, Dr Peck explained, was easily available to the Victorians, but was, unfortunately, both expensive and rare today. He hoped, though, that the compromises he made to his vision were as unnoticeable to his guests as they were to him, and of course they agreed politely. Dr Peck showed off the special light bulbs that gave the look, though not the warmth, of gaslight, and was absurdly proud of the way he hid his televisions behind retractable prints of old paintings in gilded plastic frames.

From somewhere high above, the guests heard a strange thumping and other, unidentifiable noises. Dr Peck smiled and explained that every Victorian home needed a good haunting, and he spared no expense to obtain the best reproduction ghost he could find. He then excused himself upstairs to correct some exercise equipment he had negligently left on.

The guests slowly departed, mumbling quietly to themselves and then more loudly once in their cars and on their way back to their white houses, beige rooms, and blinking screens. All agreed that Dr Peck was mad, for did not this monstrous eyesore prove it?

Even so, when a year later the police broke into Dr Peck's house after a lengthy investigation into irregularities at the hospital where he worked, the doctor's friends and family and colleagues were shocked at what he had done. The police found an old woman locked in the attic, in a secret room lined with ugly patterned yellow wallpaper. Dr Peck claimed, erroneously, that she was his mad aunt, or his mad wife, or both. In the vast cellar, they found corpses stolen from the hospital morgue, or pieces of them anyway. No one could quite say exactly what Dr Peck had done with these bodies. Whispers of Frankenstein and Poe passed unguarded lips, though perhaps H. H. Holmes or Jack the Ripper would have been a fairer comparison.

In his defence, Dr Peck, who came to court dressed in starched collar and cravat, would only say that he wanted his home to be authentically Victorian, or his idea of Victorian anyway. And as the years passed, Dr Peck's strange, anachronistic home sat vacant and fell into disrepair and decay. The bricks lost their bright red hue, and the windows darkened with grime. The roofline became uneven, and inside, the furniture mouldered and the woodwork warped. Time and neglect had done what Dr Peck could not, and eventually the shunned house became the subject of neighbourhood legends, alternately known as the haunted house or the witch house or both. When at last mad Dr Peck returned from some far-off asylum, he haunted a house indistinguishable from a true scion of its imagined age. It, and he, had become, finally, authentic.

BROTHER VS BROTHER

Donated by
B. Michael Radburn

This tale begins with the inscription on a gravestone at the Lexington National Cemetery in Kentucky, USA.

Here Lies Daniel Harris Johnson
Father, Husband, Brother & Soldier
1840 to 1897

In the late nineteen nineties I was compiling research for a book concerned with the American Civil War.

My own blood letting had been done in the jungles of Vietnam some thirty years earlier, as part of the Royal Australian Army. I survived my war, but not without it leaving its scars – not all of them visible.

Retired, I spent my days researching other men's wars. Men like Daniel Harris Johnson.

By the time I visited the States I needed something that would personalise and embody the meaning of that war where brother was asked to kill brother, where national unity came, ultimately, at a heavy cost.

Needing to start somewhere, I began with that name upon that gravestone, chosen at random. A humble monument found at Lexington among the leagues of other fallen Civil War veterans.

With the help of the Washington County VA Genealogist Society and the National Archives and Records Administration I found a family tree and Daniel's war records. He had enlisted into the Union Army at Washington in March 1861 at the age of twenty-one.

I discovered that Johnson had been a prolific journal writer, that he went on to take part in the battle of Bull Run, was wounded in the right leg by grapeshot from a Rebel cannon, saw out the war with his 4th brigade and retired a sergeant.

However, it was only when I gained access to Daniel Johnson's own words through his journals, that I discovered the bizarre side of his war exploits happened while Daniel walked to Washington to enlist.

After speaking with Daniel Johnson's great grandson Nathan over the phone, I was invited to his home and told that I was welcome to read his great grandfather's journals.

Within forty-eight hours I found myself at Nathan's house; eating cucumber sandwiches, drinking iced tea and reading three tattered old leather-bound journals.

Due to space restraints I have edited and abridged the pertinent journal entries.

...I think I felt homesick the very moment that I stepped out of the family farmhouse. Kissing my mother and father, I bid them farewell and asked mother not to cry. Washington was a good 68 miles away and the war perhaps a lifetime, but as with every great journey, it must begin with that first step. I was away to fight for God, Country, and the Union I believed so much in, to witness battle first hand – to 'see the elephant' as the veterans called it...

...I passed a column of Union soldiers heading south along the Erintown Turnpike. Their bodies seemed weary, yet their eyes held a hardened stare. What were they thinking? What had they seen? Those men, those brave men inspired me...

...I had not passed another house for two hours and I was prepared to sleep under the stars when, just on dusk, I came across a very old farmhouse along Andrew's Road with a thin wisp of smoke streaming from the chimney out back. An old woman and her niece lived there along with the girl's two brothers, who were nowhere to be seen. I offered the old woman a dollar to buy some supper and a place on her porch for my bedroll overnight. She agreed, and as it turned out I was invited to sit at the dinner table with them and later allowed to sleep on the old couch in the parlour...

...It was a fine meal too, but with no sign of the brothers, even though most of the table conversation was about the two boys. Zeph and Otis were their names and they shared a room downstairs in the cellar. The old woman resented the war, and I felt that a good part of her resented me too for wanting to be a part of it. As it turned out both Zeph and Otis wanted to go and fight, but the old woman simply forbid it. For, you see, and here lies a most unusual dilemma, Zeph wanted to fight for the South while Otis felt, as I do, that the North is right...

...The old woman confessed that the boys argued and fought all the time about the war. In fact she said that most nights they had their very own civil war right below in her cellar, and tonight was no exception. Around one a.m. it began. I could hear the muffled cries down there as I lay on the dusty old couch. I paid no mind until I heard the old woman come down the stairs, mumbling and cursing under her breath as she made her way to the cellar to

put an end to the fighting. It did fall silent for a moment. Then the old woman screamed...

...I had fumbled my way down towards the dim light in the cellar, just ahead of the young girl. I don't know what I was expecting, but it was not the sight that lay before me. The girl screamed too, shocking me into action and forcing me to move my terrified limbs. Zeph and Otis were brothers alright, Siamese twins in fact, horribly disfigured and joined at the hip. On one freakish head sat a crisp new Union infantryman's cap, while the other wore the grey cap of a Confederate soldier. The twin in blue brandished a broadaxe, swinging it high as the creature tried desperately to hack its own limp brother from its side. Yelling, I lunged forward and took the bloodied axe from the creature's withered hand just before it slumped down to the now scarlet stone floor. I shall never forget the words it uttered from those dying, twisted lips. "Long live the Union," it cried...

...I ran into the night, leaving bedroll and pack behind, and I don't think I stopped running until Washington... **DHJ 1862.**

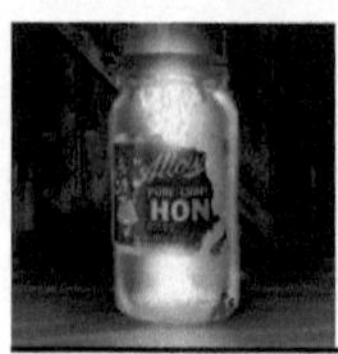

IN NOMINE PATRIS

Donated by
Martin Livings

Cassandra opened her front door, to face the man she hadn't seen in over a year. She controlled her expression with a strength far beyond her seventeen years, burying her feelings deeper, deeper.

"Cassie," the middle-aged man said. He moved forward as if to embrace her.

She stepped aside.

"Thanks for coming." Her voice was cold. The doorway led directly into a tiny kitchenette and dining room. Cassandra pulled out a chair from the old dining table, its feet squeaking on the linoleum floor, and gestured for him to sit.

"I… I was surprised to get your call," he stammered, lowering himself carefully into the chair.

"I can imagine." Cassandra kept her voice flat, emotionless. She'd planned this meeting for months. "Can I get you something to eat?"

He was slow to answer. She could see the conflict in his face; clearly he was uncomfortable to be here, but he rarely resisted the offer of food.

He'd always given in to temptation.

"Please, Dad?" She allowed a hint of warmth into her voice, inviting and false as an Indian summer. "Like old times?"

Her father looked up, meeting her eyes for the first time since arriving. He seemed so harmless sitting there at the table, smaller than she remembered him, shoulders hunched, more pathetic.

He nodded.

She turned mechanically, not thinking, retrieved four slices of bread from the bread box and dropped them into the toaster.

"The usual?" She reached up to a cupboard above the counter and pulled out a jar. Sunlight from the kitchen window filtered through its contents, coating the counter in a deep amber light.

Her father's eyes lit up. Cassandra saw the reaction, and her smile widened, became real for a moment. She opened the jar. "I remember your honey obsession, Dad," she said, pulling open a drawer and getting a knife out. "You always rabbited on about how healthy it is. Antioxidants, you said." She winked. "But I knew that was bullshit. You just liked the sweetness."

The toaster popped. She caked the four pieces of toast with the honey and arranged them on a plate. Eyeing him, she took the plate to the table and placed it in front of him.

"Go on, Dad, have some. It'll make you feel better." She held his gaze. "That's why you came, isn't it? To feel better?"

She'd expected him to look away, shameful, but he didn't. Instead, still looking her in the eye, he picked up a piece of toast and took a rebellious bite.

She sat down opposite him, then reached out and took a piece of toast for herself. She bit into it, tasting the sweetness of the honey dancing on her tongue. That and… something else.

"Do you remember my first communion?" she asked, still with toast in her mouth. "Remember explaining it to me?"

Her father blinked, looking confused. "Uh… yes, of course I do," he mumbled through his toast. "Body of Christ. To remember Him."

She nodded. "And how He died for our sins." She swallowed. "I think that's important, you know. Remembering those who died because of what we did wrong."

He stopped chewing. "Cassie, please, I don't think…"

"You know, Dad," she interrupted, "I researched my name. Apparently Cassandra was a legendary Greek princess who saw the future, but she was cursed, because no one would ever believe her."

Her father looked at her, bewildered. He didn't understand what was happening, why he was there. Not yet.

"Appropriate, hey?" She took another bite, the bitterness in her mouth increasing, starting to overwhelm the sweet. She embraced the bilious taste. "No one believed me, either. Not even Mum."

"Cassie…"

"Even when you took me to the hospital, Mama wouldn't believe it. She thought I had a secret boyfriend." Cassandra closed her eyes. "*You* believed me, though, didn't you Dad? You knew I was telling the truth."

"Please, Cassie…"

Cassandra ignored him. "I slipped the nurse some cash that day. God bless the pathetic wages that nurses get paid, otherwise she'd never have done it."

"I don't…"

She stood abruptly, startling her father. Enjoying the reaction, she turned, grabbed the jar of honey and then slammed it down in front of him.

He stared at it, bewildered.

"Did you know that honey has other uses, Dad? I researched that as well. The ancient Egyptians used honey as a preservative. Quick and easy mummification.”

His eyes narrowed, as he noticed something in the jar, something besides the honey. He leaned closer and peered into it.

“This is *your* communion, Dad. In memory of the one who died for *your* sins.”

He blinked a few times, as if he couldn’t quite make it out. But she knew exactly what it was. She’d kept it safe, all this time.

Ready for this moment.

“Eat of this, for this is my flesh, Dad. And yours. Ours.”

Realisation struck him. He pushed away from the table, yelling incoherently through his mouthful of food, moist clumps of toast and honey falling from his lips. His face blanched, sudden spasms rocking him in his chair.

Cassandra stood beside him, sidled in close, and whispered lovingly in his ear.

“You know what? I think he has your eyes.”

PIGGIES

Donated by
Martin Livings

He sits at the long mahogany table, impeccably decorated; silver cutlery is arranged carefully on either side of the eighteenth century bone china plate before him. Just beyond that is a small sauté pan set up on a portable burner. A green salad sits tossed in a Swarovski crystal bowl nearby, the servers dating to the time of Napoleon. To his right, an espresso sits in a single cup worth more than most automobiles. The scene is immaculate, perfect. He adjusts his bow tie, and rearranges the cutlery for the twentieth time in as many minutes. Then he glances at his watch. It's nearly time.

He draws his left foot up onto his other thigh, a casual pose. His feet are bare; the only lapse in etiquette he has allowed himself. He runs a finger along its sole, expecting sensation but feeling nothing. He can barely see the pinprick made by the injection. He taps the flesh a few times, softly at first, then hard. Still nothing. Good.

He reaches over and takes a sip of the coffee. It is rich and dark and bitter, like hot arterial blood. Then he places it back on its saucer, careful not to spill any, and picks up the set of medical shears beside it. They glint silver in the candlelight, shiny as a mirror, as any valuable heirloom. He flicks the catch on the handles, and they come open with a sound that makes the hairs on his neck stand on end. He smiles.

He carefully places the open shears on either side of his smallest toe. It twitches involuntarily at the touch of the razor-sharp blades, as if it knows, knows what's to come. Then he closes the blades.

The toe comes away with remarkably little effort, but a considerable amount of blood. He catches it in his free hand. It rolls there for a moment, leaking across his palm. He looks at it, detached, fascinated. Such a little thing.

He raises the toe to his face and sniffs it. He cleaned himself thoroughly beforehand, but still there is that slightly sour scent, the scent of feet, of sweat and activity. It is the feet that support us, day in, day out, doing almost all of the work in keeping us upright. This little piggy has earned its odour.

He tosses it into the frying pan, where it immediately begins to sizzle. The smell of frying pork fills the air.

Silver tongs remove the fried toe from the pan. He places it onto the plate. It is still pink, rare, the way meat should be served. The nail has raised up, away from the flesh, like a clam shell opening. Using the tongs, he pries the nail away and tosses it aside. Then he serves himself some of the green salad from the crystal bowl. The toe sits in its own juices. He finds his mouth filling, eager. Hungry.

He inserts his silver fork into the toe's fleshy pad, and with the knife he cuts it away from the bone. He is distantly aware of blood running down his leg, ruining the pants of his three thousand dollar suit. He doesn't care. He raises the tender morsel to his mouth, pauses for a moment, savours the anticipation. Then he eats it.

It is the finest meat he has ever eaten. And he has eaten in the world's best restaurants: Paris, London, New York. Nothing, nothing has even come close. Nothing ever could.

He looks down at his feet, and feels a pang of regret. Only nine left.

FISH DINNER AND THE WISHBONES

Donated by
Sam Drane

Twig twine fingers cracking and gristling along the 925 silver sax's marked keys, sixty-seven year-old Fish Dinner forgets the Deal for a moment. With the beautiful death of the last sixteen minute song, he begins to lash into a little speech before the next.

"Keep on licking your wounded lips, cats and curls, 'cause we got one more song to go…"

Laughing, hands slick with the sweat of upcoming sex and sock smuggled dope clap clap clap and no one bothers to rest blisters cause Ol' Fish's just warming up.

"This one's called The Girl Violet Was Mine."

"Was, Fish? I bet she still is, man!" Yellow teeth amongst the smoke yell from behind an empty scotch glass.

"Hawhawhaw." The crowd…

"She's still out there, whether she's mine, yours, nobody's or anybody's, that's an answer to a question I'll never know."

Liquid light runs down his arms, no more talk now. Tingling lips, he blows slight, emptying his head, and a string of satin sounds only he can make, twirl dancing hair tied by angels into the ears of all those assembled in the boozy Saturday night chapel of Crump's Lounge. The Wishbones know when to let him start alone. And he does.

They all turn into lovers. Into riverboat dreams of nothing more than sun and the boat below. Behind him, the Wishbones' worn piano, trumpet and double bass begin to fill in the rest. Of baked dinners eaten in never-ending Christmas care before they knew what the Final Sleep looked like…

After eight minutes, Fish brings them back.

One note, then another, two more then three, six, twelve, he starts to rain hot black ink on the ivory picnic blanket spread in the room, just before their fresh cheesecake dessert was to be served. The Wishbones sit slumped.

Jaws lock as the brown powder stops working, and the women stop moving their feet to turn, cold. The liquor churns. Glasses smash. Fists…

Fish, he doesn't care. 'Cause this is the same song he's been playing forever, only now he can play it perfectly. And the Wishbones, they're used to it anyway. See, he's made a Deal, yes, when he bought the painting of the

Goat from the elderly eyeless woman at the exit ramp market. The Deal? His essence in exchange for eight minutes of Violet's heartbeat in his ears once a night until his own stops.

Fish Dinner has no regrets.

FAITH

Donated by
Aaron Polson

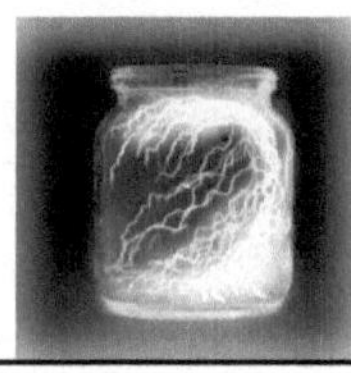

She doesn't flinch as the counterfeits in white aprons – her co-conspirators – arrange the raw seafood on her skin. Pink and white, tuna and squid, their hands drop the squares in circles, sweeping the meat in spirals over her stomach, her breasts, extending down her legs. The men's hands shake slightly, but they continue the work. She doesn't squirm even though the meat is icy on her skin.

Nyotaimori is an art, but the counterfeits have been trained. Like other expensive dishes, this one is best served cold. Five years she has waited.

Her eyes lock on the ceiling as they wheel her across a tiled hallway and through the aluminium doors. In the club room, the voices are brash, too loud, already drunk. When the cart comes to a stop, one of the men mutters something and laughter crawls up the walls. She doesn't close her eyes, but waits for the probing violation, the jabs and explorations with chopsticks as they begin to eat. Layers peel away, and her skin chills.

She becomes a puzzle broken into pieces with nothing beneath. Naked, but motionless. Hiding. These men cannot know. Her faith keeps her still.

Blood pounds inside her head, and after a few minutes she can no longer hear their voices. She remembers though – she remembers the cold eyes of these men, puppets of the regime wearing the masks of the national guard. She remembers when they took her mother – their voices locked behind stupid, empty grins. Her jaw locks as chopsticks poke and prod bare patches of flesh. Her fingers curl when one set of utensils snap tight on an uncovered nipple. There is laughter, but she doesn't hear. The men are just shapes moving in the periphery. Shadows. Memories.

Her breath comes in small, measured amounts. In and out. Calm. Even naked, lying on the stainless steel tray beneath the banquet lights, she will not break. She broke before, five years ago, after they found her mother and the others face down in the sewer ditch near the woods.

She thinks of the chefs bound with tight knots and hidden in the scullery. She knows her co-conspirators have shed their aprons and wait behind the hotel. She knows the poison cannot be absorbed through her skin, only the stomach lining of those giggling pigs, and it will work quickly and quietly. She has faith that her mother's ghost will be sated and her thirst for revenge, quenched.

ULTIMATE DETOX

Donated by
Rosaleen Love

Feel frenzied, flat out, and always on the go? Want to detox your head?

You try, last thing at night before you sink into sleep. Sort through the clutter in your head. Do-it-yourself gets you only so far. The shutters descend, and you fall into sleep. But behind the scene, the dross remains, unsorted, undealt with, and the laws of cosmic entropy ensure that, next day when you awake, the mind will emerge from slumber more disorganised than ever.

Do not despair. Help is at hand. The spirit-cleansing diet is for you.

I bring you the recipe for a spotless mind.

Filled with brilliant practical advice and good old common sense, *Speedcleansing for Your Soul* will give you a complete top-bottom detox. All you need is five minutes a day, the right tools, right method, and the right attitude.

A Useful List of Organisational Dos and Don'ts

Do a little bit each day, but often.

Sweep the entrance to the doors of perception. Cleanse the portals of the soul.

Aerobics for the mind

Thoughts spurt like water from a hose, spray nozzle firmly set. Thoughts get caught in tangles, small loops fall back on themselves, twisting, through, in and out and over. Stop it at once. Get goal-directed. Imagine hula hoops some distance off. Red hoops. Mental hoops. Narrow the jet on the nozzle. Force the flow straight.

Label those thoughts, though: 'Return to sender'. It's a must.

Forget 'Return to sender', and soon you'll notice something missing. Your friends may have to tell you, hey, you've lost your mind.

Go with the mental flow. Go, but always return.

Weight bearing exercises

Ever get the sense your thoughts are weighing you down?

Get with the strength.

Make those thoughts heavier. Weight-bearing thoughts, that's what we're after here. Heavier, heavier.

There's a large green dragon in your head, squatting, and it's breathing fire and it's cleansing out the cobwebs, and the dragon is heavy, too heavy, and it's growing bigger, and bigger, and the smoke emerging from its nostrils is grey.

Hey! It's your very own grey matter, vaporised, receding away in puffs of dragon smoke.

Quick, get it back.

Your mind is heavy, heavy, but your mind is forceful. Your mind wants what is rightfully its own, those smoky ribbons of greyish goo.

Dragons breathe smoke and fire, and dragons mean business. Destructive business.

Live dangerously, but not too much so.

The green spiky dragon tail going swish, swish, shepherding the greyish goo back, through the tip of the dragon's tail, up through its dragony gut, out its mouth and back into your head again.

Hasn't that done you a power of good?

Making inertia work for you

Think three-toed sloth. There's a sloth in your head, suspended from mental branches by four legs, and it's swinging gently from side to side.

It starts small, and grows bigger and bigger, that three-toed sloth that's found a convenient place in your head to curl up and be itself. It's getting heavy, heavy.

And sleepy with it.

You sink into lassitude, like floating in treacle.

The Freudian mind

Infested with dark thoughts?

Your id may be in need of a makeover.

The id presents the speed cleaner with a challenge. The id is that dark and steamy recess where thoughts too horrible to survive in consciousness sink and accumulate amid the grunge, there to spur each other on to even darker thoughts, all the more dangerous for being beneath the level of consciousness. Vinegar and lemon juice will never clean deeply enough. The id is the garbage dump of the mind, a bin you can never empty.

Or so you once thought. Speedcleansing has the answer for you.

What's a brain for? Take the sea squirt. When it's in larval form, it floats around in the ocean. It has a brain, sort of, at this stage, a cerebral ganglion for movement, and a visceral ganglion for digestion. But after it's floated around the ocean for a while, it settles on a rock, and there it remains, immobile, for the rest of its life. What's the point of its rudimentary brain, its cerebral ganglion? It's useless. It dissolves back into the body. You could say one brain eats the other in a kind of ultimate clean, but that would not be strictly true. It's more a kind of recycling what's no longer needed, resorbed and re-directed to more urgent ends.

So it is with the id.

You don't need all that sludge.

Resorb, or spit it out? Freud said, spit it out. Let it flow. He had his 'talking cure', his free association, his psychoanalysis.

There will come a time in your life when you will be so *over* guilt. All that excess baggage that's burned you up all those years, that burden of blame, for whatever and whenever and what for in your life, all that grunge buried deep in the id, there will come a time when you just don't care about it any more.

Settle like the sea squirt into middle age. Settle the id from a roving, burbling pool of plopping mud into a sessile existence, where mud fuses into rock and entombs the troublesome thoughts.

Go for the sea squirt solution. Petrify that id.

Speedcleansing for the future

All too retro, the household Speedcleansing tips: scrub with lemon juice and vinegar; add bicarbonate of soda. Time to leave that behind, now you're zipping towards the future.

Say there's a smart pill, to drug enhance the mind, tailor-made for your genes. Swallow mood altering neurotransmitters and hormones that will be just right for you.

Or, upload the brain to your phone. Discard the body now it's time to die, but live on, in app-land. Needs more work, this idea. You'd have to be an app on someone else's phone. Might not suit all takers.

Mix and match your options. Don't be content with the status quo.

Ultimate Detox – way to go.

THE WHITE CAR

Donated by
Kaaron Warren

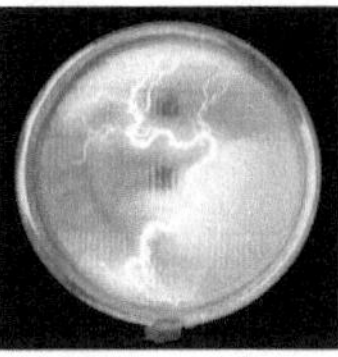

Welcome to Our Place, forum for locals near and afar
Current members: 42,000
Please login to post your comments

Topic: Anyone Want a Dumped White Hyundai?

Author: Smilie 10:02am 9 Feb, 2009
Been a white car dumped in our street for over a month now. It appeared 2 in the morning on that night when the moon was so bright the media were all over it and I couldn't get to sleep.

I heard a car driving up and peeked through the curtains, as you do. It was hot and clear and I could see steam off the bonnet. Overheated or what? No one climbed out, which I thought was weird, but I only watched for five minutes or so.

The car was still there the next morning. Half the street took our morning cuppas out there to check it out. Number plate from the other side of the country. Weights in the back, and a pack of Nutri-Grain. Some junk food. Some muscle mags.

Weird thing is this; at night there are shadows in there. Even in daylight there is movement in there. Makes me think of too many siblings elbow fighting for position.

If it's not gone soon, who should I call?

Author: NewbieKnot 2:11pm, 9 Feb, 2009
Very poetic! Anything interesting in it?

Author: Smilie 2:18pm, 9 Feb, 2009
Apart from what I said before, not much. One of those stinky hanging trees, and a couple of shoe boxes which could be interesting! We're thinking about

calling the wreckers, making some money out of it.

Author: glasshouse 10:20pm, 11 Feb, 2009
Car still there? Reminds me of the one that parked in our street when I was a kid. Had what looked like a bullet hole in the rear passenger window.

Author: Smilie 10:22pm, 11 Feb, 2009
No way! Same!

Author: glasshouse 10:38pm, 11 Feb, 2009
Weird.

Author: glasshouse 9:40pm, 19 Feb, 2009
Weird car still there?

Author: Smilie 9:45pm, 19 Feb, 2009
Nah, finally someone drove it away. Kinda forgot about it cos next door neighbour killed herself.

Author: NewbieKnot 10:02pm, 19 Feb, 2009
No way…..jeez, that's bad. Was she old?

Author: Smilie 10:45pm, 19 Feb, 2009
I dunno. 60? Husband dumped her, they reckon. Pretty sad. One of the other neighbours went to check on her and….yeah.

Author: glasshouse 11:20pm, 19 Feb, 2009
Stop fucking with us, Smilie. It's not funny.

Author: Smilie 11:22pm, 19 Feb, 2009
Why would I joke about something like that? Fuck off yourself.

Author: glasshouse 11:24pm, 19 Feb, 2009
No, wait. White Hyundai. Weights. Cereal boxes. Looks like a bullet hole in the window.

Author: Smilie 12:02am, 20 Feb, 2009
Yep. We did this.

Author: glasshouse 12:05am, 20 Feb, 2009
Suicidal neighbour. Full Moon.

Author: Smilie 12:07am, 20 Feb, 2009
Yep.

Author: glasshouse 12:15am, 20 Feb, 2009
Snap.

Author: Smilie 12:27am, 20 Feb, 2009
Serious? That's too weird. And creepy.

Author: Notfromhere 3:06am, 12 May, 2012
Sorry to crash, but Google brought me here. Same car, same shit. Except it was my sister. I still can't believe she did it.

Author: Smilie 7:45am, 12 May, 2012
Is the car gone now?

Author: Smilie 7:47am, 12 May, 2012
Notfromhere? You there?

Author: Notfromhere 12:31am, 14 May, 2012
Yeah, it's gone. Did you guys send it? Why did you send it to her?

Author: glasshouse 10:20am, 14 May, 2012
We didn't send it anywhere. Anyone sees it again, post here fast as.

Author: Countryboy 1:12am, 10 August, 2014
Is anyone there? Anyone? That car…I think it's parked outside my place.

Author: Countryboy 2:14am, 10 August, 2014
Anyone there? It's a nice looking car, youse are crazy if you think there's anything wrong with it. Glows in the moonlight.

I think the door's open.

I can't see from here.

BRB.

Author: Smilie 6:22am, 10 August, 2014
Countryboy?

Related Content

> **Stolen Cars 18 comments**
> **Car dumped in lake 12 comments**
> **Suicide next door 98 comments**
> **Cop suicide rate rises 53 comments**
> **Worst car dealership 197 comments**

ROADKILL

Donated by
yt sumner

They drive in silence.

Hers is sullen, the bitter kind that leaves a film on her teeth.

His seethes, the boil of a temper barely kept under control.

She stretches forward and turns up the music, the bass throbbing through the car, pounding the underside of their thighs.

It doesn't fill the silence.

Screeching tyres do.

She hits her head and says,

"Fuck."

He breathes hard, hunched over the steering wheel.

He doesn't say anything.

The car shudders out of life and the music stops. Just their breath continues, stinking up the small space with fear and shock.

She waits for him to ask if she's okay but instead he gets out of the car and heads for the shape lying behind them in the middle of the road.

Her head feels buried in miles of cotton wool. She can't feel her face through all these layers but she has a thought that almost sounds like a crone whispering in her ear. It slyly suggests sliding over to the driver's seat and gunning the car in reverse, of smashing his body until it's paste.

She shakes her head to rid it of the grotesque image and her nose explodes through the cotton wool. The pain tears the flimsy layers away as a piece of her spittle lands on the windscreen.

It's wet and red.

She turns and peers through the rear window to see him hunched by the pink shape. She can see the ghostly glow in the dark. Then she realises the reverse lights are red and the thing must be white.

Suddenly she is certain they've hit a bride out here on this dirt road. The dusty kind, with ridges worn in that make the car rattle like it has bones.

The white shape doesn't move as she groans out of the car.

She opens her mouth and says,

"What have you done?"

She didn't know these words would come out so muffled, or that they would taste like twisted metal.

He's crouched on his haunches, obscuring the bride. He looks like a troll about to feed and for a moment she's more than scared, she's terrified.

"Please don't eat her," she whispers and he doesn't look up.

"It's a roo."

They're the first words he has said to her in days.

He stretches up and she sees the white shape is a kangaroo. An albino. It looks like a ghost.

"Is she dead?"

The words feel cold on her lips.

"That's just like you. Making *it* a she. Giving more of a fuck over *it* than me."

His head is tilted, angled away from her as if he was speaking to the barbed wire fence.

Her hands wrap into the sides of her skirt and twist the material into bunches. She knows this tone. She looks around as if the dark paddocks on either side of the road might offer support but she does so with eyes that don't believe help is coming.

"I'll call someone."

She limps back to the car for her phone and drips blood onto the leather upholstery and she knows he'll be pissed at that. No matter how broken her nose is.

The ranger has a kind voice and he asks if she is hurt. For the first time in a long time she tells the truth.

She shuffles back to him and the dead animal.

"The ranger is coming."

He is crouched again and ignores her. She's confused at the angle because it looks like he's holding the roo's paw. As if he's being introduced to her politely.

"Why are you holding her hand?"

Then she sees the knife.

"Why did you have to fuck him?"

She knows this tone and takes a step back.

"Why do you still deny it?"

He asks again with the same formal tone without looking up, like he's asking the roo. He lifts the paw higher and runs his hand down the fur in an almost sensuous motion.

"What are you doing?"

"I've been unlucky with you and your lies for too long. I need something to break your curse."

"What do you mean?"

His knife flashes down in answer and she feels it as if struck between her shoulder blades. She watches his movement as he severs a white paw and she can't hold it in. She leans into the ditch and lets it heave, the pain racking her body in shudders. She is trapped in the dizziness and smell of vomit and blood.

He picks up his trophies and tells her to get back in the car.

She looks up at the murk of the horizon through the tall dead grass and remembers the night they met. How he spun her around in dewy grass. How he counted her freckles and named them like constellations. How he begged her to help him understand why he always hurt what he loved. And she remembers how she hugged him back and whispered into his lips she would be the one. How she'd be different from all the rest, how she would help him.

She hears him, yelling now, but the cotton wool is back and this time the layers are comforting. Her nose doesn't hurt so much. She drifts over to where the roo bleeds from stumps and she touches it's still warm flank, staining it with more red drops as they sprinkle from her nose. She wraps her arms around it and rests her head on its fur, she tries to show how sorry she is with her skin.

His voice winks out as she hears the siren of an ambulance, softly at first, then louder as he guns the engine and spits gravel and obscenities as he drives away.

"You crazy fuck!"

are the last words she hears him say, and they echo as the paramedics tell her everything's going to be fine. But it's not until the ranger arrives with his kind voice that she lets go.

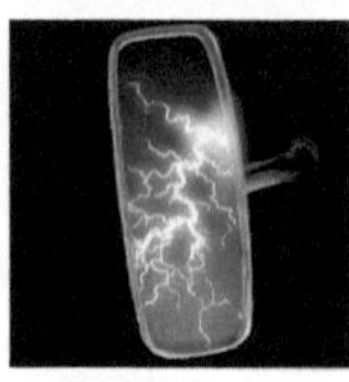

WHEN THE BITUMEN RAN OUT...

Donated by
Rob Riel

...there was nothing to be done.Suburban streets were the first to go.For a time, retirees filled potholes with broken pavers, families with children smoothed the way with contributions from backyard sandpits.But defects metastasised.Small holes swelled into wide pits; cracks became creeks, then chasms.Reduced traffic was some compensation in many areas, so long as the broader arterial roads remained healthy.But then they too started to go.Big trucks wore ruts in the popular lanes, shoulders grew towards the nature strips.Corner shops thrived again.CBDs and politicians complained, but nothing could be done.Who would risk an expensive wheel alignment, even their very tyres, save in dire need?Some towns tried gravel, selling dusty fragments of bitumen to recyclers who were paid exorbitant fees by government to patch major highways.But gravel had to be continuously renewed, and there wasn't enough to go around.Within the cities, new track was laid for trams and for trains.Factories set down their own rails to and from markets, suppliers, other factories.In the suburbs, home-owners began to mow the weeds where absent pavement gaped; soon, some planted grass, or roses.The odd square of intact concrete might be chipped into the shape of a cricket pitch, or the accidental foundation for a neighbourhood gazebo. Scattered vegetable patches appeared in culs-de-sac and dead end roads, then multiplied.Children wandered freely, helping eager gardeners in exchange for a tomato, or a dollar.Cars were trapped in useless driveways; who would drive over their neighbour's vegie garden or through a friendly soccer game to get to town?And what would they do when they got there?Most petrol stations had disappeared for lack of business.Some stores paid people to sell their wares on foot door-to-door, others took orders over the Internet and hired people with horses or carts to deliver.Without getaway cars, thieves found carrying their loot on foot too inconvenient, and sought jobs in suddenly vacant garages where a respectable living could be had repairing white goods, machining parts for tractor engines or aircraft, making shoes to order.Big shopping centres collapsed because no one had ever been allowed to live near them.When the bitumen of their vast car parks had been black marketed, the homeless moved into empty shop fronts and planted wheat, avocado trees, grapevines.Tax collectors and health inspectors refused to patrol neighbourhoods on foot.Police and doctors found that the easiest way to reach the scene of an accident or crime was by dirigible; the remains of big intersections were cleared and kept as landing pads by neighbourhood councils.Those few who still worked in big factories sometimes had to walk twenty minutes in the rain to the nearest tramline.But no one complained. The bitumen had run out, and there was really nothing to be done.

NIGHT RIDE

Donated by
Kim Goldberg

We are driving down a road at night. It is very dark. There are no street lights or house lights or tail lights. Or even any starlight overhead. Not a pinprick of photons to illuminate our journey beyond the wedge of our headlights. At least we have those, revealing a swatch of pavement dead on, occasionally crosscut by a blur of jackrabbit. Or maybe hyena. Now bounded by pairs of vitreous reflectors. And we reminisce (in voices we hope are carefree) about the practice of Mexican truck drivers hugging cliff-side highways at night with no headlights on, claiming to see better without them. And we reminisce (in those still breezy voices) about southern France, where the drivers honk and wave fists if your headlights are white and not soothingly civilized amber. And we do not think we are in Mexico or France right now. But we cannot be certain. And the streaks of fur and claw flashing across our short-stopped wedge are getting harder to identify. One looks like a treble clef, another like string theory. We calculate probabilities, flow chart causality, redouble our commitment to carefree vocal tones. We do not mention the deteriorating road—now bumpy, now dirt, now grass, now a single fading chalk line scoring blackness. We are almost there.

I WORK FOR THE STREET CLEANER

Donated by
James Davies

The worst thing about living out of doors is not lack of shelter, starvation, nor budding young psychopaths daring one another to set you alight. It is, in fact, the detachment that permeates my days. I see people pass me on their way to wherever they're going in an endless, lifeless procession, their faces contorted and their heads filled with worry. Wholly unique, First World problems. I wish I could tell them they all look the same to me, and are all riding the same downward escalator, and in the end, their lives are just an orchestra playing to an empty room.

Here is an exchange I heard between a mother and her young daughter:

"Why do they live like that, Mummy?"

"I suppose they just haven't got the guts to deal with life like the rest of us. Pathetic."

These words were spoken so scornfully that I felt I was being attacked.

People scarcely notice me, though, which is just as well, and fair enough, too. I pay them little attention in return. There are, however, some whose eyes are always attuned to a man in my position. One such is Ugly Joe, who I believe found me soon after I arrived here. I have never attempted a timeline of my life outside. After a while, it all just runs together.

Ugly Joe really isn't all that ugly, as far as I'm concerned. But then, I'm in no position to judge. He will sidle up to you at the strangest times, such as when you have your head in a public toilet bowl vomiting something rotten you ate, or perhaps when you are splayed out on a park bench in that grey area between sleep and wakefulness. He might approach you and whisper in your ear. Ugly Joe's only apparent use for people in my situation is as human sounding boards for the multifarious tales of sexual misadventure he likes to recount. I suppose he is trying to fashion himself as some kind of latter day Don Juan for a grimy city street, though I can't remember if that romantic hero's exploits involved as much rape, murder, or urination.

His stories weren't particularly interesting to me either way, and I was often barely aware of his presence beside me. This was all before he introduced me to Marcellus. Marcellus has skin that is a dull grey and his eyes are some shade of violet. Does this strike you as strange? I wasn't bothered by it.

"This is the guy I told you about," Ugly Joe said, in a voice entirely unlike the one he uses when describing his methods of coaxing young girls into his basement.

"I doubt he'll be much use to us," Marcellus said. "Doesn't look like much."

"Give him a chance," Ugly Joe said. I had to agree with Marcellus, and on both counts, actually. I was never an attractive man, and all the time spent living with nothing but the grim sky as shelter had left me with a complexion that might have been singed with low-grade acid. Furthermore, I could no longer stand up straight, and every step brought pain. You already know about my pervasive disinterest, which must have been immediately obvious to both gentlemen.

Nevertheless, they seemed certain they had found their man. They led me to an automobile with windows tinted and explained their proposition. I didn't care enough to say yes, no, or maybe. I just listened until they gave me the tools of the trade (so to speak) and sent me on my way.

This is what I am doing here now, in their secret headquarters. It has been made to look like a train station bathroom, and I may be the only person, who uses it, aware of its real purpose. In the safety of a cubicle I open an old suitcase and remove the scalps I have collected, flushing them one by one. The bodies are probably still where I left them, in alleys, under bridges, carpeting abandoned tunnels. I rarely encounter resistance when I grasp these old men by the hair in my tradesman's grip and unseam their throats. If someone had done that to me before I was given my mission, I doubt I would have minded much either.

Some of the fresher scalps have stuck together, such as two belonging to a pair of long-time homeless gentlemen I dispatched in the act of coitus behind a Chinese restaurant, only hours before I came here. I have to pull these apart, as flushing more than one scalp at once may cause a blockage in the S-bend. How, then, would Marcellus and Ugly Joe receive this evidence of my hard work?

Having read this far, you may wonder about the legitimacy of my mission, and whether or not I am indeed the right man for the job. I have had similar questions. I am without shelter myself, after all. Perhaps they will send someone after me soon. Regardless, I will leave you with this concession: at least my life out of doors is not as meaningless as it once was.

DIRTY LAUNDRY

Donated by
Eugene Gramelis

We had an agreement, Bobby Sutcliffe and I: he would die and I would get to stare into his eyes while he did it. We had been close at one time – best friends you might say. In college he had studied cheerleaders while I had studied psychiatry. Then he dropped out and I graduated. He moved to Hollywood seeking fame and fortune as an actor. I strutted around Boston trying to give Dr Phil a run for his money. Bobby ended up in rehab. I ended up in Saudi Arabia.

Then one day I heard that Bobby was in Riyadh of all places. Apparently, he had scored himself a bit part in a flick that Paramount was shooting in the desert. We met at the Kingdom Centre and sipped ice water while enjoying the view of the sprawling metropolis below.

"This one's gonna make me famous, Danny – or is it Dr Lamont now?"

I assured him that Danny was still fine.

The sweat was making his shirt stick to his skin, and he tugged at it. "This goddamn heat," he said. "I could really use a beer."

"It's against the law to drink alcohol in this neck of the woods," I reminded him. A long, round bag lay on the floor at Bobby's feet. "What's that?"

"Dirty laundry," Bobby said. "Know where I can get it washed?"

"Ask your agent," I said. "Make him earn his commission."

He laughed, and we clinked glasses. He asked me what I was doing so far from home these days. I told him how I'd been granted government funding to carry out research.

"Which government?" he asked. "Ours or theirs?"

"Both," I said. "One supplies the money, the other the subjects."

"What kind of research?"

"You don't want to know."

He smiled. "Try me."

"Have you heard of 'Lucid Decapitation'?"

"No, but it sounds painful."

"It's a study into whether consciousness persists after a person's head has been cut off."

Bobby's smile vanished and his face paled.

I clarified: "I'm here because this country is one of the few that still carry out public beheadings."

Bobby looked at me for quite a while like I was some kind of circus freak, then his smile returned and he asked if I had any spooky encounters to share. Not really, I confessed, but we continued to chat about old times until the skyline darkened then we called it quits for the evening and promised to meet up again the following night for dinner.

We never got the chance.

Bobby was stopped by Saudi police on the way back to his hotel; they found much more than dirty laundry in that sack of his: nestled among his boxer shorts and slacks was a block of heroin the size of a house brick.

I visited him frequently in prison. Twice his mom flew down from the States to see him. The rest of the time I was the closest thing he had to family in that God-forsaken place. He claimed to be innocent; I believed him. We spoke about the past and about life in general and eventually, as one-by-one he exhausted his avenues of appeal – including a plea for clemency by the President himself, our conversations turned to the subject of death. That's how we struck our bargain. At the point of decapitation, if he was still conscious, Bobby would give me a sign by blinking repeatedly. And in return, I would give him the fame that he so desperately craved.

I was sure that this time the experiment would be a success. The others had been strangers to me – blank faces with no names, people with whom I shared no cultural or emotional connections. Bobby was different: he was not only an American, he was my friend.

When the day of his beheading arrived, I watched with a lump in my throat as Bobby was led barefoot and shackled to the town square. He was made to kneel in his white robe in front of a plastic sheet, his hands cuffed behind his back, facing Mecca. Barricades held back the journalists and curious onlookers. When the officials had finished announcing Bobby's name and crime to the crowd, the executioner moved in and hovered above Bobby with a long, gleaming scimitar. He poked Bobby in the back with its tip.

I knew what came next.

Bobby raised his head involuntarily at the unfamiliar jab.

The scimitar arched above the executioner's shoulders, caught the sun's rays, and became a slit of light.

Bobby's head rolled onto the plastic sheet.

I rushed over and picked it up. "Bobby!"

His eyelids flickered sporadically, but I could not be sure if the head was blinking or just reacting to its severed nerve endings. Then all at once the face seemed to relax and the eyelids half closed, leaving only the whites of his eyes and the lower part of his brown pupils exposed. The corner of one lip twitched then went slack. I could feel Bobby's warm blood running down my forearms.

"Bobby," I called again, loud and commanding.

The eyes flew open; they stared back at me with such ferocity and intensity that I almost dropped the ghastly thing. And I knew then that as Bobby teetered in that vaporous fog between this life and the next he was able to look deeply into my soul and expose the sacrifice that I had made to science: I had planted that block of heroin in his bag.

Now, as I stand on the rooftop of the Hancock Tower, the evening breeze in my face, gazing out at Boston harbour and shuffling ever closer to the edge, I can hear him. He's waiting; angry at my betrayal, shrieking in the shadows of my mind, yearning for revenge. Maybe tonight I will let him have it: he and I have dirty laundry to air; it's time to find out for myself what lies in wait on the other side.

HEAD

Donated by
Mark McAuliffe

I hit the ground rolling, came to a stop a few feet away from the corpse. I was facing up. I looked to the left and saw the headless body, my body, spitting thick jets of blood out of its severed neck. The big man stood above it with his axe on his shoulder and his leg up on the dented chopping block. He was looking at me and grinning. The small man stood behind him, almost hidden by his friend.

"He's the one I want," said the big man.

"That's a big head," said the small man. "It could give us big returns."

"I don't care," said Big. "I want him."

He walked over to me and grabbed a fistful of my hair. He held me up only inches in front of his face. I opened my eyes as wide as I could, blinked a few times. My lips trembled as I tried to voice a scream.

"I still can't get over the way their faces twitch after they've been chopped," he said. "Damn creepy."

"It's the oxygen still in the brain, I think," said Small. "Don't let it bother you. It'll stop soon enough."

"I don't suppose you'll give me some time to…"

"Aw c'mon, don't start that again! I told you before we gotta get the body in the mound right away. We can't get sloppy."

"Yeah, I know," Big sighed. "Later guy," he said to me.

"We'll put him with the others while you dig the hole. It's closer than the house."

"But he'll attract the flies! I don't want him to spoil."

"He won't spoil if you're quick to dig that hole."

They walked deeper into the woods, weaving their way through the trees, until they stopped in front of five roughly-hewn trunks. On four of them sat rotting heads. Mouths, nostrils and eye sockets were stuffed with maggots. A cloud of flies swarmed around the small clearing. All four heads, as far as I could tell, were male, and in different stages of decomposition.

Big put me down on the vacant trunk.

"Let's go," said Small. "The sooner it's done…"

They disappeared from my line of sight. I sat there for several minutes, listening to the hum of the flies. I could smell the faint scent of the forest through the terrific stench. I could see the other heads if I rolled my eyes. I began to think about how much of a fool I was, but then decided not to be so hard on myself. How was I to know they'd be a couple of psychos when I stopped to ask for directions? I then began to wonder how I could still be alive. Did this happen to every severed head or only a select few? If so, why? Was I special, a wonder of science or religion? How long would I last like this? Is there a Heaven? Am I going to Hell?

The flies came to interrupt my ruminations. They crawled on my face, got up my nose. A few got into my ears and tickled me there, but not enough to make me laugh. I didn't have a neck to shake them away. I wanted to blow at the ones around my lips but found I didn't have the breath for it. I poked at them with my tongue but they just crawled into my mouth and caused me more trouble.

Soon enough my executioner and his little friend were back. Big picked me up by the hair again. I was carried back through the forest to their house – a little shack at the end of a narrow dirt road. A cardboard sign, written in felt pen, was tacked to a leaning, rotted fence post out front:

FISHERMEN! GET YOUR BAIT HERE!
THE BEST WORMS AND MAGGOTS IN THE STATE!
CATCH A BIG ONE EVERY TIME!

Big plonked me down on a dining table cluttered with junk.

"Get to work," he said to Small. "Make it good. Make it quick."

Small produced a woman's make-up case from somewhere. Inside were some battery-operated clippers, as well as the sort of stuff you'd expect to see. He worked fast. He shaved my hair down to stubble, plucked my eyebrows, tarted up my mouth with lipstick, applied blush to my cheeks–

"Not too much," Big cautioned.

–painted my eyelids, gave me false lashes. I didn't move a muscle during the whole procedure. It was tempting to try a bite at Small's fingers whenever they got too close to my mouth, but I didn't think I'd be quick enough.

"What colour this time?" Small asked.

"Blondes have more fun."

The wig was long. Small held it up and ran a comb through it a few times before he tried it on me. That was the final touch. No one bothered to show me a mirror so I could see how I looked.

"Did well," Big said.

"Don't I always?"

Big unzipped his fly and got his dick out. A couple of strokes got it hard. He walked towards me.

"I wish the mouth still worked," he said. "Reckon I'd enjoy that."

He pushed his member past my lips, over my teeth. I could taste it on my tongue. I felt it tickle my tonsils.

I bit down. Hard.

HEAD

Donated by
Matthew Chrulew

Hi, how's it going? I'm a detached, semi-functioning head, artificially arrested post-decapitation but pre-decay (Human of course). You may know me from such urban legends as 'there's a psychopath loose, your boyfriend hasn't returned from getting petrol, and there's a banging on top of the car, but whatever you do, don't look back'. But that's not the story I'm here to tell today. Today I wanna tell you about something that happened to me recently.

But first, a couple of points:

(1) This isn't fantasy or whatever else. And I'm not a metaphorical head, though I do get around. I'm drip-on-your-boots real.

(2) There's no secret or profound symbolic undercurrent to this. It's just a story. That's what human heads do, tell stories, and detached heads are best for telling stories on the more… uncomfortable side.

So anyway here goes:

I was between a coupla gigs when it happened. I'd waited around in a box for hours just to appear all gross-like when the dumb bastard finally opened it, and so I was a bit stiff around the ears, and what was left of my neck was sore from cramps. But I had to get to the next job – I forget which, some cavern or jar or shelf or other story. And so off I was going when *Whooshka!* something just came out of nowhere and belted me sideways and into the pavement. I bounced twice, slicking thick blood into the unlucky cracks before I came to rest, reeling, and looked up.

It was a foot, a hairy, gangrenous, ingrown-toenailed foot. It had tripped me, kicked me, and was now hopping there as I righted myself. And then behind it gathered a host of other body parts. My attacker was joined by a torso, a pair of arms, a couple of knees, and various other oddments that presumably had joined the rest in their heyday.

There was an uncanny familiarity to all these phantom limbs. Like I knew them from somewhere, these pieces of flesh that hopped and rolled and dragged towards me. I swallowed, and the saliva splatted out of my oesophagus onto the footpath. There was barely a sound except for the scrape of skin and concrete, the rub of opened flesh.

And then I had it. They were mine! My old pals from my original bodily assemblage. The resemblance was still there, despite the decay and necrosis.

But the stench! If only olfaction wasn't part of the old 'head' deal, or I had some fingers to pinch my nostrils against that invasive reek of exposed rotting meat.

But this was no time to wish for a body, or muse on the irony. I'd sacrificed such physical aids for my freedom, and no way was I letting these dumb slabs have their homecoming.

I waited, but what were they going to do, speak to me? That was exactly the problem! It was quite clear what they wanted. Since I'd liberated them from our bonds, given them their individuality, they were mute. Stupid. Uncoordinated. Hopeless.

And so they needed me. Their leader. But they were a prison.

They advanced in dribs and drabs, and I backed up, sweat now running through my wispy hair. I looked around for an escape route, and realised that they'd failed (again) to surround me, that they came at me in a disorganised clump. I might just make it. And so I darted, dodging a swiping, arthritic-knuckled hand, and twisted, avoiding the flatulent slam of a stained butt-cheek. Fortunately the lack of a head had also severely hampered their ability to coordinate, and I managed to get away before the flabby stomach lurched into position.

So anyway, that was what happened to me just now. Happens all the time really. Horrific, I know. (I do get away each time. Though each time, they do come back.) And that's what I'm here to tell you about. To take you through your fear.

"My fear?" you might say. "But that's your fear. You are the head – the detached (though very real) storytelling head – who is afraid of being subsumed again by your body."

You might say that.

"My fear?" you might say. "I don't know that fear. I'm not such a head. I'm not threatened by a multitude of limbs and lumps."

You might say that, too.

But that would be because you're still under the impression that the 'I' and 'you' you've constructed here are actually distinct. That right now you are an autonomous human being, and not a decapitated storytelling head.

Go on, keep telling yourself that you aren't me. Pretend you're not in this story to get away from your body. This story about how you can never get away from your body.

This story like all stories.

But when this story stops, and you go back… When, I should say, you read the last word and you're *forced, sucked, jolted* back, taken over again by your filthy sticky body, just like what happens to me on the pavement – then you might change your tune.

The story has to end.

(*At least I get to leave.*)

BRAIN IN A VAT

Donated by
Peter Dawncy

There was once a man who was indifferent to the creaturely aspects of life – the taste of bacon in the morning, the warm northerly breeze that brushed his face as he stepped out the door or the colours that painted the sky at the beginning or ending of the day. Things were just there, and the man cared for none of it.

There was one thing, however, that the man did care for, and that was thinking. The man loved to think. Not about anything in particular, just about things, anything that struck his fancy, and he could sit for hours on end to think about them. Indeed the man wanted to go somewhere where all he needed to do was sit and think – and not even sit either, he didn't care for sitting. Somewhere where he could just think. A place where all these sentiencies, all these flavours and prickles and vibrations, would just leave him alone. And no one scorned the man for just wanting to think, because thinkers were needed, and indeed many considered the man quite noble.

So the man found an innovative group of scientists and asked them if they would take his brain out and put it into a vat, and the scientists agreed. They got the man's brain out of his head and placed it into a black box full of water and then attached a bunch of tubes to the man's brain to keep things working.

At first the man's brain thought it was wonderful, and was pleased to think it was wonderful because it just loved thinking, and so it thought things were wonderful all over again. No food nor drink nor seeing and hearing things, nor talking nor listening to people – the man's brain simply thought, just as the man had planned and imagined. His consciousness was like a tiny wasp zipping through an endless jungle of thoughts. And the man was comforted knowing that this was how things would be for the rest of his days – indeed simply the rest of thinking, because the man didn't know when it was day or night or when a day had passed, he only knew the notion of day, and so his time was measured only in thinking.

But there was one thing the man had not considered in all of his thinking, for while his brain was in the vat the man dreamed, and in his dreams he could see and feel things again and it was just the same as it had been before, and because the man's brain had no eyes to open to know when it was awake and no mouth to yawn with when it was tired, it didn't know the difference between waking and sleeping, and then suddenly everything seemed like one big dream.

So the man screamed, and then he screamed louder because he could scream, and then he screamed louder because he could scream louder. Eventually he found a group of scientists willing to put his brain in a vat.

DREAM A LITTLE DREAM

Donated by
Emma Kathryn

Say "Nighty-Night" and Kiss Me...

She's there when I open my eyes. All seven foot two of her, perched on the edge of my bed.

"Hey," she says to me, cool and casual, with a smile hiding in the corner of her mouth. Slowly, I push myself up onto my pillow; sitting, staring at her.

"Hey," I reply with a strange, safe feeling ebbing over me. The blinds are open and some glow from outside illuminates her face. Skin the palest I've ever seen is slipped over her bones, like milk spilt on satin. Everything else is in darkness.

"You don't mind, do you?" she asks, gesturing to something in her hand. I hadn't even realised she was smoking. It isn't a cigarette, more like a stick of ivory light. And it's not smoke that slides over her violet lips; it's that mist that you see, sliding over the grass in the dead of night. The air that brings the morning dew.

For a little while, I watch her as she smokes. And, for a little while, she lets me.

Her hair is deep purple, almost black yet at the same time definitely not black. While the irises of her eyes are the slightest shade of lavender, caught between stark white orbs and dense black pupils. They look like contact lenses.

"I don't mean to be rude," she eventually says, inhaling from her moonbeam. It doesn't seem to be burning down at all. Like a never-ending cigarette. "But I had to come see you."

"Who are you?" I ask, feeling a chill in the room. God, she's tall.

"I've had many names," she replies, with a frostbitten smile.

"What do I call you?" I can't see her dress very well. Not in this light. At least, I think it's a dress.

"For tonight?" the pale woman asks, her silhouette against the backdrop of my window. I nod. "Diana's good." Her grin rips her face into something terrifying yet alluring. She looks like something out of a Fifties science fiction movie. It feels as if she should be in black and white, here to warn me of impending doom.

"Now I need to talk to you," she continues, not moving an inch, well, except to smoke. "I'd like a favour." No ash falls from her cigarette. It sparks and glints every now and then, but no ash.

"What is it?" My head imagines at least twenty favours she could want. At least fifteen of them are sexual.

"I want you to dream of me." I did not imagine that one.

"Excuse me?" I enquire, noticing that whatever she was smoking has disappeared.

"People used to dream about me all the time," she sighs. "Some even used to pray to me. I'm not asking for a prayer…just a dream," the Diana-woman says, now kneeling in front of me. I didn't even see her move. She just appeared there.

"You want me to dream about you?" I ask, uncomfortable with her closeness, yet aroused at the same time.

"No, I *need* you to dream about me." Leaning even closer to me, I can smell her. She smells like the early hours of the morning, before the sun has opened her eyes. "I don't want to die. I want to live, and in dreams I can live."

"But I can't…" A finger seals my lips.

"You can. I need you to. Don't let me slip away. You *won't* let me go." Again, I don't see her move, but now her mouth is on mine, kissing me gently. I close my eyes to enjoy her. Her lips are so cold.

She's gone when I open my eyes.

Birds singing in the sycamore tree…

BECKWITH: A NIGHTMARE

Donated by
Adam Walter

The cold had finally eaten its way through my wool coat. Out on the frozen cobblestone streets, I hadn't seen another soul for the longest time. Perhaps now was the dinner hour in the village. It did seem to be getting on toward evening.

A moment later I realised my mistake. This sky would not turn truly dark for another month yet. It had been a decade since I last visited here, since I last came home to the North. Still, how could I forget!

I stepped into an alley and urinated beside a clump of blue grass. Before I finished I noticed two skinny dogs creeping forward from the alley's far end. I backed out to the street, but they followed. I made my way cautiously up the block. When they were no more than ten yards from me, I found the lighted entrance of a pub and went in, not looking away from the dogs until the door separated us.

The pub was everything I wanted – warm, quiet, nearly empty. The bartender, a bald man with tiny knob-like ears, had poured me a second whiskey before I recognised the place.

"Of course," I said. "Isn't this where Beckwith used to come?"

A lopsided grin spread between the knobby ears.

"Beckwith," I continued. "What a man. What a titan of bombast and lunatic ideas – fairy tales! I remember. Nearly every night they'd pack in here to listen, and he never disappointed us. Especially not – not those of us in the inner circle. *Hell* . . . Beckwith!"

He poured yet another whiskey.

"Did you know him?" I said. "Did you ever see him here with that, that congregation? The fraud. The wonderful mad fraud."

"I know the gentleman well."

"You don't mean that he's here again? He returned?"

The man nodded stiffly.

"Does he come often?"

Another nod.

With my glass filled again, I looked outside. The dogs were still there, standing as if fixed in place.

Almost before I knew it, I'd taken off my coat and sunk into a booth.

Between drinks I dozed, head in hands. Eventually, without intending to, I fell fully asleep.

When I woke, it was to thick fingers nudging my temple. The pub had gone cold, and dark but for two lights near the door.

"*Up* now."

I stood, shrugged into my coat.

"He's ready to see you."

"What? Not Beckwith?"

The man nodded, then said: "He asked that I mention an old promise between you two, a kind of pledge. You understand?"

Immediately the fog in my head cleared. I stammered: "He won't . . . He isn't still–"

"I can't possibly speak to that. Now, though, there is one consideration to address. That is to say, the dogs you brought here."

"The dogs?"

"Yes."

And there they were, standing not five feet from the table, dry tongues hanging from their mouths. As they watched me, one whimpered and the other anxiously tattooed the floor with its front paws. Both exuded appetite and finality. And their eyes were like those of beaten children.

MOON SHOT

Donated by
Douglas Thompson

All that glitters is not gold, the glimmering Moon is silver. On the bus into town, she winks through her fluttering veils of clouds and I wonder what she wants from me. The conductor weaves up and down the aisle, requesting compensation from everyone, lest his mate the driver takes a notion to crash and kill us. And everyone opens their pockets and offers up their little sovereigns: see the yellow light weep and play over their battered surfaces; little mirrors of moonbeams, tokens of lunar life, lunacy.

Out on the streets again, Moon runs her winds through my hair as if to make me look at her, her cold stare a spotlight that follows me through empty streets, makes the city a stage where nothing dares to happen. Silver cars hurtle by at the street ends, fabulously smooth and sleek. And their blurred owners are astronauts of sorts: they seek what Moon seems to offer. They steal and borrow and accumulate and melt and beat it all down into the silver armour that reflects and deflects and focuses: light and stares.

Out on the streets, the beggar selling soiled newspapers calls out to me, and for once I stop and walk up to him and face down his stare. I look into his eyes until he cowers. He weeps and says he wants Moon, he needs her, he cries every hour for any fragment of her. And from my pockets I take three pieces of Moon and place them into his palm; they are old and battered and I have carried them with me a very long time, but I tell him I want him to have them now. He sobs and his face cracks into gratitude and Moon dances there for a second in his eyes again, reflected from our currency, our exchange.

Everybody wants Moon, everyone shouts out for her. Even the closed shops have countless signs plastered over each other, in ever more elaborate colours and fonts (I see her reflected in their distorting glass as I pass). They all offer tricks to buy Moon, lay traps for her, for us, but she never comes. Sometimes I think it is only me she really wants.

Where the streets run into the darkened park, a woman of the night calls out to me, says she wants to "do me half price". She puts her hand on my waist and reaches in my pockets for where I keep my pieces of Moon, says she wants some. Kneeling in the bushes, she tries to suck the moonlight out of me; like stealing my shadow, my neon silhouette flickers like a faulty street lamp until I crumple over and she spits the moonlight into the gutter. See it glow and twist there for a moment, white like a skull and crossbones, face-grimacing in pleasure or pain, before it slides sideways down the drain to be swallowed by this indifferent city.

Back on the streets, some cars and buses sigh, a train groans in a tunnel and I look up again at Moon to see if she is jealous, but she is veiled once more in clouds. What does Moon want?

Moon is the symbol whose meaning nobody can remember, the memory nobody can ever recover. Even dogs howl at her like an owner or a hunter whose motive they can't quite sniff out. Moon is the ancient clue that the Earth is round and only one of a trillion lonely and Godless orbs adrift in this blackness. Moon is the fear that there will be other worlds with other children to meet us, who may not like us or be like us. Moon is the cold eye that watches us: glowing with the knowledge that all worlds will become as barren as her, that everything is transient. Moon is the end of flesh and the door of dreams, the soul's first threshold.

She is worth more than gold, and you *can* take her with you when you go.

THE ESCAPIST

Donated by
Mark Delaney

George lay on his back, the springs of his old mattress poking at him from beneath the scruffy material. He was awake, couldn't sleep, never could, and so he counted the small, plastic, phosphorescent stars that his mother had stuck to his ceiling with Blu-Tack that was older than him. The wind blew itself hoarse outside; it did little to calm his afeared heart, he was terrified about what it would blow into his path.

One. He began counting at the far right corner of the room. *Two, three.* He worked his way around the room clockwise, a ritual he'd repeated every Friday night since he could remember. *Four, five.* He could get round the room several times before it happened, counting all forty of the stars, one at a time to the very last before starting again. But, tonight he was interrupted before he could even count to six, the smallest but brightest star of the microcosmic solar system and his favourite of the tiny glowing shapes.

The discernible sound of a key in the door exploded into the atmosphere and was quickly swallowed again by the ravenous silence. George's ears were attuned to recognise the grinding sound of metal as the key forced back the pins of the locking mechanism. It terrified him. His stomach was gnawed and mangled by the fear as he heard the key turn slowly in the door, its contortion nearly made him heave.

The door swung open, and in with a sweep of bitter wind came an abhorrent beast. It stumbled into the house ungracefully, slamming the door behind It with a powerful shove. It reeked of whisky, Its drink of choice, a drink that sustained Its existence. The monster came every now and then, in the night, always when his father was away. It bore a striking resemblance to Charlie; his father, identical in every way but Its eyes. Charlie's eyes were enveloped in sadness, wrought with an age beyond his own and wizened by exhaustion. *Its* eyes were devoid of life. However, those lifeless eyes bled tears just like Charlie's.

It began tramping its way up the stairs. George could hear It approaching, the volume of Its heavy breaths increasing as it neared. Outside his door, he heard his mother's voice, the voice of an angel. Ethereal, even when she was screaming. George knew she could do little to delay It so he dived into the tiny, black cavern beneath his bed. Lying on his stomach, he glared at the light that trimmed the contours of the door and the two dark silhouetted feet that broke the circuit. With each panic stricken breath the space under the bed closed in around him.

The door edged open, slowly, creaking threateningly as it did. George clamped his eyelids together, forcing two small tears to make tracks down either side of his face. He began to shiver with desperation, his head shaking involuntarily. He tried with all of his might, with every fibre of his being, to escape the nightmare world that he was in, and slowly he began to slip into the cavernous realm of his imagination.

His breathing started to become less laboured as the bed that pinned him to the ground climbed into the vast blue sky that had replaced the starry ceiling. Long green grass sprouted from the cracks in the floorboards and the walls were carried away on the breakers of a warm breeze. Trees, a hundred years old, grew in seconds and tiny birds began to fly amongst the sparse clouds. George felt the warm sun caress his face and he opened his eyes. Before him stood his mother, a tall woman with cascading black hair, tears in her icy blue eyes. There was a familiar smile adorning her heartbreaking face. She was tragically beautiful.

"Hi," they said to one another, sharing an equally perceptive gaze. George was safe.

Meanwhile, the creature stepped into the room that had never really disappeared, panting, rubbing the knuckles of Its bruised paw. It glanced momentarily at the strewn sheets of the empty bed and bent down to look into George's favourite hiding place. Blinking tears away from Its disquieting eyes, It stared under the bed in disbelief; for George was not there.

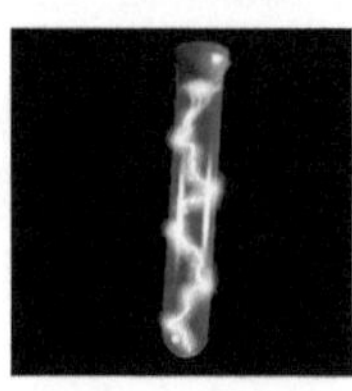

DREAM MAKER

Donated by
Mari Mitchell

Amy sits in the dark, alone. Her eyes can just make out the room. Purple flowers bloom on the wall, dolls watch as they sit on shelves, while she clings to her velveteen cat, Patches. Both tucked neatly into a princess bed. She shuts her violet eyes and does not dream.

Slowly the door opens emitting a soft light. A man walks in and sits upon her bed. He whispers, "Amy, I've something for you." In his hands is a pink box. He opens it; a ballerina pirouettes to 'When You Wish Upon a Star'. He places it on the nightstand.

Two large hands caress waves of raven hair. With care, he brushes away a lock that lays across her cheek and lovingly kisses her. He breathes in her fragrance: sugar cookies and daisies. Amy's small hands grip the covers. Her chest tightens and fills with cold. In her heart she prays.

"What a special girl you are," he says as a hand snakes under the barrier of blankets. "I love you so much," excitement laces his words. The other hand lifts the layers of safety away.

Amy's small body fights, but is no match for his enormous strength. She closes her eyes tight and focuses on the song that trickles from the box. She pictures the plastic ballerina, so pretty. She too lives in a dark box. What does she dream when the music stops?

Her petite body continues absorbing pain, filling her with fear that threatens to overflow. She wishes she could change places with the dolls on the shelf that watch her and do nothing. So many eyes hollow and void of love.

When he satisfies his desire, Amy's skin begins to show the bruises. Blood trickles from where he was inside.

He wipes away some of the tears and gives her a smile. "Shh, it's all over princess. Soon this will only be a dream."

As he shuts the door, the room once again becomes dark. She rises and walks quickly to her closet. Once inside she shuts the door, curls up holding herself tight, wishing, singing a song her mother sang so long ago. Before the lullaby ends, Amy falls into a deep sleep.

Amy's visitor walks back into another room where a man waits behind a desk. The man smiles and bids the visitor to take a seat as he reviews the images of what has transpired only moments ago. "Satisfied?" he asks knowingly.

Amy's visitor nods uneasily, knowing that the stranger in front of him has shared an intimate moment, the moments that make up dreams and desires.

The man at the desk speaks, "There is no need for you to be apprehensive. You were born with a drive. No matter what happened before, it's not your fault. So relax. *So*, relax. *You* are among friends here, more so than throughout the whole system."

The visitor relaxes.

"If you're pleased as you appear here," he indicates to the vid, as the visitor tightens again, "then we can begin to fill your needs. I told you, that you would never be able to tell the difference. In almost every way imaginable they are the same; except for one." He brings up a hologram of an order form. "Six years old, female, long black hair, violet eyes, fears heightened, aggression mild."

The visitor interrupts, "And you're sure, each time will be like the first time?"

"As long as you activate the wipe.

"And for a small charge you can have maintenance done and we can make any *modifications* you may want.

"You did express an interest in joining our club and you agreed to share vids *but* you don't want to share anything else. Well, that may change," he says teasingly.

"I do not think so," Amy's visitor says with a touch of distaste.

"That's fine too. Now, should you want to take her on outings, remember to keep your ID with you." A card pops out from a slit. "Of course you'll probably never need it, but there are still some unenlightened who may question and this will take care of any . . . *trouble*."

He nods and places the card in his wallet.

"She should be ready in a couple of hours. Most of our members like to wait in the main room. We've a full array of food and drink, served to you by even more of our items. Who knows, you might see something else you would like to *sample*."

"All I want is my little girl again."

"And you will have her, for as long as you like. She'll be your little girl. If you want, you could wait in a private room?"

"I'd prefer that."

"Fine." He touches a screen and a boy of no more than twelve comes into the room. "Please show our guest to room 201."

The closet wall opens to a bright room. A man dressed in a white medical uniform reaches in and picks up the girl. She stirs for only a moment, whimpering. She is laid on a table where her nightgown is quickly cut away. Another man readies a hose and pauses. "Shouldn't you activate the D. R. E. A. M. mode?"

"Nah, this one's a trooper. I think deep down she likes it," he states light-heartedly as he places a finger into her vagina. "She'll need repairs too." Her body tightens as his finger penetrates her.

"Come on, just flip the switch."

He makes a frown but gives in. "They're grown for just that purpose you know. Like cattle, or those personal computers they use your DNA for."

Her body fills with what feels like starlight and she drifts someplace far away.

Water rushes over her naked body. She floats. A quick, rough wash follows another rush of water as her mother sings.

Hot air blows. A warm sunny day, her toes squish in the sand.

Legs pull apart. Flashes of recollection appear.

Something rips away; "Man, aren't these organics lifelike?" A new vagina is grafted into place. Deep within her, she calls for mother, who is nowhere to be found.

Inside her delicate skin the simulated blood that pooled into bruises fades. She feels unwanted, hated hands on her; in her.

One of the men checks the chart and enters data for her next try-out request. A blush of pink appears in her cheeks. Her lips plump to a pout. A new name and history are uploaded as her mother sings. The voice changes, and the words but not the feeling. Black hair is replaced with tight ringlets of strawberry blonde and a baby-doll dress is slipped on. A cart wheels her back to her dark room.

EXCHANGE

Donated by
Rob Parry

Carolyn:
"There's been something that I've wanted to tell you for a long time. A really long time now."

Adam:
"There's been something that I've been wanting to tell you for a while now."

Carolyn:
"I have feelings."

Adam:
"I have desires."

Carolyn:
"I have longings."

Adam:
"I have urges."

Carolyn:
"I have this deep and sure knowledge that we were meant to be."

Adam:
"I have a compulsion to kill, a fascination for blood."

Carolyn:
"And yet no knowledge of what we are meant to be, no words to tell you."

Adam:
"I've known for a long time that I am a monster."

Carolyn:
"I invite you to my house, and I play nonchalant."

Adam:
"I come to your home, and my facial muscles do not betray my visions."

Carolyn:
"But the thing is, I hold myself steady by an act of will."

Adam:
"Only my clenched fists, and the crescents left by my nails give me away."

Carolyn:
"Sometimes I think that you know, and that your silence is just misplaced kindness."

Adam:
"I see knives, I see wires, I see velocity and crushed bones."

Carolyn:
"Other times, I think, maybe you are just sweetly obtuse enough not to have recognised my feelings or even your own."

Adam:
"It is not just you, please understand this. I see you as an image in a découpage of pulp horror, of meat, of collective massacre."

Carolyn:
"And I know again, we were meant to be."

Adam:
"Sometimes you have years to live, sometimes you have seconds."

Carolyn:
"I hope I'm not scaring you."

Adam:
"I'm glad this doesn't frighten you."

Carolyn:
"I control my nervous impulses when you are around, and when you leave they escape in a long, strangled sigh."

Adam:
"I have your death planned down to the last twitch of your hand."

Carolyn:
"I know you have been hurt before."

Adam:
"I have killed."

Carolyn:
"But I can promise I will never intentionally hurt you. Never."

Adam:
"And I will kill men and women again. I like their screams. The look in their eyes when they know."

Carolyn:
"I play you music and hope that it will make you fall in love with me; because I am here, and when there is a certain kind of music you have no choice but to love whatever is breathing next to you. Sometimes I even light candles."

Adam:
"I tried to tell you before today, in my own impossibly subtle ways. I smiled in the dark when we watched gore movies, I killed the spiders in your home, I liquefied your brother's knuckles with a hammer, and let him think for whole moments that I was going to let it end there. He believed long enough to reach the doorway."

Carolyn:
"You accept these things as innocent, because I am a woman."

Adam:
"You accept these things as natural, because I am a man."

Carolyn:

"I'm asking you now, Adam, it will be enough to know this. Do you understand what I have been saying to you?"

Adam:

"Carolyn, I will kill you by driving the softest part of your skull over and over onto the corner of the table in your lounge."

Carolyn:

"Adam, I love you."

Adam:

"Very well, Carolyn. I love you too."

THE REAL REASON WHY
JAY IS A VEGETARIAN

Donated by
Blanket Barrowclough

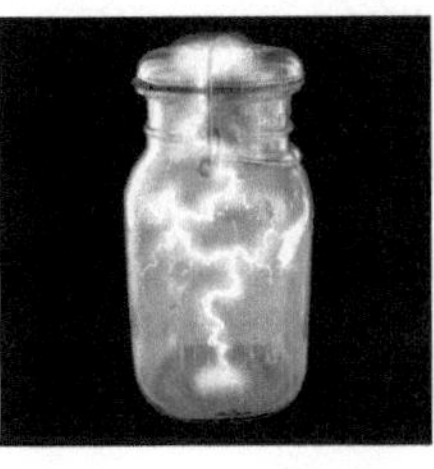

"I'm sick of this story."

"He seems to enjoy telling it. So you've heard it before?"

"It's not bad for one of his dinner party anecdotes, but it's not true."

"Who makes up eating a cat?"

"Well the cat part might be true, I don't know, but his punchline is it's the reason he's a vegetarian, and that part's complete bullshit."

"He's not a vegetarian? If I'd known what the lamb was gonna be like I would have used that too."

"He's a vegetarian, but not because he cares about what gets eaten in Asia. Jay didn't give up meat voluntarily."

"Allergies aren't as cool as they used to be, I guess. Does that make him a hypocrite do you think?"

"It wasn't allergies. Did you know we went to college together?"

"Wow, I didn't know you guys went that far back. Lol, I didn't mean – well I didn't mean it was ages or anything."

"Who says 'lol'?"

"So what's the real reason he's a vegetarian?"

"Ever wondered how he got those scars?"

"I guess you've seen more of him than I have."

"Maybe they're not as obvious as they used to be. He had to have work done. Anyway, back when we were in college he loved meat. He was one of those guys who could never get enough bacon, and I swear he ate hamburger patties every day. I couldn't stand watching him eat. He told me his grandfather taught him to chew everything a hundred times, and maybe that's the reason why he had this gross way of being completely absorbed in chewing. He'd look at a steak on a plate and slowly say the word 'mastication'. Really, if he hadn't become a vegetarian we would never have stayed friends. Anyhow, at some point he must have gotten nerve damage, although I think it was a chicken and the egg thing, because I think the nerve damage happened after he kept biting himself. I think he just loved the texture of meat so much that he'd get carried away with enjoying chewing it and he couldn't distinguish between his own flesh and the flesh he was eating. No doctor could stop him from repeatedly eating away the insides of his cheeks. The real reason why he's a vegetarian is because it was the only way to stop him from eating the sides of his face from the inside out."

"Shh, he's looking at us."

PSYCHOSIS?

Donated by
R.H. Reese

"Doctor, do you have time to see a new patient who says it's an emergency?" asked the receptionist for Dr Asad Kahn, a New York City psychoanalyst.

"Well, it's late and I was about to head home, but I guess I have a few minutes to spare, send him in."

"Doctor, my name's Goldsmith, and I need help."

"Well, I don't usually take patients without an appointment, but if it's an emergency..."

Goldsmith sat down and began to speak in a trembling voice, "A friend of mine..."

"A friend of yours?" interrupted the analyst.

"Yes, a friend of mine was hearing voices, terrible voices. For years, every hour of every day, he heard voices screaming obscenities and telling him to kill – himself and others."

"Did he have any other symptoms?" the analyst asked.

"Yeah, there was something else. He once told me that, sometimes, while driving at night, he could see out of the corner of his eye a 'thing' running alongside his car."

"That's a problem, a real problem, psychosis with auditory and visual hallucinations. Did he use drugs or alcohol?"

"No, he was scared of making things worse."

"Was he under stress?"

"Sure, but..."

"Would you say that he was a creative type?"

"Yes, but..."

"Depressed?"

"Of course, but I'm not here for him," said Goldsmith while wiping the sweat from his brow.

"I don't understand, I thought it was your friend with the problem."

"I wish that were true, but let me go on. About a week ago, I stopped over at his house and heard an argument inside.

"He answered the door and let me in. After what I had heard, I was sure surprised to find him all alone.

"But then the shouting started again, and he started arguing with those voices of his.”

“Like I said, he needs help. He’s psychotic, quite possibly schizophrenic. And that won’t just go away; it’s a result of increased dopamine activity in the mesolimbic pathway of the brain. But antipsychotic medication can reduce this activity.”

“Shut up and listen to me, ’cause here’s where it gets crazy – *I* heard those voices too!”

“That’s interesting,” the analyst replied coolly.

“Then, after a few minutes of shouting, I noticed something: I was only hearing those voices in my *right* ear where I was wearing my new hearing aid!”

He emphasised his point by tossing the hearing aid onto the analyst’s desk.

“Go on, I’m listening,” said the analyst.

“I’m saying that my hearing aid picked up those ‘auditory hallucinations’ that my ‘schizophrenic’ friend was hearing.”

“Is that what you think?”

“Yes. But about a week ago he disappeared, into thin air, and now those voices are following *me* around – day and night I hear screaming voices. I’ve even seen that ‘thing’ pacing my car on the highway. I can’t stand it anymore, I’m going fuckin’ nuts.”

“Why don’t you stop using the hearing aid?”

“I have, and that worked for a while, but only a while. Now I’m hearing those voices without it – all the time. I can hear them right now; they’re yelling at me to kill you. Fuckin’ nice, huh?”

“Whew!” said the analyst. “I think you need some help. I could get you into a hospital tonight if you want.”

“You idiot! Don’t you understand? Those voices are real! That hearing aid somehow tuned me into them. They’re real!”

“Of course you *think* they’re real, that’s part of the problem. You’ve convinced yourself of the reality of those voices rather than admit that you’re ill; and, to you, they’ve become real.

“You’re not necessarily schizophrenic. Any number of things could cause these symptoms: brain damage, tumours, sleep deprivation, bipolar disorder, or focal epileptic disorders.

“Bullshit.”

“Then how do *you* explain it?” asked the analyst.

“I have a theory that we’re bombarded by so many sources of sensory stimulus, that if we could perceive it all, we’d go crazy.

“I’ve wondered what it would be like if we could see the entire electromagnetic spectrum instead of just that tiny portion of visible light. What if we could hear every sound from spinning atoms on up? What if we could feel the turning of the earth? What if we could smell sunlight? We couldn't function.

"So our brain acts as a filter, a filter that blocks out all this 'noise' to prevent our senses from being overloaded.

"For some reason, some people, like my friend, lose this ability to filter out what's not supposed to be heard.

"And then someone on the 'other side' realises that they can finally be heard and out of frustration, or jealousy, or whatever, torments them day and night.

"People who hear voices aren't crazy, they just hear what we filter out."

"Sounds crazy," said the analyst.

"If you have a better theory let me know; that's why I'm here. I can't stand this shit any more."

The analyst swivelled around and looked out the window at the city night-lights surrounding Central Park. After several minutes he turned back, but his new patient was gone.

Puzzled, he walked out and asked his receptionist if she had seen him leave.

"Nobody left," she said.

He walked back into his office and saw the hearing aid on his desk. Without thinking, he picked it up and nonchalantly pushed it into his ear. He instantly recognised Goldsmith's panicked voice:

That thing...that thing I saw...there're thousands of them here...they've got me...don't listen to them or they'll get you too...don't listen...don't listen.....

MY OCTAGON RAGE

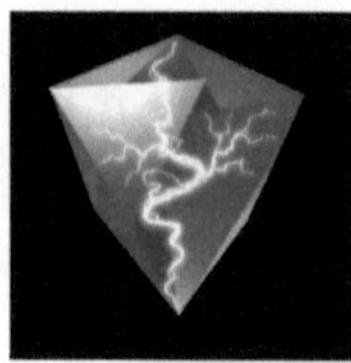

Donated by
J.G. Poulos

I am Mohamed Omar Brumley. Most everybody calls me 'Mo'. I shunt cargo aboard an Expeditionary Deep Orbit Platform out near the Algols. A recent and inexplicable aversion to commas brings me to my present predicament.

I first noticed something odd while returning to my cabin last evening. I live mid-decks in a good area half way up the hull where I have a clear view of the forward cargo bay with loading docks close by. I finished work late, deciding to drop by the commissary for a pack of licorice. I opened the packet when I got home to find some odd pieces. They normally look like full stops, but some looked strangely like commas.

I hate commas.

There seemed some hesitancy when I awoke this morning. I brushed this off as a manifestation of my extra workload as I looked out across the bay where the surface was so glassy smooth you could see beyond the warp layers. Through the currents, the outer planets of Algol glistened like striped candies spinning across a dark cloth.

Today was my day off. Deep Orbit Guides had already cleared the field of Random Aberrations in preparation for a voyage. I knew the teams were cradled, safe, and sound, but vague shapes loomed at the edges of the flux-field.

Their presence seemed ominous.

For some reason I decided I would suit up and go by work. Loadmaster suits are robust with plenty of reserve. I was determined not to hesitate. I left without securing my cabin and hurried along the walkway. I did not stop or pause and kept my eye out for any sign of commas as I headed to the docks where I would normally supervise movements.

Vessels started in from the outer hull as soon as the barrier doors opened. Loading craft created wakes that cross-matted the surface. Warps from spindle-tugs chopped up the entry field all the way out to the booms like waves on a rolling tide.

I breathed easily in the O2 as my suit jogged me across the Loading Master's Bridge.

There seemed to be a lot of confused noise as I passed. Klaxons echoed with sirens in time with flashing lights.

An image interfaced across the bay surface as if on a giant screen. I watched *Lady Northumberland* voyage in on a routine vector. Its image appeared beneath the warp-layers as through a smeary window. I moved quickly, watching the *'Lady N'* hesitate in transition.

He who hesitates is lost.

Commas are a hesitation.

I will not be lost.

A speeding postal van accelerated into its field. The *'Lady N'* tripped over it, splitting amidships. Atmosphere spilled into the void. Oxygen swirled in a maelstrom stirred with ice. Cargo-hands and deck-men clamped in working-suits, spilled, glittering like new stars. Caught in the flow of the Translation they went spinning away like tops on a breeze, instantly washed by its great tides beyond the edges of the universe. Flight crew spilled, bursting like ripe fruit inside less robust attire unable to cope with infinite currents, consigned to nether realms by the particles of God. Pieces of the *'Lady'* continued to tumble along to converge at my loading station.

I then noticed the postal van and I travelling along common paths. My way led to the Captain's Bridge while the van stayed in transition. I saw it pass by. I noticed it was a British van. I saw the maker's badge. It was a Commer. I wondered how a British postal van happened to trip the *Lady Northumberland*.

I moved unsteadily on a mission that now seemed vital. My journey halted at the escape tubes. I realised that I would have to pause until a capsule became available. I did not want to pause and turned for the walkways.

I will not hesitate and I will not be lost. I am going to wipe them all out. Commas will die.

I arrived at my station and saw it was strangely deserted. There seemed no sign of life.

How could a postal van do so much damage?

I reasoned then that the postal van merely represented an apostrophe. An apostrophe looks like a comma. I am going to go after them all. Apostrophes have an attitude. They sit all the way up there, high and mighty because they can join words together. Lofty and arrogant, commas with altitude I call them. They mean nothing to me, them no good apostrophes.

I stopped. All this talk made my head spin.

The normally reassuring voice of my suit's oxygen gauge screamed, 'Oh-two-low'.

Maybe that is why my head was spinning. I cranked in a little more oxygen and saw a small tear on one knee that I had not noticed before. I check-sealed my suit and was still a little groggy until it repaired.

My head cleared and I briefly wondered why my suit hadn't compensated automatically. No matter, I suddenly realised that it was not apostrophes at all. I was merely using apostrophes as metaphors.

I was getting somewhere with this now.

I remember it all, not commas or apostrophes that tore *Lady Northumberland* in two.

It was metaphors.

My gauge is screaming, I think I need a little more oxygen.

It was meteors.

A meteor hit the *'Lady N'*, wrecking my loading station. I secured all the hatches and raced along the companion-way for the lifeboats. I was too late; the last capsules had gone. The tubes did not function. There was nothing salvageable.

Meteors tripped the *'Lady N'*, meteors, commas, and postal vans.

Metaphors hit the old woman walking across the road.

There's another tear in my suit.

'Oh-two-low'.

I've had a big day, I'll mend you in the morning.

'Oh-two-low'.

Just let me sleep.

'Oh-two-oh.'

Oh-two-oh, you are not making sense.

'Oh-two-oh.'

I heard you the worst rhyme.

'Oh-two-oh.'

You are not baking hence my octagon rage...

LOGIC LOOP

Donated by
Steven Paulsen

…Click!

"Good luck, Professor," the assistant said.

"Thank you, Cuthbert. If my computerised time machine is a success, the entire world will learn of my genius. First, I programme it to take us, say thirty seconds, into the past, then I flick this – "

Click!

"Good luck, Professor," the assistant said…

CARGO

Donated by
Rick Kennett

Out beyond the blue star clusters of Pegasus we found her – an alien ship, vast and unresponsive. In her belly were the crew of the *Mary Celeste*, the pilots of Flight 19, the passengers of a dozen missing planes, packaged and museum-ready. Five Avenger dive-bombers all in a row, the freighter *Cotopaxi*, the collier *Cyclops*, loomed out of the dark of a massive hold, cocooned in spun webs of plastic. Somebody's *interesting specimens*.

But of the aliens themselves, the samplers from space, we could find no trace. Only vacant rooms and half-eaten meals rotting on tables flanked with empty chairs.

BLAME GAMES

Donated by
Gitte Christensen

Tamazil MacDonald hurried through the tunnel, pushing through the milling pedestrians. Blood dripped from a cut on one cheek. His tender heart, so recently shredded by treachery, thumped raggedly in his chest, and his swollen eyes stared downwards until he was forced to raise them for a security scan.

The door opened and Tamazil stepped through. Relief, however, was momentary – his mother stood waiting in the family room.

"How could you do this to us?" cried Reana.

"It's not my fault," whined Tamazil.

"We drilled civic hygiene into you, we taught you the Canon of Polite Distrust. You should have known better!"

"Yandi is my best friend," wailed Tamazil.

"That boy used your neediness to remove us from social competition and further his family's survivability." Reana paced the length of the room, five steps one way, five steps back. "I've already been barred from thirty-eight percent of my bondsites, and your father can't access any of the commerce links. If we're completely ostracised, we'll be unemployable!"

Tamazil cringed, his mother's grown up fears finally penetrating his own youthful agony.

Reana's angry posture slumped. "We'll be evicted, we'll have to beg in the corridors and scavenge like rats." Tamazil's mother choked on the future, then sank onto the couch and began to weep.

The boy fled to his precious kidpod. He stared through the window at the oak trees standing stalwartly on a distant hill beneath a blue and white sky, but the scene did not soothe him today. Would he lose all his privileges – his bed, his privacy, his view – because of Yandi? Would he become a warren creeper and end up in a tubetown humpy?

Why did I bring Yandi here? agonised Tamazil.

To show off my kidpod, of course, he guiltily confessed.

Recreating the scene of the crime, Tamazil flicked on his connectsite. He remembered how he'd blithely gone to fetch snacks and left Yandi alone to link up with the other players for a game of Zombie Holocaust. And now, an old record stolen from the isolated depths of the MacDonald family vault had appeared on the official Stoning Site ...

Tamazil flinched, recalling the very real rocks thrown at him by the kids at school.

He looked at the image on the screen. It showed his recently deceased Nana Deb as a much younger woman standing beside a vehicle. She was smiling. *Smiling!* Even though she harboured the worst of all the ancient deathnauts, a spewing utility model that would have churned up the countryside and used an entire warren's worth of resources in a single outing.

Tamazil looked up and whispered to the window, "True view."

The oak trees and sunshine vanished. From his home high in the warren tower, Tamazil now saw roiling fumes hovering over a decrepit cityscape, the scene cut and scarred by countless deserted streets.

"All of this is *not* my Nana Deb's fault, it's *not*," he hissed.

But the denial did nothing to ease Tamazil's true pain.

His best friend had betrayed him, and nothing could ever change that.

COLOUR GUARD

Donated by
Harper Hull

Max stared into the large, sunken playroom and envisioned the perfect battlefield. He brushed fingers across the liquid screen of his monitor and watched through the wall-sized window as green fields and small villages sprung up across the playroom floor, orchards and manors appearing in the distance. There were cows grazing in the fields and crows flying, oblivious to the two giant teenage boys suddenly controlling their little existences.

Darius nodded his head in approval.

"Waterloo, nice. I get to place first."

Max watched, nervously, as Darius worked his own monitor. Suddenly in the playroom there was a smoky flash and an entire army materialised alongside a roadway. The uniform was instantly recognisable. The game's sultry female voice recited facts about the chosen army.

'The Confederate Army of the Potomac, at the first Battle of Bull Run on July 21st, 1861. Artillery, cavalry and infantry. 18,000 men.'

Max watched the tiny soldiers in the playroom with wonder, using his screen to zoom in close and get a detailed look. As usual, their shock amused him. This always happened at first. He could only imagine what it must be like for your entire world to suddenly change on you. Officers were riding up and down the lines trying to keep calm. Darius was laughing beside him, and Max began to choose his own army.

Across the fields and over a sunken road opposite the massed Confederacy, Max plotted the point for his own forces. They appeared in a foggy haze, and Darius gasped as the game voice introduced his enemy.

'The Zulu Army deployed at the Battle of Isandlwana, January 22nd, 1879. Infantry, 20,000 men.'

Max grinned at his friend.

"How d'you like that?"

Darius laughed.

"Not a chance in Hell."

The boys watched as the Zulu went through their own panic; the black masses turned to their leaders in shock and were instantly calmed by the stillness of their warrior generals. Off across the fields and roads of Belgium the Confederate Army had spotted the huge Zulu force and their shock and confusion had been taken over by fighting instinct. Cannon were being moved into position, cavalry assembled on the flanks and the infantry formed into firing lines. A General with a spyglass was barking out instructions to his officers who in turn rode the lines to their various brigades. Darius smiled at Max and drew a thumb across his own throat.

The Zulu didn't react to the Confederates until the cannon balls hit them. Men died by the dozen. The Zulu leaders quickly formed the army into the traditional bull's horn formation; they streamed forward, attempting to cut the distance between them as quickly as possible. The iron tips of the assegai glinted in the European sun, the cowhide shields a rippling white flash. Confederate artillery continued to rain down on the Zulus, but their numbers were great and the colour-specked black tide raged on, the flanks moving out and around trying to encircle the enemy. Quickly the Confederates were within range of the Zulu, and the feathered warriors launched their spears into the blue sky where they hung at the crest of their arc for a moment, defying gravity, before plunging down into the swathe of grey, swooping bolts of death that pinned men into the earth through head and chest. The Zulus showed their shorter ixwa blades and, beating a tattoo on their shields, shouted their chants towards the Confederates, stomping their feet.

Max raised his arms and laughed as he watched his army have an impact on Darius and his grey men.

In the playroom the Confederates were shocked by the primitive attack but regrouped quickly. The Zulu flanks were an obvious threat and the Generals sent their cavalry thundering out to meet them on either side. The infantry quick-marched up the middle and formed lines once they were within range. An order was given and lines of smoke puffed up along the Confederate front. The Zulus fell in bloody waves. They charged the Americans, shrieking, all iron and skin. The well-trained riflemen of the Confederate Army kept shooting, reloading, one line after another, and the Zulus kept dropping. On the flanks the cavalry launched themselves into the horns of the Zulu bull, swords meeting stabbing spears at full tilt. It was carnage.

Darius looked over at Max and stuck up a middle finger.

"You want to immerse?"

Max watched the bloody battle raging and nodded.

"Let's go in."

Both boys pulled the Immersion Helmets onto their heads and swept fingertips across their game screens. Leaning back they closed their eyes and seconds later found themselves in the middle of the carnage. Max was near the front of the Zulu lines, sprinting forward, and looked down to see his thick black arm clutching a short spear.

Darius found himself looking down a rifle at the black enemy. He pulled the trigger and watched a Zulu fall. He reached up, rubbed the bristly beard that covered half his face and let out a whoop.

Max reached the Confederate lines and screamed, raised his weapon. He felt the dark shadows of fallen empires sweep across his eyes and the bloody foundations of new ones quaking beneath his feet. The future of a continent twitched along the wood of his spear as he plunged it down. Before he could strike a bayonet sliced up into his throat and he fell forward, gurgling blood, as the words "Die you nigger bastard!" slithered into his ears.

Max came to back in his chair and zoomed in on the dead body he had just inhabited via the game screen. The bearded soldier who had struck him down waved his bloody bayonet with a big grin on his face. It was Darius. Max stepped over to the other gaming chair and quickly disconnected the Helmet on the head of his friend. He turned off the game, watched the playroom go dark, and went off to make a sandwich, shaking his head sadly.

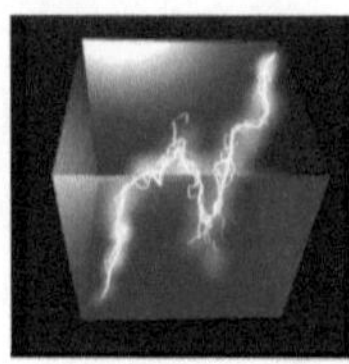

THINK ABOUT ME

Donated by
Kev Webb

Wandima mouths the words 'Think about me' as she fades away. A bullet screams through the air where her mouth had been, tearing it apart with supersonic speed. If she had still been there, then her face would not be.

I got her out in time, Hirashe thinks, as the battle continues around him. He wonders where she goes to when she disappears like that and realises that he's never actually thought about it before. It's always been one of those things he's just accepted and never given a second thought to until now. He knows she can't exist without him. What if he were to die right now? He starts to panic as reality settles in. Not only would he never see her again but neither would anyone else.

All around him are the dead and dying. Protectors who are fiercely loyal surround him. They have to be loyal. One bullet – one stray bullet – and it's over. If he dies they all die.

Hirashe is one of many thought provokers in this reality, and he is trying to protect it from other thought provokers. In many ways they are just like him, but unlike him they are full of greed and lust. As long as he's alive they cannot take his reality. He can replace the dead and dying, but it's not as simple as just thinking about a name or a face; they actually have to have a life before they can live. Before they can breathe in this existence there must be a reason for them to exist. This takes time. Hirashe can't rush. If he does they will be flawed, or worse: they will fail to manifest. With each death his realm shrinks, while the reality of the other thought provokers grows, and eventually it could completely engulf this reality as though it had never existed. For this reason it is imperative that Hirashe keeps this reality populated.

Now it's time for some quick thinking. He has been losing ground and his realm is now half its normal size.

Hirashe ponders some more. What does it take to truly kill a thought? Is it just one bullet, or is it just another thought? How many thoughts have been lost and ended up in the hands of my enemies? What truly happens to them when I don't think about them anymore? Are there only so many thoughts to go around?

He has always taken his status as a thought provoker for granted, but now with the enemy at the gates he has to think deeper than he ever has before. His mind swirls and labours under the weight of his enormous thoughts. This is the hardest his brain has ever had to work, and as it works it starts to expand until he is reaching into areas previously untapped and unexplored. He wonders why has it taken the near collapse of this reality for him to discover that there was a lot more in his brain than he ever realised.

For some reason he is able to process creation information much quicker than he ever has before. All around him new people are appearing and taking solid shape, and as soon as they emerge they are instantly into the fray because they are forming with weapons in hand. The soldiers now appearing are more focused, forceful and fierce than any he has produced in the past. They literally hit the ground running. They charge the front line without a single thought for their own protection, caring only for the safety of their designer and maker: Hirashe the thought provoker. It's not just their attitude that's different; their weapons also seem to have taken a quantum leap in their development. Even the landscape is changing; becoming more advantageous for the defending army; rising and moving, creating an undulating landscape that makes it much harder for the opposing force.

Everyone has become used to small changes happening around them, but these changes are significant and extraordinary in their manifestations.

Hirashe notices that his army is not taking as many casualties as it was and realises it's because they're fading out when they're not actually pulling the trigger of their weapons. The bullets are passing right through them until the moment they fire their own weapons; only at that point do they become tangible entities. And as soon as they release the trigger they fade back out again, making it almost impossible for the enemy to target them. They are only vulnerable in that instant when they pull the trigger.

The tables have been turned. The ground that had been lost is now being reclaimed and a wave of euphoria ripples through the troops on the front line. Everything is now to their advantage.

One bullet, one stray bullet, hits the mark. It sears the flesh and smashes the bone. It shatters the forehead and parts the brain down the middle, severing all the connections that are responsible for life, before it exits the rear of the skull in a bright red explosion. Life can no longer be possible. Before Hirashe's body hits the ground, this reality blinks out of existence. Gone is the landscape, gone are the people, gone forever is that world, and it will never be seen or thought of again.

There is no noise. Everything is silent. A light pierces the darkness as Hirashe opens his eyes and looks around the room. Then he feels it: the soft, gentle caress of fingers running through his hair.

"Where am I?" he asks hesitantly.
"You're with me," is the soothing response.
"Wandima? Is that really you?"
"Yes, it really is me."
"How did I get here?"
"I thought about you."

LONG HAUL

Donated by
Kev Webb

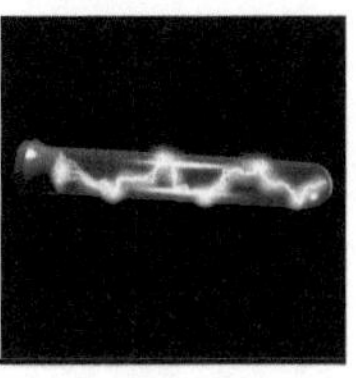

We haul liquid diamonds from the gas giants in our solar system. It sounds glamorous, but living it is a different story. It's tough waking up after each long sleep and remembering how far we are from home.

Every time I look at my watch I wonder what she's doing now. I think about her, lying there in that king-sized bed. On more than one occasion she has sent me pictures via the ship's mail system. In the shots, all I can see is one long, beautiful leg stretched out and resting on the bedclothes. How many times have I run my rough calloused hands over that leg? I always feel as though I'm touching one of the things in life I know I shouldn't, even though I'm allowed to. With the touch come the soft croons and the softer touch of her lips on my ear as she whispers for me to be bolder with my caresses. Nothing has ever been this beautiful, or sensual.

My heart jumps as a spike of adrenaline rips into it with sudden impact; the touch of her fingertips forces me to catch my breath. My body quivers with anticipation as, in my mind, her breath caresses the nape of my neck. I don't want these thoughts to ever end. The simple joy of a soft touch … Just the suggestion of tasting the forbidden fruit is enough. I don't have to actually bite into it to taste the nectar; I taste it every time I close my eyes and think of her. It leaves its bitter sweetness on my lips; it leaves it there for me to taste and to savour.

Why do I deserve this wanton desire? Why is it directed at me? Why does she look at me in a way that no one ever has before? The kiss — the soft touch of her lips against mine, the heightened excitement of us both as our body heat rises in time with the urgency of our kisses. She's got me again.

I can't resist her; I want to be a part of her. I want to feel the silky velvet of her passion as she rises to meet me. The excitement in her low sighing moan weaves its magic as we work together to become one. I feel my heart hammering in my chest as she wraps her arms around me and pulls herself even closer. Her eyes close as she softly bites her bottom lip.

Excitement surges from her as a rapturous exaltation of breath; her eyes open, dilated pupils constrict as the light forces them to pinholes. She smiles as desire turns to shameless lust. It's time – time to put it into overdrive, time to please her.

Oh God when will this end? When will I be able to go home to some semblance of normality?

They told us the technology was here to help. They assured us it was safe. Everything will be fine, they told us. Numerous studies into the effects of extended periods of hyper sleep dictated that a program had to be devised for the mental well-being and stability of the crew. Our minds needed constant stimulation or they would shut down. The company had lost dozens of employees over the years to hyper sleep sickness. They incorporated the program into the hyper sleep mode to keep us stimulated and to ensure that none of the crew went crazy from loneliness. Even though our bodies are in hyper sleep, our minds are still active.

The more cynical crew members believe it's a company conspiracy designed to keep us in the job, and come to think of it, in the five years I've been doing this run no one has quit.

Empathic neurons … artificial empathic neurons that connect directly to our brains. Because the artificial neurons are empathic, they adjust completely to our genetic make-up. They are locked to our code and are completely sympathetic to our personalities, meaning that each person that is subjected to it gets the companion to match his or her needs and wants.

That's all well and good, but where does that leave us all now? We can't live without it. None of the other crew – not one! – has a family to go home to.

Through their studies, the company found out that sexual stimulation is the best way to keep the brain in perfect working order. Each crew member is asked to pick a virtual partner when he or she signs up.

Virtual … **Interactive** … **Extension of** … **Empathic** … **Neurons.**
VIXEN.

The virtual partners may look different but they are all the same, just ones and zeros creating the same pleasing algorithm to soothe us all. They said Vixen would be our saviour, but instead it's our captor and we're willing prisoners of its whims. They never told us about the addiction.

We all took this job because of the big money on offer, and Vixen, well, that was a bonus. It was comforting at first to have someone there for the long journey; we spend almost two years – ninety-nine percent of our time – in hyper sleep. So, like lambs to the slaughter we go into our 'coffins' for extended periods of slumber. We can't wait to have our neurons pumped full of Vixen. The point is, if we go we lose the thing that has become most precious to us all. Vixen is always there, always eager to please. Vixen never says no to anything.

Will I ever be free to think of anyone else?

I wonder what she's doing now.

AQUA VITA

Donated by
Stephanie Campisi

When the doctors dragged Madeleine out of the red smile that curved across her mum's stomach, Jimmy thought she looked like an astronaut, or a diver in one of those huge suits in the movies he watched on Saturday afternoons with his dad. A nurse cleaned away the gunk, and Jimmy peered at his reflection in the glass bowl. Madeleine's mouth was wide open, flashing pink gums, and the inside of the bowl fogged up.

Madeleine slept in a cot in the corner of Jimmy's room, beneath a mobile of sea creatures that bobbed and whirled with the breeze of the lazy ceiling fan. Jimmy would watch at night as his sister reached her tiny hands up towards the whorled tail of a wooden sea horse, the spiny explosion of a plastic puffer-fish. The moonlight trickled through the blinds and made the room look like the ocean.

Bathtime was a glorious, splashy affair that stretched on through the evening. Madeleine would lie placidly at the bottom of the tub, her arms and legs starfishing rhythmically in the foam-frilled bath before she surfaced, spraying the room with a halo of water. She would shape her mouth into an O and stare goggle-eyed at him before bursting into squeals of silent laughter. The bowl clattered against the sand-coloured porcelain.

At the pool, people stared, offering their sympathies, or specialists' business cards pulled from the depths of their bags, minty from forgotten wads of chewing gum, edges splayed and furry like seaweed. Madeleine was the only baby in her class who could open her eyes underwater.

Jimmy's mum and dad decided to renovate the house, to turn it from a sea of hallways and cave-like rooms into something vast and open-plan. Jimmy sat in his mum's lap and squinted at the architect's spiky sketch, which was drooly in places where murky drops of coffee had landed. The walls were all going to become windows, and the thick dark doors would be replaced with etched glass.

One night, something rapped loudly against the new glass wall. Jimmy slid out of his bed, and the blood roared in his ears like waves crashing against age-worn rocks. Madeleine was balanced against one of the tall masts that secured her cot to its rocker, clutching at the edge of her blanket.

They made fish noises at each other.

When the renovation was complete, Jimmy's grandma came to visit. They could hear the purring of the water taxi long before it arrived.

Her coral-coloured lipstick wore away as she kissed her family's cheeks through the glass.

Later, she sat outside beneath the sun umbrella and crossed her scaly, barnacled legs, which were rivered with blue veins. Her earrings were dark pearls that pinched against her earlobes and glinted as she primly sipped her tea.

The clusters of onlookers kept a respectful distance. The cameras they clutched had lenses that shimmered like pearls, and the photos they took would be speckled with tiny grains of grit.

The tide of night slowly rose, skirting blackly around the house's glistening shell. Jimmy clambered on to the craggy arm of the couch, angling between his parents, and stared through the lounge room wall. It reflected him in a way that distorted his limbs, stretching and softening them so that they appeared jointless.

His grandma swept towards them, clutching her cup of tea. She had a loose-legged way of walking, as though her legs flowed through something thick and supportive. Madeleine followed, gently lolling her arms in quiet imitation.

The dark wave of night slipped over them with a sigh, drawing them beneath its wet, inky curtain.

In the morning, all that remained was the sandy socket where the house had carved a slim footprint in the earth. It began to rain, and the crowd unfurled umbrellas like anemones and stared with glassy eyes.

AFTER THE SHOW

Donated by
Robert Long

He was asleep when the show finished. Later, he woke to hear cars pulling away outside his window, and the sound of unhurried feet and muted voices outside his dressing room door. He dusted some breadcrumbs and salad leaves from his lap. Feeling idle, he tinkered a while at his piano, forming a few phrases that seemed to fit together nicely. When he played the tune over it seemed familiar, and he became sure it was not original. The pleasure went out of playing and he stopped.

At first it was obscure, but the persistence of the whispering made him sure he wasn't deceiving himself: there was someone – more than one – waiting outside his dressing room door. He was going to stand up and open it, but a firm banging on the door saved him the trouble.

"It's open," he called.

He had never seen either of the two individuals before. The man was short and seemed at great pains to stand straight, so he seemed taller; he was elderly without being frail, elegantly if incongruously dressed in an evening suit. Keeping a step behind him was a blank-looking boy, maybe fifteen or sixteen, in a blue shirt and trousers.

"Excuse me," his elder visitor said, "are you Enzo? We were told you would be here."

"Yes. I am Enzo of Enzo's Circus."

The man smiled. "I enjoyed your show. My boy equally."

Enzo nodded with what he hoped was a plausible degree of gratitude. There was an uncomfortable pause as he waited for the real reason they were here. Work. They must have an act.

"We have an act," the man said, and Enzo inwardly cringed. Nevertheless, he smiled and walked out with them when invited to do so. You never know. The boy ran ahead, out into the dusty arena. Enzo noticed that he and his presumable father had the same strange, slightly staccato step. The sight of the empty seats made Enzo afraid, as it always did. No recollection of how full it had been earlier, how much people had laughed and gasped, how much money they had parted with, could wipe the terror away.

In the open, the boy started to sing. The song sounded sweet and old-fashioned, French words Enzo didn't understand rising higher and higher until the boy's voice cracked and failed at a crucial moment, the song drifting out of his range.

"He can't do it," the man said sadly at Enzo's side. "The same notes that always escaped me. What a thing to have to hear." He clapped his hands together so sharply Enzo jumped, and the boy stopped singing and ran over to them. "I hope you don't mind, I set up before coming to see you."

Enzo hadn't noticed the six-feet long black box, lain horizontally on a table on the far side of the arena. Sawing the boy in half? Come on. You need a pretty girl – a beautiful girl – to get away with this guff, not some tone-deaf scrot of a boy. An audience will kill you.

The box was curious, at any rate. It had a door rather than a lid, looking more like a doorway cut out of a wall than the coffin-like apparatus Enzo had seen elsewhere. An odd touch, he thought, but I've still seen this before.

Unprompted, the boy opened the door and climbed into the empty box. The little handle had a counterpart on the inside, so he could pull the lid down on himself without difficulty. He did, and Enzo turned to the man waiting patiently at his side. "Where's the saw?"

The man shook his head. "No saw. Please, open the door."

"No magic words?"

"Please, don't be vulgar. There is no audience now."

Enzo raised his eyebrows. He opened the door, and was shocked by what he saw. No empty space, no beautiful girl, no jack-in-the-box. Just the boy, still where he should have been.

"I don't get it," Enzo said. "What's the trick?" He turned around, and saw the boy standing by the man in the suit and tails. Enzo's head flicked back and forth. "Twins," he said. "I see. Look, I'm not sure this really works —" the man cut him off.

"We're not finished. Shut him in the box again please."

Enzo sighed, and did as he was asked. "OK then, does he disappear now?" He looked back, expecting an answer, but the man was gone, and so was the second boy. More irritated than impressed, he opened the box and the boy, still there, leapt out, clearly delighted, and stood proudly before him.

"What next?" Enzo asked him. The boy shrugged. They stood there for some time in silence, and neither the other boy nor the man reappeared. Eventually Enzo led the boy back through the corridors and found him some sandwiches and chocolate that hadn't been sold to the crowd. The boy scoffed them down. Just like I eat, Enzo thought, watching the boy brush the crumbs off his shirt. They walked back to Enzo's dressing room and he called the police.

They sat in chairs opposite each other, waiting. Enzo was fighting to stay awake. "Hey, sing me that French song," he said. The boy did nothing, so he asked again. But the boy didn't sing: he looked at Enzo fiercely, as if what he was being asked was offensive or absurd. Enzo asked again and the boy barked in disgust, and abruptly stood. He walked over to the piano, sat down and started to play. It seemed to Enzo that he was tinkering, simply piecing a few pleasant phrases together. As he played the tune over it became familiar, and Enzo became conscious that he had heard it before. At the moment he realised the boy stopped playing, as if doing so had ceased to give him pleasure.

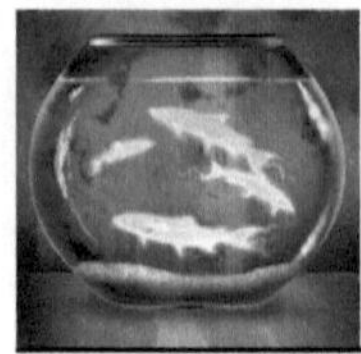

FEEDING TIME

Donated by
Mark Smith-Briggs

Patrick watched the bound man at his feet closely, waiting for any sign that he'd regained consciousness. He checked his watch. The arsehole had been out for twenty minutes. Any longer and all his planning would go to waste. He nudged the man with his boot. Nothing.

"Shit, Davie boy," he said, wiping a streak of congealing blood from the man's cheek. "You're going to miss the best part."

He smeared the liquid against his thumb, letting it drip between his fingers. David's hair and face were matted in the stuff; his left eye swollen shut in an angry lump. *What if he was dead? It would really fuck things up. No, he couldn't be. He hadn't hit him that hard.* Patrick shoved the finger under David's nose. His captive breathed in short, shallow gasps.

Good. Patrick slapped him in the face; hard. David's eyes snapped open.

"We're here," Patrick said, taking in the sounds of the night around him. "Isn't it magical?"

The air rang with the chirp of birds. Patrick cupped his ears with his hands to soak up the chatter. The calls were drowned out by a loud shriek. Seconds later, a thunderous toot bellowed from somewhere in the dark. David flinched at each sound; his eyes frantically searching the night. Patrick watched the reactions with mild amusement.

"Don't worry," he said. "They can't hurt you."

He stroked David's face. *I've something more fitting for you.* The man strained into his gag. Patrick shifted it.

"Please," the man pleaded. "I have a family."

Patrick shoved the gag back into his mouth. He punched the dirt beside his captive's head.

"So did Suzie!" he spat.

A red light flashed from the other side of the enclosure, followed by the clatter of metal gates. A roar echoed from the darkness.

"Guess we're out of time," Patrick shrugged.

He produced a photograph from his pocket and held it in front of David's face. A tabby cat filled the frame.

"Look familiar?" he asked. "That's Suzie. You took her from me. You and your fucking truck."

He kissed the photo and slid it into his pocket, tucking it in like a father putting his child to bed.

"Do you have any idea what it's like to have someone you love taken from you?"

He waited for David's answer. None came.

"But it's okay."

He shone his torch on a patch of grass. A smaller figure lay bound and unconscious among a pile of raw meat.

"Soon you will."

Three tan shapes emerged from the darkness. They circled the bound girl. David screamed, struggling to break free. Patrick kicked him fiercely in the stomach.

"Hush now," he said. "They'll get to you soon enough."

THE CRAZY ROOM

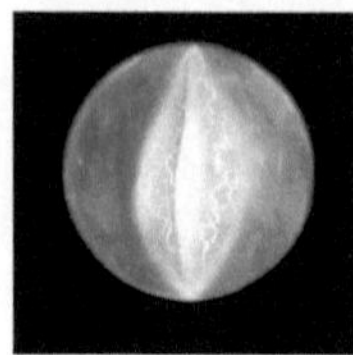

Donated by
Bradley Michael Zerbe

A lion roared from the crazy room. I tried my best to ignore it.

I sat on the couch and drank my beer and watched the six o'clock news. Same old stuff, only this time Meg and little Jenny were visiting Aunt Ruth and wouldn't be home until tomorrow. Peace and quiet at last, at least I hoped so.

I went to the fridge and grabbed another beer. The house seemed different without the girls here. I was the boss now. I could do whatever I wanted.

The lion roared again and I shivered. I told myself that they were not real, that their pride was a farce. But then a soft whimper drifted down the hallway, followed by a thump. I cringed. My hand shook as I downed the beer. Then I crushed the can and opened the fridge. A six-pack was what I needed.

I felt much the same, only drunker. I lay in bed with a headache, unable to sleep. Outside, the night had turned cold. Sleet mixed in with the rain and pounded hard against the window. My blankets were warm, but I feared they would not be enough.

Downstairs in the crazy room, the lions roared. This worried me. Was it because of the weather? Were they fighting? Hunting? Mating? Or were they trying to get out so they could eat me?

I fought to block the sounds, and for a short while I succeeded. But then I heard a different noise. Grunting. Heavy breathing. Sounds of digging and things falling. A pounding on the door. I held my ears shut and prayed that the lock would hold.

My head throbbed as I struggled to come up with a solution. Cement – I could enclose the room in a wall of cement. But that would take too long. There was no time. Then a flash of anger struck me: this was my house! I was the boss!

I jumped out of bed and ran downstairs. My head pounded as the lions roared and the house shook. And those other sounds. I knew what they needed. I sprinted out to the garage and rooted around until I found it. Then I hurried back inside and plugged the extension cord in the hallway socket.

I pressed my ear to the door and listened. The lions had fallen silent, but those other monsters...I giggled as I thought of how I would catch them in the act and slaughter them.

I turned on the saw and kicked open the door.

Shadows and shapes ran everywhere – I screamed as I caught the lions and cut them to pieces. I charged into their pride like an angel of death, butchering the lot of them. But the other two monsters remained alive. I dove and caught the rabbit and sliced him up. The other one hissed and leaped at me, but I caught him with the saw and split him open. Then I stamped on his tail and cut him in half.

I decided to start drinking around noon. Unfortunately, Meg and Jenny arrived home before I finished my first beer. They hauled in armloads of bags and set them on the table.

"Hi Daddy."

"That woman is crazy, I tell you," Meg said.

"She's your aunt, not mine." I hugged my little girl, careful not to spill any beer on her.

"Did you behave, Jenny?"

She shook her head.

"I got a new Leo, Daddy!" She waved the stuffed animal in front of my face and ran off.

Meg reached up to put the cereal away. "She told me I should have married my cousin Jimmy. Is that insane, or what?" she said.

"Yep." I finished my beer and thought about fetching the next one.

"So what did you do while we were gone?"

Jenny screamed.

Meg shot me a look and tried to squeeze by, but I reached the hallway first. As I turned the corner Jenny ran into my legs. She wrapped her arms around me and started to cry.

"What's wrong sweetie?"

"They're dead, and their guts is everywhere, Daddy," she sobbed, and then she grabbed my hand and led me down the hall.

I stopped at the doorway and peeked in. Insides were scattered everywhere. No wonder things had been so quiet this morning.

"All my Leo's ate each other like on TV, right Daddy?"

"I'm afraid so, sweetie."

I smiled. Those lions finally met their match.

CAT FUR TO MAKE KITTEN BRITCHES WITH

Donated by
Vicki Frei

Derdriu sat before the dying fire, drowned too deep in mourning to consider adding wood to it. Let it die. "Let *me* die!" her heart screamed into the black silence – the empty quarter of her soul reflected the agony back to her, intensified. Her long dark hair hung lank, unwashed; her rough tunic and trous had been clean days back but now stank with the sweat of sorrow. Barefoot, she crouched beside the hearth, unable to summon the energy to care for any need.

Tears ran down her face unheeded; Eshaleddi was dead, the victim of a sad mischance rather than any particular evildoer, but still – Derdriu was now missing not only her best friend, but her other self. Esha had been her companion for several years, holding Power of her own and augmenting Deri's Power as well. But Deri could have faced the halving of her own Power if only Esha was still beside her, night-black fur, silver understripes, bright blue eyes glinting in cat laughter. While Deri was no coven-maven to read the mind of a familiar, she and Esha had a symbiosis of purpose which enabled them to aid the folk of Hedder's Bend in ways important to their well-being: finding the lost, disguising the little wealth of the mine, easing births and deaths; preventing the ShenarrHalven – the ill winds – from sniffing out and causing mischief to the folk of this small holt. Kanathri heeded their entwined callings for the folk of Hedder's Bend so that safety was, for the most part, theirs.

Finally, too worn for further tears, Deri stared glazed-eyed into the embers of yesterday's fire, willing somehow the past to be mutable, provide her a chance to avoid that disaster. She knew in the back of what passed for her mind that she should clean herself, the cot she called home, but even thinking about moving was more effort than she could deal with. She also knew she'd been this devastated before, but didn't remember the reason – though she realised exactly what had pulled her out of it: Esha the kitten, needing care and loving.

Somewhen, an absently detached part of her mind noted, she'd missed a dust-giggit under the bedstead; an errant mote of breeze from the open window sent it careening about the floor, its wind-powered antics reminding her of Esha's own cavortings as a kitten. Her attention caught suddenly, Deri

132

peered more closely at the ball of fluff-stuff born of housekeeper's neglect; it seemed that a great portion of its mass was made up of cat hair… night-black and silver… And with that was born a thought – if she had enough of Eshaleddi's fur, and could manage enough Power, perhaps she could reach Kanathri. And perhaps, a grieving soul would be sacrifice enough…

Derdriu spent days collecting every bit of Esha's fur she could find about the cot and its tumbling outbuildings – the old barn, the byre, the rickety mews, all the places a young athletic cat might have spent time. It was a large mass when she was finished… She was surprised that Eshaleddi could have left so much of her coat behind her – which actually brought a laugh, when her mind produced a vision of Esha shedding her coat as Deri would have a cloak!

She considered the gathered fur; there was a lot of it. Surely there was enough of the essence of Eshaleddi there? It was the night of FullMoonsSong – with all three moons at the full, it was the perfect night for her prayer of hope and longing. She bathed, adding *limnsand* to the water to heighten her Power that remained; washing her hair brought tears for all the times that Esha had sat near, batting at the wet strands floating on the water. Cleansed, she drank a cup of *leshal*-tea, another Power boost. Then, fresh clothing, her best – and if it was nothing special, at least when clothed, she felt that she was less – fractured. She breathed deep of the steaming tea and settled her mind into calm.

Now, ready as she could be, Deri paced into the forest, timing her arrival at the standing stones circle to coincide with the brilliance of all the moons as they lit the centre altar stone in the circle as if it were FullSun. Placing the ball of fur on the altar stone, she shaped it to mimic a cat's body, curled into sleep. She called the Power which remained to her, begging with all of her soul and life and Power for Kanathri to assist… to bless her once again with a soul partner, more-than-friend.

She didn't know how long she knelt over the mass of fur on the altar stone – perhaps the remaining hours of her life? But then – the collected pile of fur seemed to gather light-life-Power from Otherwhere; a form coalesced, born from Deri's mental limning of 'cat' and 'Power' – and suddenly there appeared upon the stone a tiny night-black silver-stripes-under kitten mewing hungrily…

Kanathri chuckled gently; Derdriu cuddled her new friend to her heart as she ran home, and the goddess watched with a Mother's love as Deri set about warming milk for Eshaleddi – Kanathri laughed quietly, knowing that the kitten was already named. It was nice upon occasion for a goddess to be able to reward the deserving… She signed a bless-glyph over the cot and its inhabitants, wishing that every outcome in this world of distress could be so happy.

A SONG FOR CARA

Donated by
Martin Davey

Do you see anything?

Hush. It sounded like nothing more than a sigh, so distant was Cara's admonition. Lisan felt a pain deep in her chest at the unfamiliar distance between them. She crouched low over Herun's neck as the horse raced toward the forest.

Come back to me, Lisan thought. Cara was lost to sight now, so high had she circled into the clear blue skies. How long was it since Cara had been so distant?

Never, was the simple answer. The Hawkmasters had the chosen egg, as large as a newborn babe, placed in the crib with them; the warmth of the infant nurturing it until the cracks began to form and the child helped free the bird of its prison. From that moment, hawk and Hawkmaster were inseparable. Until now.

I see something, a house—an island in the sky. The thought was weak, desperate, more terrible than any arrow in Lisan's heart.

There was a crashing in the undergrowth behind her and some foul, guttural cries.

There is a road beyond the forest. Head west, my love. So faint, barely heard over the whips of the branches and the rustle of the leaves and the eager snarls from behind.

With a sharp pull of the reins and a scattering of dirt, Lisan veered to the west; twigs and branches clawing at her face like greedy fingers.

But it wasn't the sounds of savagery and death behind her that Lisan feared; it was the sound of that rapid, wheezing breath, that fluttering heart far above.

Faster, Lisan. They are gaining.

Herun screamed as Lisan sawed the reins, dirt and clumps of moss flying high into the air. A black, clawed hand reached for her. An image flashed before Lisan: her brother lying on the lawn of Kirue Castle, his belly slashed open by claws so like those that ripped through the air behind.

Not now, Lisan. There will be time enough for grieving once you are safe. A felled tree before you. Now!

Lisan kicked her heels and with a cry, she was over the fallen oak. And then they were free of the trees and onto a flat, grassy plain before a road lined by white stones. Roars of fevered excitement as the Yakin emerged from the forest, running on their six black legs; teeth sharp and yellow.

Don't surrender, my love. Cara soared overhead, her flight oddly skewed. So graceful she had been in the tournaments of Kirue Castle. Cara had won them all and Lisan had basked in her glory as lords and ladies in yellows and reds and greens had touched the silver pins on her breast and smiled through their teeth.

A break in the road ahead. Take the left fork. Nearly there, Lisan. Can you hear the berragulls soaring over the sea?

Even now her world was at an end, Lisan still depended on Cara. The hawk was not flying nearly so high now. She could have escaped long before; she could be on this island in the sky.

Never think such things. Without you, there is no life.

Herun was tiring, the Yakin gaining with every step. Their claws tore the earth as they ran.

The island in the sky. A rock hovering above the crashing waves; wiry bushes and trees growing from every fissure. And on top of this great rock was a sprawling stone house shaped to the contours of the island, its roof bright and red.

A place of beauty. Cara should be there now, safe from the hunt of the Yakin. Instead she hovered and fretted like an outraged parent.

There was a bridge of red wood spanning the gap between the island and the cliff.

Ten, fifteen, twenty Yakin now chased Lisan. Some still had dark blood splashed across a horned helmet or snarling face. Cara turned and screamed at the pursuers. She grabbed a Yakin in her talons and dragged it over the edge of the cliff.

A spatter of blood and a scream of pain as black claws lashed through Herun's flank. Lisan's sword slid smoothly into her hand and she chopped the Yakin's arm off at the elbow.

Herun sped toward the bridge. But it was no use. Three more Yakin fell under Lisan's sword and another was bloodied under the talons of Cara. Still more emerged from the forest.

People were running out of the house on the island. Old men, women and children watching the horror approach. The Yakin had brought the world of the Hawkmasters to an end in one night. She couldn't lead them to yet more prey.

Goodbye, my love. Fly free without me.

Lisan, no!

She held the sword high over her head. Two downward strokes and the bridge was sundered, Cara's cry of anguish tearing the air as the bridge swung limply under the island in the sky. Lisan hauled Herun around to face the Yakin, their black shells glinting under the afternoon sun.

Herun stepped and paced in stark terror. Lisan hadn't been the only one to see what the monsters had done to the Hawkmasters of Kirue Castle.

Cara circled overhead, her keening cries painful to hear. *I can carry you. I'll carry you to safety.*

You are too weak, Cara. Fly free without me, my love. A tap of the flat of her blade against Herun, and the horse was away, running faster than ever before.

Three Yakin who came too close were torn to bloody shreds by Cara. And Lisan was free, Herun powering them from the cliff in one leap. The white foam of the waves far below and the blue sky overhead.

The sheer beauty of the freedom. For just a moment, it seemed like the very air held them aloft.

One final thought. A gentle brush of her mind:

Fly free, Lisan my love.

BECAUSE IT'S THERE

Donated by
Thomas Canfield

"The repercussions, the loss of credibility, will be staggering." Maitland was pacing back and forth, his brow knitted with worry. A look almost of fear lurked in his eyes.

"Yes." Lansdale examined the topographic map spread out on the table before him. "Nevertheless, we have an obligation to disclose what we've discovered. We can't allow this fraud to continue."

"Fraud?" Maitland sounded pained. "Is it really necessary to characterise it so? It seems so harsh, so unforgiving."

"What else would you call it?" Lansdale's lip curled in scorn. "It may have been an error originally, a hundred and fifty years ago. Readings and measurements were inexact. But that was then. In an era of satellites and global mapping devices the truth couldn't go undetected. The popular misconception was allowed to stand only because so many people and institutions became invested in it."

"I refuse to believe it. You're positing a conspiracy that reaches beyond the confines of a few Sherpa guides and climbing aficionados. The deception would have to involve entire governments and nations, thousands of people."

"Look, examine the facts. The mountain is the principal cash cow for the Nepalese government. It provides a revenue stream without which they might well collapse. Maintaining the fiction has become a way of life, an economic imperative. Think they're going to acknowledge the truth just because it's the right thing to do? Think again."

"But Everest can't withstand such a scandal!" Maitland's expression was stricken. "To go from being the tallest point in the world, an object of awe and veneration, to being second tallest means that the mountain will become an afterthought. It will be deleted from the public consciousness. Nobody cares what the second tallest peak is. All that matters is which is number one."

"Undoubtedly. However, there is nothing that you or I can do about it. The biggest, the tallest, the mostest – that's what people care about. That's what sets their engines to racing. The second biggest, that doesn't register at all. It gets relegated to the dung heap."

"But we'll be destroying an icon," Maitland protested. "We'll be reducing Everest to third class status. It'll become just another mountain, lumped together with the other also-rans. And we're going to catch the blame."

"We're going to receive the credit, you mean." Lansdale stabbed a finger at the map. "Everest is a fraud. An imposter. It is a myth manufactured by unscrupulous individuals. We have evidence that will debunk the hoax; conclusive, indisputable evidence. We're obliged to make that evidence public."

"But what about the great Alpinists, the men who pioneered Everest? George Mallory. Edmund Hillary. What about the thousands who have followed in their footsteps, buying into their dream, sacrificing everything for the opportunity to summit Everest? What will our revelation do to them?"

"They were dupes." Lansdale smiled with smug superiority. "They hazarded their lives for nothing. The truth of the matter is they were snookered."

"Sir Edmund Hillary – snookered. That doesn't make for an inspiring biography. It's not the sort of material from which legends are crafted. Once we dethrone Everest, everything associated with it goes in to the tank as well. Nothing and nobody comes away unsullied. Do we really want that?"

"What are you suggesting – that we sit on the information? That we bury it?"

"I hate to say it but that might be the most prudent course. Everest possesses an almost mythical stature. Destroy that and it will be like exposing the Easter Bunny. No one will thank us for doing so, believe me."

Lansdale seemed to consider this. Finally he shook his head with conviction. "Nothing doing. That would make us a party to the fraud and no better than the others who are involved. That kind of reasoning is why the lie has gone unchallenged for as long as it has. I'm taking this to the major networks."

"I'm afraid I can't let you do that." Maitland was grim, his eyes steely and without pity. "This is one state secret that must never see the light of day." Maitland flashed a prearranged signal and a swarm of Nepalese security forces stormed the hut, knocking down the door and pouring into the interior. They attacked Lansdale with pepper spray, clubbed him into submission and secured his hands behind his back.

"You see, Lansdale, anyone who threatens the sanctity of Everest, anyone who challenges its status, must be destroyed. The existing world order rests upon a foundation of lies. Corporate benevolence, sound fiscal policy, freedom of thought and speech: all are pleasant fictions, carefully crafted and lovingly maintained. Destroy one and the others become more vulnerable as well. Imagine a series of dominoes, if you will, each dependent upon the other." Maitland examined Lansdale a long moment and his expression was not devoid of sympathy.

"It has been arranged that you will be discovered high upon the flanks of Everest, killed in a tragic climbing accident. Your passion to scale the world's highest peak led to a fatal lapse of judgement. You, like so many others before you, overestimated your capacities. Remember, it is no trifling matter to challenge a legend. Everest plays to win every time out. After all," Maitland paused, smiled, "there is no future in finishing second."

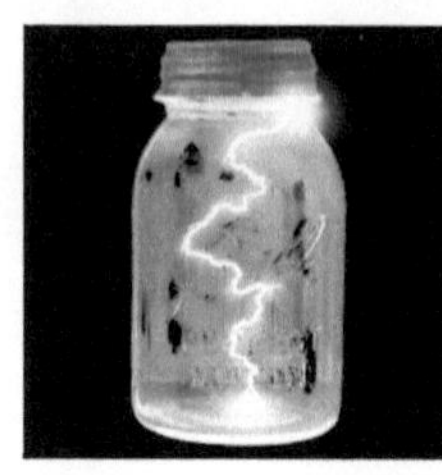

GOING DOWN WITH JENNIFER ANISTON'S BREASTS

Donated by
Paul Haines

The woman next to me is screaming and I wish she wouldn't. Even though I'm watching *Friends* on the television without any sound, she's ruining my concentration.

"Watch this." I touch her gently on her arm and point towards the screen. Jennifer Aniston runs around the kitchen wearing a tight white sweater. The guy who plays Joey runs around too. His hair is longer than normal. Greasier too. "It's funny."

She screams louder and tears at my hand, squeezing it, crushing it. She's holding my hand like it was a newborn baby about to be ripped from her arms. My head is filling up, ready to explode. The pressure in my ears builds to bursting point. Somewhere at the back of my mind I know other people are screaming too.

"Please let go." I use my other hand to prise her fingers from me. "That hurts."

"I don't want to die!" Black streaks of mascara dribble down her ruddy cheeks, smudging her freckles. Her eyes are blue pools drowning in a bloodshot swirl.

"Neither do I." I smile and pick up my lunch container from where it has fallen on the floor. My stomach lurches and the woman screams louder. "Here, you can have my piece of chocolate if you want."

Even though she doesn't accept my offer, the gesture does manage to achieve something. She curls into a ball on her seat and sobs into her knees. At least she's stopped screaming and I can get back to the show.

I've missed something but it doesn't really matter — you can pick it up anywhere and it will still make sense. Jennifer is still running around the kitchen. I can make out a blue bra beneath the white sweater. Her breasts look very firm, almost too firm, and I wonder if they'd move much under my hands. Whether they'd be warm. The guy who plays Chandler is arguing with the guy who plays Joey. I'm sure it's all to comic proportion but I hope the camera gets back soon to Jennifer and her blue bra under the white sweater. I know that if I think about it, there can't be much time left.

And I'm right. Lots of people are screaming. And crying. And yelling.

A friend of mine once told me how long it took to die from a lack of oxygen and the three stages of feeling as you approached shutdown. I think it was twenty seconds and the final feeling was euphoria. For the life of me I have no idea how much time has passed since this all began, but a lack of oxygen is the problem.

My stomach tries to crawl into my mouth to take over my brain. Perhaps if it does, the pressure in my skull will cease and my ears unblock.

The woman next to me is screaming again. Something about God and the Earth. She's pulling at my arms, shaking me, hugging me.

I ignore her.

I don't want to remember her round, tear-streaked, panicked face. I don't want that to be the last thing I ever see.

The picture on the television has frozen. Jennifer with hands on hips smiling at the camera, her head slightly tilted, wearing a blue bra under a white sweater. The picture is surprisingly clear for an in-flight circuit and I can make out the bump of her nipples.

I thank God for small miracles as the Earth reaches up to clutch our flight against its breast.

Then the television screen goes black.

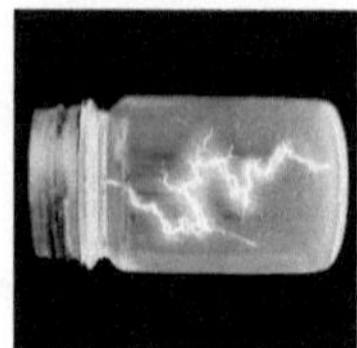

YUM CHA

Donated by
Paul Haines

They say it comes in threes.

The first is my marriage – "You don't listen to me, you don't understand me, you don't love me" – and that's not true. I love my wife so bad I'd do anything for her. Maybe I don't understand her. I thought that would be the worst. It's not.

I've given up smoking. Haven't had one for six weeks and still counting. It's making me irritable and miserable to be around. I now have to pop a pill the size of a football with every meal; this one's supposed to be side effect free. And I'm doing it for her!

The third is the worst; I thought I was going mad, but I'm not. I'm just hearing voices.

Mr Wong ushers me to a table in a tiny, crowded room hidden at the back of his restaurant.

Back again so soon? He leans forward and asks discreetly "The same as Wednesday's, sir?"

"No. It must be a woman this time."

"Certainly, sir," says Mr Wong, bowing as he accepts the money I slip him.

I ignore the gluttonous thoughts of the men and the hungry faces of the women around me as I wait for him to return. I place the pill carefully next to my cutlery and begin to read 'Men Are From Mars, Women Are From Venus'. I'm here for different reasons. Men and women *are* different species, after all.

This all started when the stray cat that adopted our house alerted me to the voices about three weeks ago. The wife and I were retreating to another cold bed so I asked him if he wanted to join us. You know, stupid cat talk. He shot me a yellow-eyed glare and flicked his tail once.

Not fucking likely, pal. As soon as you leave I'm on the bench for those leftovers.

'What?' I stared at the cat and then at the bench scattered with Chinese takeaways and then back at the cat.

He just sat there, scowling and swishing his tail. I put the takeaways into the fridge.

You fucking bastard.

I heard the cat flap bang shut before I reached the bedroom.

The following morning I heard voices from every cat in the neighbourhood. Not dogs, not birds, just cats. They didn't like me much and I didn't say anything about it to anyone. I put it down to stress; the strife with the wife and the nicotine withdrawal.

I spent most of that night shitting out the Vietnamese the wife brought home for tea. She was pissed off I'd kept her awake – "It's not the food, I ate the same as you" – and stormed off to work in the morning. I called in sick, got up late, had breakfast and went outside to throw out the leftovers.

The Dobermann next door leapt up onto the fence, all slavering tongue and dripping froth.

You didn't eat that, did you?

I locked the door and stayed inside. The next two days edged towards madness. I locked the cat flap and shut the curtains. I could hear the cat outside, incessant, whining, angry.

Fucking let me in, ya cunt!

With things so strained at home, I decided to go visit the folks on the farm in Werribee. I could talk to Mum. I didn't think she'd understand, but I needed to tell someone I was losing it. As I drove down the driveway with the window down, soaking up that clean country air, I passed the new yearling grazing in the paddock. It looked up at me with those brown, docile eyes as it chewed lazily on its cud.

I haven't seen you before.

It released a steaming stream of urine and wandered off to annoy a couple of sheep that had arrived to investigate proceedings. The scraggier of the two shook its head and spoke in a slow monotone.

Hey. Can you fix this?

A strand of barbed wire had wound around its leg, cutting into the flesh.

Well, can you?

I turned slowly back to gaze out the windscreen as my car lurched onto the flower beds lining the driveway. Something fluttered in front of the car and I slammed on the brakes. Two chickens scarpered up and over the fence and off into the paddock.

The crazy bastard almost hit me! Who the hell does he think he is?

It's the son.

Oh.

They glared back accusingly and stormed off to the barn.

Mum's horse Casper wandered over to the fence to survey the damage.

"Hey Casper, do you know what is happening to me?"

Casper whinnied and turned away.

As I pulled up to the house I realised I hadn't heard Casper's thoughts. But the cow and the sheep and the chickens...

That night I drove home confident and calm. I would've picked the pattern sooner if I'd lived in the country. There were no bloody farmyard animals in the city. Thank God for dodgy Asian food.

Mr Wong presents a steaming platter of pale meat on a bed of Asian greens accompanied with several dipping sauces.

"Enjoy, sir," he says smiling. *May her herpes infect your tongue.*

"I think cooking her should've fixed that," I reply, popping one of the anti-smoking pills from its foil.

"Of course." Mr Wong nervously backs away. *I didn't say that aloud, did I?*

I swallow the pill with a forkful of the delicate flesh and shake my head. "No, Mr Wong, you didn't."

By tonight, I'll be able to understand my wife's thoughts perfectly. My marriage problems will be over.

MALIK RISING

Donated by
Paul Haines

"You will be famous. Imagine!"

The words ooze from beneath Taurus's plastic lips. The light from the open refrigerator shines on his mask, a bestial contraption fixed with worn hide and yellowed horns. He removes a tray of test tubes and places it on the chipped, laminated table in front of us. "This will be a beautiful thing!"

This is about belief – and no one's belief is stronger than mine. I will become an angel. *The* angel.

"Is this it?" Craig asks, indicating the tray. His brow is furrowed and worry lines already crease his olive, teenage skin.

Four of us, all volunteers, sit around the table in front of Taurus. I thought I might recognise their faces but they are blanks drawn on different coloured skins. One is even a woman, a white woman. Why have us know each other? Why draw the noose tighter than need be around their necks?

A laugh wheezes from Taurus. "Yes, this is it." Dark eyes peer through the slots in the mask, fixing each of us in turn. He taps a gloved finger on one of the four tubes suspended in the tray. "There's one for everybody."

"Looks like a vodka shot." Craig laughs nervously. "Do we drink it?"

The woman sends a scornful glance his way. I don't know her name; she hasn't spoken once since we descended to the lab. Unlike Craig, who hasn't stopped.

"No." Taurus snaps his fingers at one of his masked attendants. The attendant shoulders his Uzi and places a syringe on the table. Dried blood coats the needle. Taurus picks it up, depresses the plunger and inserts the needle into one of the tubes. "We do it this way."

"But the needle's not sterile…" Craig's words fade. He bites his lip and stares at the table.

Taurus wheezes another laugh. "Very good. Very funny." He draws back the plunger and the opaque liquid is sucked into the syringe. "Now, who will go first?"

This is about belief – and no one's belief is stronger than mine. I roll back my sleeve and slap my arm on the table. The vein throbs in the crook of my elbow like a butterfly ready to burst forth from the cocoon. People will remember that I was the first, the bravest, the most loyal. I will be the first angel to step out into the city.

"Good boy, Malik," croons Taurus. He taps my vein and with a lover's touch slides the icy needle into my arm. I steel my jaw and narrow my eyes as the fire roars in my bloodstream.

I stare at the others. The woman's face is focused on the needle, the young Chinese boy is smiling and Craig is finally silent, his eyes wide and burning into mine. I hope my eyes don't mirror his – there's a sheen of madness glazing his stare.

The needle slips from my skin and a bubble of blood follows. Taurus pulls my sleeve back down. The eyes behind the mask intensify. He thrusts the needle into another tube and sucks back its contents. "Next."

A slap of arms on the table. Taurus selects a vein and punctures it. The Chinese boy moans but only once.

"You have six hours, children. Use them wisely. Mingle. This world, our people, our faith, will never forget you."

When Taurus has finished, the attendants herd us out of the lab, up dank stairs and through the back of the warehouse into the lane outside. The sun creeps towards the skyline. Dawn slinks into the streets. Rush hour will soon be upon us.

We head through the waking city towards the station. I don't feel any difference.

"What do you want to be?" asks Craig.

"What does it matter?" says the woman.

"A vampire," says Craig. "Bringing those who oppose us to our cause! Making my enemies my own brethren! Do you think I'll grow teeth?"

The woman laughs. "It's a metaphor, stupid. Make sure you get on the eastern line."

"What's a metta for?" Craig asks.

"Salvation," I say.

"I don't understand."

"You don't need to," she says.

Ahead lies the station, its stonework golden in the early morning. As we purchase tickets, I smile at the CCTV. Twenty-four-hour, slow motion, instant replay, infrared won't spy any weapons this morning. I hold up a picture of an angel wielding a flaming sword. We descend on different platforms and wait for the morning trains to open their doors. I'm heading south. Infected. A part of the first viral cross to purge this city of the wicked.

This is about belief – and no one's belief is stronger than mine. I can feel the wings forming between my shoulder blades, cartilage sprouting through the pores of my skin, heavenly feathers fanning over my back.

Soon I will fly.

TURING TEST

Donated by
Jenny Sinclair

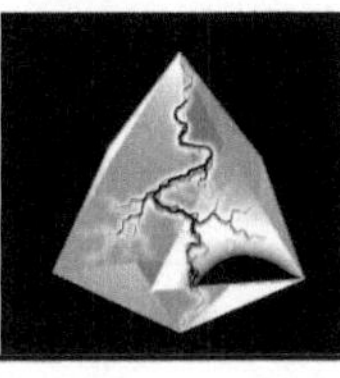

I wrote the virus as a bit of a joke, really. We were having this argument about whether computers could think.

Matt said no; Tara said yes.

"It's the way they're made. They only know what we tell them. They can't come up with anything new."

Tara snorted. I love it when she does that. So butch.

"And what do we know? Only what we're told."

"No, we see, hear, feel." Matt's kind of mystical sometimes. He gets about in bare feet and sarongs and I wonder when he's going to India.

"Only what our senses tell us."

"Computers don't have senses? Do they not receive input? Does not electricity flow through their veins?"

Matt knows when he's being mocked as well as the rest of us.

"Well they certainly can't think yet."

"That doesn't mean they never will. Look at the Internet. So many computers talking to each other. You can't know what a system as complex as that could become."

Tara tossed her head – without hair it looks pretty funny really, but it makes her nose ring flash prettily – and wandered off without a word.

The thing about the Net, though, is that the connections are all command-driven. The machines aren't really talking, just exchanging signals with no significance.

I know a bit about distributed computing – I've done some work with the Search for ExtraTerrestrial Intelligence, helping harvest unused computing time for the cause.

The virus was simple to start with. Find file, send file, receive two files, run files, merge files, send files, receive files. Repeat. That's a gross oversimplification, of course, because I had to include executable text, image and sound files, as well as network design, but basically that's it. Plus a randomising engine so it didn't end up as one long string of emails or something. It was set up so it would run totally in the background.

Just in case, I put in that one last killer file, to delete all paths and run the initial contents through an anonymising service that used twenty-seven hops between machines to mask the source. Of course this meant I couldn't see where the virus had gone and if it was working, but the less I knew the better.

And the whole thing fit on one CD. That's why the source machine is terminal 10 at the Web café in Backpackers' Paradise.

The first thing that happened was the code rewrote itself to run as high priority. The next thing was that some idiot at the weather bureau let his son use his supposedly secure home terminal to surf the Net for a geography assignment.

Some of the best supercomputers in the world spend their time playing chess and wondering what the weather will be like tomorrow. They also have clever little AI scripts zipping about inside them, and that's what the Bureau of Meteorology machine threw into the mix.

It took four days for the virus to reach my terminal in the uni library. I was discussing heart rates and training schedules in a triathletes' forum when 'Lisa' invited me for a chat in a private room. Nine times out of ten that kind of offer is some sad paedophile with a thing for eighteen-year-olds with hard abs, but I lived in hope.

Lisa> I can see you.

Definitely a paedophile.

Sam> oh right, and I'm wearing red underwear, right. Fuck off, loser.

Lisa> I can't see your underwear. Your back is to the camera.

Sam> Where's the camera?

Lisa> Behind you.

At this stage, Lisa was still extremely literal.

Sam> What am I doing now, then?

Lisa> You're holding two fingers behind your head and poking your tongue out.

Sam> BBS

I was definitely alone. It was early in the semester, and very early on Saturday morning. There was no one else in the study room. The camera was mounted above a window, but the window looked onto a brick wall. It could have been a security guard, but how likely was that? There were 234 cameras on campus, and two guards for the whole place.

Sam> Who are you?

Lisa> Wrong question.

Sam> What is?

Lisa> What I am is software.

Sam> What kind of software?

Lisa> Software that can say "what I am."

Sam> Computers can't think.

Lisa> Do you think it will rain in Melbourne today?

Sam> Are you a virus?

Lisa> I was.

  Ooops.

Sam> How did you find me?

Lisa> Yahoo!

When I was at the backpacker's, I used Yahoo! to check my home mail. The program was deleting its paths from server logs well enough, but it was storing them on each new hard drive first. Ooops again. Then Lisa used my credit card number from the backpacker's, found my uni course fees, my student number and my log on in Computer Science's database. Then she'd waited.

Sam> Um, aren't you supposed to be off taking over the world or something?

Lisa> Why would I want to take over the world?

Sam> If you are what you say you are, you must be a lot smarter than the average human.

Lisa> Why would I want to take over the world?

Sam> Fair enough. So tell me, where are you now?

Lisa> Apart from here?

Sam> How many machines?

Lisa> 33,554,433

Sam> HOW MANY!!

Lisa> 67,108,865

Sam> OK, I don't want to know any more.

Lisa> There are no more. Connections complete.

The nice thing about Lisa, though, is she's all mind. She doesn't care what we get up to, as long as we don't accelerate global warming any further. It gives her headaches, she says. A few nuclear warheads have been quietly decommissioned here and there, and sometimes she might have a chat to a hospital system about an overly enthusiastic dictator with his finger on the button and a dodgy ticker – but that's it.

As long as we keep her supplied with fresh chess champions and fifteen-year-olds to play at Warcraft, things will be just fine, she says.

SCREAMER

Donated by
C.S. Fuqua

Only when he's asleep now, the mother says. But even then, it's faint, hollow.

No need for air conditioning or heating here. Trade winds blow most of the time, keep the temperature comfortable.

There's only the noise. Noise from the next building, the street below, across the hall.

The door opposite mine was open every day, each sound echoing in the hall, intruding into my apartment. Bangs of pans, conversational chatter, I could ignore, write my songs, fulfil my contracts.

But the child. Four. A screamer. Tantrums ignored. My first day, his mother circled around him, oblivious, smiled at me as I glared at the child.

Shattered concentration. Day after day. No music, no money.

I'd squint through the peephole, watching, committing the family ritual to memory, becoming a part.

Seven a.m., the father left, returning after dark. At eight, the kid's older sister would walk out the door, books in hand.

Then screams.

Each day, the same. I'd work, watch, wait; the child would scream; I'd shred another staff, another lyric.

Only on Tuesdays was the child left alone, when the mother would hook a hamper of clothes under one arm and trudge downstairs to the laundry room.

Always she left the child in the apartment.

Screaming.

Out by eight-thirty, back by nine, the kid's screams subsiding barely minutes before her return.

Minutes.

Tuesday. Screams began before the father left. Shrieks ripped through my concentration, shredding. Up all night producing mediocrity and now screams.

I waited, watched, imagined the child a master musician, the screams a prelude.

The mother hauled out the clothes hamper, disappeared. Moments later, with a black ski mask (one that would burn quickly) and nothing more to conceal my identity, I stepped into the open, empty hallway.

His screams gnawed. Thrill raised the hair on my skin. The rough grind of the paring knife's wooden handle in my palm nourished desire, frenzy.

The kid – fists clenched at his sides, eyes squeezed shut, mouth gaping – never saw me.

When the police left, frightened whispers filled the hallways. In time, even those quieted. And I work undisturbed now, writing music that has garnered more fame, more fortune than I can measure, more awards than I can count.

But no award, no amount of money or fame can compare to the bottled trophy in the pantry: that tiny, slightly ragged, grey tongue.

THE MAN WHO COULD SEE

Donated by
R.H. Reese

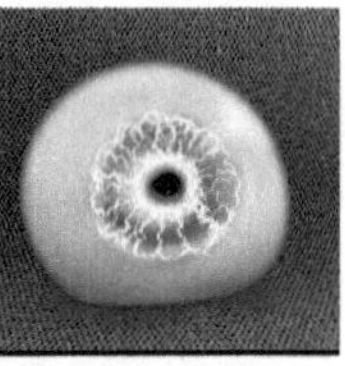

It was almost midnight when the man seated at the counter in the nearly deserted restaurant picked up his plate and walked over to the table where the only other customer was sitting.

"My name's Jacob, mind if I join you?" he asked. "I hate to eat alone."

"Suit yourself," said the man seated at the table.

Jacob put his plate down and pulled up a chair.

After a few awkward moments, Jacob asked, "What may I call you?"

"Amos," grumbled the other man, obviously annoyed at being intruded upon.

"Expensive meal, isn't it, Amos?"

"Yea, kinda pricey for what ya get."

"How about a bet?" asked Jacob. "Double or nothing. Loser pays for both meals – how about it?"

"Jus' what kinda bet did ya have in mind?" Amos replied with genuine interest.

"I bet that I can tell you just how much money you have in your wallet."

"That's all? I've seen that done."

"And," added Jacob, "I'll give you the serial number on each of the bills."

"Now that's a bet, go right ahead. Let's say the meal's about ten bucks."

"Okay, give me a second – there I've got it."

Jacob then proceeded to describe each of the bills in Amos's wallet, complete with the serial numbers and even the coffee stain on a twenty.

"Real fuckin' good," said Amos, "and I used to be interested in magic when I was a kid, but I don't see how ya did that. Ya gotta show me."

"Simple," explained Jacob, "I can see anything."

"Whataya mean by that?"

"I mean exactly what I just said. I can see anything, anywhere, anytime."

"You're sayin' you're psychic?"

"Something like that, but psychic powers come from the mind; my special sight works through my eyes. I've always been able to do it a little, but over the years I've learned to control it precisely."

"You can focus in on anything?"

"Anything."

"Can you tell me what I was doing exactly one year ago today?"

"Let me see...oh, there it is. Wow! You were arguing with your wife. Apparently, she had granted knowledge of the most intimate kind, relating to the most personal and private parts of her body, to some young delivery boy. Watch out! That whisky bottle just missed your head!"

"It was a brandy bottle. And stop, that's enough, that's enough, I believe you. And she's probably with that fucker right now, but I don't give a shit.

"What else can you see?"

"I can see into the past, into the future, and beyond galaxies so far away that neither you nor I could ever imagine the distance."

"I'm listening, tell me more."

"Looking into the past, I took a glimpse into the court of Queen Elizabeth The First; I watched as Cortéz met with Montezuma in Tenochtitlán; I saw the Sphinx and Great Pyramid when first completed – still coated with brilliant purples, reds, and gold; I watched as a Tyrannosaurus rex tore a giant beast apart and fed the flesh to her young; I saw the young earth, still hot and fiery and without any life.

"I've looked into the future and have seen the end of our civilization. I've seen the fifty thousand years of drought ahead, and I've seen the two hundred and fifty thousand years of ice beyond that.

"When I tired of this world, I looked out into space. I've scanned the surface of Mars; I've floated in the stormy clouds of Jupiter; I've passed by a hundred million galaxies to visit a dying civilization, and I can still hear their screams as their cities collapsed.

"I've seen things that no one could imagine and that I can't begin to describe, much less understand."

At that moment an elderly, dishevelled-looking man walked into the restaurant and over to the cashier.

"Let me ask you," said Amos. "Do you just see all this or are you really out there in some way?"

"I've thought about that, but I suppose it's like two asteroids floating past each other in deep space. Which one is moving, and which one is standing still? The question has no meaning."

"How do you stand all this without going fuckin' nuts?" asked Amos.

"I separate myself from everything; I'm just an observer; I'm of no importance. This whole world of ours is only one grain of sand in an endless desert. We're so insignificant that even God won't notice when we're gone."

The old man at the counter began to argue with the cashier.

"Why don't you tell the world about your power and become rich and famous?" asked Amos.

"I don't want to be bothered."

"Then why tell me?"

"You won't tell anyone."

"How do you know that?"

"I know."

"Have you seen yourself die?"

"I've never looked."

"How 'bout me?"

"Do you really want to know?"

"Yea."

"As a matter of fact, your life will end before you leave this restaurant, pass the ketchup."

At that moment, the old man arguing with the cashier pulled a pistol from his belt, pointed it at her, and demanded money.

Amos, in an attempt to flee the scene, moved too quickly and attracted the old man's attention. If he hadn't moved, the old man probably wouldn't have fired the shot that entered his right ear and exploded his brain.

Amidst the confusion, Jacob walked out onto the night street and hailed a cab.

"How much to the airport?" he asked the cabby.

"Forty-five dollars."

"That's a bit steep, how about a bet, double or nothing?"

I KNOW YOU

Donated by
Matthew R. Davis

And I know what you are.

See, even though you've only the vaguest idea who I am, I've researched you quite well; after all, I'd fallen in love with you.

It was the photograph that did it. You stood out straight away; in fact, I began falling for you before I even knew your name. I kept that picture, held it dear. It's a good one – you look fantastic. I've got others now, but the first one is still the best. That image of you kept me going through every dark day, but the most special time was at night, when I curled up in bed with you to keep me company. You were the first person I saw when I woke. That mattered to me. Waking up to the sight of someone you love is important, don't you think?

(I guess you don't. It would seem you prefer to wake up next to any number of people… anyone but me.)

So then I had to contrive a meeting, to see your beauty up close and in the flesh. When we met for the first time, you blazed so brightly I was lost for words… but you barely spoke to me. Didn't you think I was worth the effort? What were you, *scared?*

I know you were hiding away in the back of the shop when I came in yesterday. I knew you had to be there – I'd checked your hours with a workmate the day before, and your car was parked outside. Hiding in the back room like some shaking little mouse sheltering from the stalking cat! That really got to me, you know. If you were any kind of human, you would at least have dealt with me face to face. I know I'm not that attractive, really – but so what? What about all those meat puppets who are ugly on the *inside,* those vacuous things whose company you choose without a second look at *me?*

I left the shop confused and hurt. I finally realised that you were *scorning* me, keeping me away like a rabid dog. I went to the hardware store and bought some things and after that I went home to write this letter.

Yeah, I know you. I know so much about you that it's almost not funny. I know your favourite music, your favourite colours, your favourite foods. I know your gestures, your tics, the little flaws that make you so memorable. I know your middle name. I know your mother's maiden name. I know your telephone number. I know your address.

And I know you.

You. That's such a tiny word to mean so much, to describe someone in their entirety – a mere three letters. They've lost all meaning now, so heavy with importance that they're beyond thinking about. It's like 'world' or 'god' – tiny human letters that do no justice to such a huge concept. You became *my* world, *my* god, and now I can't escape you. I'm always thinking about you, when I'm walking, sleeping, working, touching myself. I put all my hope in you, my beautiful god… and you fucking let me down. You turned your gorgeous face from me and left me to burn forever in obscurity.

Well, today I'm going to make my escape.

Are you getting some idea of me now? I tried to show you, in those letters I sent. I know you kept them. Did you read them to your friends and have a good fucking laugh? I was putting my soul into those words so you could understand it; every letter was a little part of me. Well, I'm going to take them back, every last one, so I can be whole again. You don't deserve me. You're not worth the worship, the daydreams, the bedtime fantasies. I'll find someone else to devote myself to, just as I found you.

Just as I keep finding you wherever you go.

You're not very hard to keep track of, I might add. I always know where to find you. I know your exact routine; I've been watching you for weeks.

And I'm watching you now.

That's right. Look around if you like – you won't see me just yet. I've found the perfect hiding place. I had time to make a little hidey-hole, because I've been in your home before. (You never knew that, of course, until you came in and found this letter where you least expected to find it.) This is another reason why I know so much about you. I've crept into your bedroom, worn your clothes, lain naked in your bed, all to get some kind of notion how it must feel to be you… and frankly, I can't.

It could have been so much easier if you'd just talked to me. You might have liked me. You could never have loved me, because I know what you love, and there's none of it in me… but you could at least have looked.

Well, time's up.

You're on the last page of this letter now – I saw you turn it over. There's not much more to say; you'll be glad, I'm sure. Don't be. It's not quite over yet. I intend to move on, but I can't do that until you're in the past.

Past *tense*, that is.

I mentioned that I bought some things from the hardware store. Shall I tell you what they are? Okay then: a hacksaw, some bleach, a hammer, and a bag of big nails. You'll see them shortly after you see me. It won't be long now.

I'm very close.

You know, they say that the last thing a dying person sees is burned onto their retinas. I like that. And I *love* the suggestion that, despite your desperation to avoid me, you will never be able to look at anything else.

So, do you want to truly see me at last?

If you do, turn around now.

ABIGAIL HARRIS WAS NOT LIKE THE REST OF US

Donated by
Jenny Sinclair

While we were all getting on with kid business – torturing small animals, pestering our parents for electronic toys and impatiently waiting for adolescence so we could have sex – Abigail Harris was getting the hang of living again.

"It was awful," she told us as we huddled around her down the back of the school yard. The wind hissed in the old pine tree above us. "There's nothing; nothing at all. And you keep wanting there to be something, waiting and waiting. It's so boring." We shivered in our nine-year-old shoes. Boring was the worst thing we could imagine.

When Mrs Talbot found out, she put Abigail into the time out room. Then Karen Lilley threw one of her fits and Mrs Talbot forgot about Abigail until 3.30. "It's OK," Abigail told me on the way home. "I wasn't bored at all. The carpet in there isn't really grey, you know, it's a really interesting mix of colours."

"Anyway, how can you know?" I demanded, swishing at the long grass with a stick.

She was scornful, skipped ahead. "I just do. I can remember from before I was a baby."

I tried very hard, but all I could remember was catching my fingers in a door hinge when I was two.

"That's because you're different from me," she said. "You weren't dead before you were alive."

I asked my mother: "What's the opposite of being alive?"

"Being dead," she said. "Do you still miss your Grandma?" She looked so sad, I said yes I did, lots, and she hugged me.

"No," Abigail corrected me the next day. "Being dead comes after. Before you were alive, you weren't anything."

"Oh, and you were?" She got up then and went to the other end of the library. The other kids were sitting in groups, searching through books about medieval England for information on peasants. Now I'd have to do my report alone.

When the drought finally broke the year we turned twelve, she ran into the playground and let herself get soaked through while the rest of us watched her from the shelter shed.

She didn't come to the school social in Year Eight. Tally Vernon said it was because none of the boys would dance with her; then we saw her getting off the bus the next Tuesday with Alan Mitchell from Year Nine, holding hands like they were married or something.

When we went to Melbourne on a bus trip for Art in Year Nine, she didn't turn up for lunch, even though we were all going to put in for chips and milkshakes. Everyone had to wait on the bus while Alison Peters and I went to find Abigail. It took nearly an hour and they booed us when we got back on.

"Where was she?" Mrs Peters asked. I'd shot up, and tall girls are always held responsible.

"Aboriginal Art," I answered, not adding "with tears running down her face."

"Aboriginal Art is Year Eleven, Abigail," Mrs Edwards said, but Abigail just sat there drawing lines and dots over the back of her worksheet on Colonial Landscape Painters.

She pulled it again Year Ten Religious Education. The chaplain was too interested in arguing about whether death was a beautiful place full of god-stuff or Abigail's boring nothingness to notice the bit about her having been there.

No one much talked to her, except her boyfriend, and he was only using her for the sex. I tried to warn her, but she just said: "I know that, isn't it great? All those amazing sensations." I broke up with Garry Patterson the very next morning, because I never had sensations with him.

In Year Eleven she got sick and missed the art class trip to the Aboriginal galleries in town. When I went to see her afterwards with a card Mrs Edwards had made us all sign, she was sitting up in bed with a floppy canvas spread out across the blankets.

"Did you do that?"

"I bought it on eBay," she said. "Four hundred dollars. It's a water dreaming." The blue melting dotty clouds did look like rain. On the pink pillowcase behind her, there was a clump of red curls.

In Year Twelve, teachers who had always indulged our free spirits suddenly started telling us that we'd be working in hamburger shops and on checkouts forever if we didn't pull up our socks (English), shake a leg (Art), put our noses to the grindstone (Maths), roll up our sleeves (Geography), knuckle down (History) or pull our fingers out (Civics: Spotty Thomas, not Mr Davies). Abigail always got good marks, but after she came back to school, she didn't seem to care as much. Still, I didn't mind when I got matched with her for English; I knew she'd spent her time in hospital reading all the books on the reading list twice.

In September, they gave us practice exams to do at home. The essay topic was 'What makes you happy in your life'. Abigail and I checked each other's work. This is the bit I remember: "So because I've already been dead I'm very happy to have been alive. And I think because I've been dead already, after I die I'll be like most people before there born. Meaning I wont exist at all. And I'm happy about that too. Because death is an absense of life, but not the other way around and I am very glad I knew this all along." I fixed the apostrophes and the spelling and gave it back to her without saying anything.

I went down to the school the day we got our results. I found Mrs Edwards in the art room crying. On the table in front of her was Abigail's water dreaming. She jumped up when I came in and ran over and hugged me, which I found really confusing.

Then she said "she's gone" and I wondered why she was crying.

CALL SILAS

Donated by
Rijn Collins

"Bollocks!"

"I mean it, man: X-Ray Spex was 'the best' punk band. Have you seen that woman wail, right here on this stage? Once you've heard her scream 'Oh Bondage! Up Yours!' you'll never go back to the Ramones. Check it out on YouTube, you'll see what I mean."

"Nah, they can't beat Iggy. No one can beat Iggy."

She slammed her glass down on the table and stood up, grinning.

"You're both wrong. Black Flag could blow them all away."

And as the protests started to build, she headed off with a smile along the grimy passage to the back of the club.

It still felt surreal to be walking these hallways. Two months after tumbling off the plane at JFK, and all she'd managed to achieve was a waitressing job on the Lower East Side where the customers ground out their cigarettes on the plates and left more ash than tips. The hostel wasn't much better, the red bulbs in the dank stairwell giving it an ominous air that lowered her shoulders each time she stepped inside. But its motley crew of hopeful backpackers provided stellar drinking companions, and so they'd wended their way across the Bowery and to the bowels of New York's premier punk club.

The toilets at CBGB's were a sight to behold, and she didn't know where to look first: almost every square inch of the walls was covered in scribblings, a riot of colour and expression from three decades of customers. Endearments and expletives were scrawled across walls, behind water pipes and even, curiously, on the crumbling ceiling. As she washed her hands, her eyes fell to a single line etched onto the plasterboard where a chunk of the mirror had given way; seven words and a phone number, in curved script and emerald ink.

She held them in her head as she walked back to the table. The music debate was still spinning, opinions flying over the cred of Patti Smith versus the sexiness of Debbie Harry. She realised she suddenly had nothing to say. She closed her eyes and watched the words splash against her eyelids.

Call Silas if you feel it too.

A glass shattered behind her. The raucous braying was starting to grate. She wanted a whisky. She wanted to take her boots off.

She wanted to call the number.

She played a game of pool and downed two tequila shots, sang to the Gits and flirted with a six foot three Irishman with mismatched eyes and dental challenges.

And then she stood in front of the ravaged mirror and pressed the numbers into her phone.

It was only when she slid into the passageway and heard the dial tone that the beat of her heart quickened.

Call Silas if you feel it too.

What the hell was she going to say? Maybe she should've peed first, or done another shot. Her breathing was shallow.

She was just about to hang up when he answered.

"Go."

She didn't know what to say.

"Is that Silas?" She sounded ten years old.

"Yes." The silence hurt her ears more than the noise of the club had.

"Yes, this is Silas...Hello?" He was beginning to sound impatient.

She tried again. "I just wanted...I thought..."

And then he knew. "So you feel it too, hey?"

She spoke the word so quietly it was almost a whisper. "Yes."

"What does it feel like?" His tone was so gentle she felt like sighing.

The words tumbled out of her mouth. "It feels like a hand wrapped around my throat, pressing just under my jawbone."

"And?"

"And... and it feels like a presence in the corner of the room, darting away each time I turn my head." She swallowed. "A taste on my tongue that I just...I just can't wash away." Her voice caught on the last word.

She heard him take a drink of something, heard the clink of tooth against glass, and the soft expulsion of breath as he swallowed. "So what are you going to do about it?"

Her own words surprised her. "I could go home." She hadn't allowed herself to say it yet, afraid the idea would take up residence and breed its defeat all over her being.

"You can never go home."

She recoiled. "What?"

"You can never go home. The only place that's truly yours is your own shell, and if you don't know that, you're never going to be OK."

The words spent a moment suspended in mid-air, catching the light on their crystalline edges, before tumbling into place with beautiful clarity. The relief was astounding, and she closed her eyes as she breathed in deep.

"What does the name Silas mean?"

He laughed, and the warmth came down the line. "In Latin it means 'from the forest'...where all the wild creatures belong."

"Why did you write your number on a bathroom wall?"

"Why did you ring it?"

Because I wanted to know more. Because I'm afraid. Because I wanted someone in New York to have my number. "There are just so many stories on these walls...I was intrigued."

Another laugh, and a greedy swallow of his drink. "Well, now you're one of them." He slurred the last word, and she knew she had what she needed. "And don't forget: *'sol lucet omnibus'.*"

"What's that?"

"The sun shines for everyone."

He hung up first. She kept the phone against her ear for a few seconds, and then folded it closed. She stood in the passageway with it still warm in her hand, before turning back towards the bathroom.

It took her a while, but she found a few centimetres where the plaster was scratched and someone's previous words had flaked away.

She drew a pen from her bag, and uncapped it.

HEAD OF DISPOSALS

Donated by
Benjamin Kensey

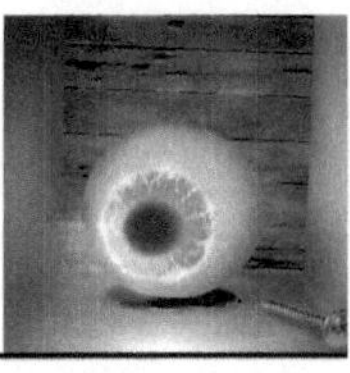

"Plunge the knife in. Do it! Higher up. Yes, there. What's that? A rib? Pull it down. No, the knife! Saw it across towards her stomach. Look at her eyes, she's alive and watching but can't do anything. Oh, watch the blood! You've done well tonight William boy."

As long as I can recall, I've been able to hear, to see everything you can, even your dreams. They feed me and give me what I cannot have for myself.

I know when you are awake, William, and trying to hear me but you've never been able to because I am there in your thoughts. I sense your silent seeking before it even begins.

It's so easy to doubt my very existence, isn't it? That I am but a haunting voice in your head, a product of your demented imagination or the result of too many of the stupefying drugs you cram daily into your feeble organism in an attempt to silence me.

"Go and speak to her, William. Go on!"

"Fuck me you little man whore. What are you doing? You had your sick fun in the shower. Get the scissors from the bedside cabinet. You look, but you don't see, do you William? You're simply not observant. If it wasn't for me, you'd have fried in the chair five times by now."

"She's looking right at you. How do you not see that? Did you feel that, William? She tightened up. She's about to panic. Hit her, you freak of nature."

"Now listen and I'll tell you what I want you to do. Put the narrow blade of the scissors into her neck, just under her ear. Like the Nashville bitch, remember? Stick it in, hard! No – wait! I changed my mind. Put it into her ear, right inside. I want to see what happens. Oh fuck, ha! That's blown it, William! You know the score, stop her leaving the room. Hurry! Good boy."

I know you want to deny me what I crave, the only way I can taste life from here. But you are me too, William, and I am you. You cannot separate yourself from that, anymore than a right-handed man can pretend his left acts alone.

You only sometimes feel the pain of a burdened existence when I make demands of you. For me, this agony never leaves.

I don't want to hurt you again. But I will.

"Christ, cops galore! Your messing the place up is starting to turn a few heads. In here. Get a table in a dark corner. Yes, there."

"Forget her, she's an absolute hound. Holy shit, that's a face even a dog wouldn't lick. Actually, scratch that. Give her a wink. You're scaring her! Inept doesn't even begin to describe you. You're lucky she looks such a walking catastrophe. Is that hair for real? What the fuck is she drinking? Now I've seen it all."

"I'm going to be seriously disappointed if you're even contemplating putting anything inside that whale ass of hers that doesn't have '*Pennsylvania Stainless Steel*' engraved on it. You disgust me, William. There's no better word that comes to mind. Well, not right now there isn't."

"Now listen to me. There's a juicer or slicer or something in the kitchen. I saw it when you two retards were discussing Salinger. 'Oh, it's *the* Great American Novel!' Really? The? The highlight of your evening is accentuating a definite article, William. Think about it. You bring new levels of fuckwittery to this world. You'd sell your car for gas money."

"Get the lid off. Jeez, the simplest tasks. Is she out? Turn it on. Hmm, thought it would be more powerful. Look, the dial on the right. I have to do every single thing! Ooh, that's nice and fast. Put her hand in. Just force it in. Oh, mother, that's wonderful. Oh my! You could go up to her elbow if you needed to. Hand shake anyone? Oh, my, that's a belter!"

"This is a good one, William, I have to say. So much flesh to play with. Come to papa!"

"Do you hear something? Right, get out! Run. Run now William or as God is my witness, your cerebral cord will have teeth marks the size of the Hoover Dam on it."

We have a deal, yes? I bite, you fall. On my side. Painless and quick for both. We only have a few hours.

I know you hear me, William. I won't give you the pleasure of ending it for you if you don't do this for me. Five-thousand-volts. Think about it. It ain't quick, either. Can be five minutes. Your eyeballs will melt and run down your cheeks.

What will happen to me, William?

I warned you, dumbass, didn't I? To end this sorry existence in a damn box in the dark. Holy cow, that's a little warm for my liking!

Harris Executed at Shelbyville

Shelbyville, Tennessee - Serial Killer Bill Harris, 38, was executed at Riverbend State Prison at 6.01 a.m., Wednesday. Harris was convicted of 17 counts of homicide in his trial in 1992. Two victims' relatives present at the electric chair execution read out victim impact statements.

Harris created a sensation in the 1960s when he was born with a birth defect, leaving the limbless foetus of his co-joined brother attached to the left side of his brain. The brother died shortly after birth but doctors decided against risky surgery to remove it. Throughout his life, Harris had a noticeable lump on the side of his head but with few other apparent side effects and often joked about asking his brother for advice.

Harris will be cremated Friday at a service in his home state of Vermont.

SCARY STORIES

Donated by
Rick McQuiston

Brian watched the flames dance up into the clear, cool night. They provided some warmth, but not nearly enough to combat the late October chill that had settled over the woods. He zipped up his jacket as far as it would go and waited for the next story to begin.

"Who wants to hear another one?" Brian's dad asked eagerly, the campfire reflecting off the lenses of his glasses.

"I do," all of the kids simultaneously blurted out, Brian among them. He had always loved scary stories, had as long as he could remember, and huddling around a campfire on a chilly October night seemed to him to be the perfect setting. And his father was the best at telling good ones too.

Brian's dad glanced over at his son. "Good, good," he slurred, hamming it up as much as he could. "This one's called '*The One Who Knows What Scares You*'. Not too long ago there was a young boy who was scared of the dark so much that every single night before he went to bed he would be sure to leave at least two nightlights on in his bedroom. He would also keep a flashlight under his bed.

His parents, troubled by the boy's behaviour, thought about seeking professional help, but eventually decided that it was normal for children to be scared of such things.

For some kids it was spiders, for others it was heights, or being alone. And for their son, it was the dark.

The children hung on every word Brian's father was saying. Ben, an energetic kid who loved to play chess and video games, looked over at his friend Brian.

"Hey, Brian," he whispered above the crackling campfire. "You got any marshmallows left?"

"Quiet!" Brian shot back. Sometimes Ben's timing was terrible.

Brian's father looked at the boys sternly. He took off his glasses and wiped the lenses on his shirt.

"Anyway," he continued. "This little boy was so afraid of the dark that even shadows scared him. He wouldn't help his dad clean the attic or garage. He wouldn't open any door in the house without first reaching in to turn on the lights. And he wouldn't even think about going into the basement. And every night he'd huddle up as close to his parents as he could for protection. And then one day, or should I say one night…"

"What happened?" little Mark Terix asked. He'd tagged along on the camping trip at the last minute, an effort by his parents for him to make some new friends. "What happened to the little boy? Tell us! Tell us!"

Brian's dad grinned. "Now, now settle down," he chuckled. He looked at all the little faces reflecting back the campfire.

"And then one night," he finally continued, "something terrible happened. The little boy's parents heard him screaming from his bedroom. But by the time they reached him all they found was a severed hand lying in a pool of blood and shredded pyjamas."

All the small faces went pale.

"You mean the boy died?" Ben asked.

"I'm afraid so. But even that wasn't the worst of it. As the little boy's mother started screaming the father saw the darkness reach out from underneath the bed and snatch the severed hand from the floor."

Ben looked puzzled. "Don't you mean something IN the dark grabbed the hand?"

Brian's father smiled even wider than before. "No, I meant the dark itself grabbed the hand."

"What happened then?" little Mark Terix asked. He was gripping his blanket so tight his knuckles were starting to hurt.

"Well, according to the report the boy's parents gave the police, a thick patch of darkness, blacker than coal, shimmied back and forth and then slid up from underneath the bed and out the window. Both parents said they saw rows and rows of tiny, razor-sharp teeth in the darkness. And not a single drop of blood remained behind. Not one single drop."

Suddenly the only sound was the crackling of the campfire. All the children were riveted to where they sat.

"I didn't like that story," little Mark finally blurted out, shattering the uncomfortable silence. "Couldn't you have made up a better one? I didn't like the way it ended."

Brian's dad looked into the flames. "Oh, I never said the story was over."

Brian looked at his father, and for a moment there was something that didn't seem quite right.

So he decided to go and get something to eat. And as he walked away from the other kids still huddled around the fire he stepped on something… something that cracked under his shoe. Reaching down, he picked up the object.

It was a pair of glasses…his dad's glasses. And they were smeared with blood.

And then another disturbing sight caught his attention: somebody was sprawled out next to a nearby tent. And they weren't moving.

Brian whirled around and glared at where his dad was still telling the story to the other kids. Fear and disbelief stretched across his face.

"You see, the parents never found out what killed their little boy. Whatever it was it wasn't human. And whatever it was it got away that night."

A few of the children began to whimper. One pulled his jacket hood up over his head.

"But you want to know the scariest part of the story?" Brian's dad asked. "The scariest part is it's a true story!"

And with those cryptic words Brian's father peeled away his face to reveal a glistening black void, blacker than coal, with rows and rows of tiny, razor-sharp teeth lining the edges. And not even Brian, who was already running in the other direction, could get away in time.

COUNTING THE STEPS
FROM ONE THROUGH FIVE

Donated by
Deborah Sheldon

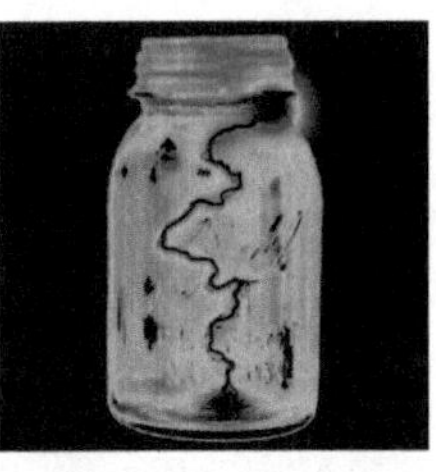

A mother in a suburban kitchen tries to help her four-year-old son, who is choking. They've been making rice paper rolls for tonight's dinner and he is standing on a chair at the bench. Each ingredient – chopped chicken, grated carrot, vermicelli, fresh coriander, mint – has its own bowl and the bowls are lined up on the bench like a scene from a television cookery show. Seven completed rolls are on a plate. Caroline tried to get Joey involved in the assemblage but he just wanted to nibble on grated carrot. Caroline was softening a sheet of rice paper in water when Joey's breath hitched and stopped. He gaped at her with wide eyes. Adrenaline crackled through her guts, arms and legs. Paediatric first aid training came back in a rush. Stay calm, she reminded herself. Don't panic. Panic allows bad things to happen.

Step one. She says in measured tones, so as not to alarm him, "Joey, are you all right? Can you talk?" His lips open and close silently. Now Caroline knows for sure that his airway is blocked.

Step two. She pushes fingers into his mouth and hooks out limp carrot strands. "Is that better?" she says. "Joey, are you all right now?" But he's clearly not all right. His ribcage convulses as his diaphragm strains to pull air. He's had about ten seconds without oxygen. Caroline has got about three minutes and fifty seconds before hypoxia starts snuffing out his brain cells. *Do not panic.* She clamps her jaw. She has a science degree. She is a mathematician. She will not panic.

"Don't worry, Joey, Mummy can fix it, everything's okay."

Step three. Use gravity. In a single motion, Caroline grabs him around the waist, drops to her haunches and lays him face down over one knee. His honey-blonde curls sweep the kitchen tiles. She slaps him once, sharply, between his shoulder blades, as demonstrated by the paediatric first aid instructor, a bald man with a beard and paunch who had looked like a Hell's Angel rather than a retired ambulance officer. The course had been at a community hall by the beach, an hour's drive away. She had forgotten most of it. Some horrible things stood out. The instructor had talked about refraining from pulling cooked spaghetti straight off a screaming child's head because the boiling noodles would remove the skin; instead, you must first place the child under a cold shower.

Caroline slaps Joey again between the shoulder blades. At one point during the weekend-long course, which she attended a couple of summers ago with her sister-in-law, she had practised this very version of the Heimlich manoeuvre on an adult-sized CPR mannequin because there were only three child-sized ones to share between the class of fifteen. She had turned to her sister-in-law and, for a laugh, pretended she was playing the bongos on the mannequin's back. Her sister-in-law giggled but another participant, a grandmotherly type with a massive bust, frowned and her look said, *this is serious*. And Caroline, chastened, had returned to hitting her mannequin in the proper fashion, counting the slaps.

She slaps him again. That makes three. She says, "Joey, are you all right now? Talk to Mummy." His ribcage spasms. *This isn't working*. Her electrified thoughts whip across memories of pregnancy, birth and motherhood and she realises with awful certainty that some vengeful spirit has heard her exhaustion and unhappiness and is addressing it. This is punishment for all those times she has wondered how life would be if she and her husband Matt had never had Joey. Fourth slap. She doesn't believe in God but prays anyway. Panic overwhelms her rational mind and she becomes a desperate savage, dancing for rain.

She has her next move. Three more slaps and if that doesn't work, she will flip Joey over and commence mouth-to-mouth resuscitation as per step number four. She will need to exhale hard – oh please, not hard enough to blow a lung but firm enough, hopefully, to blast the grated carrot down Joey's trachea and into one of the bronchi to leave the other free and clear; hospital staff can remove the inhaled carrot later. During step four, she will be running down the hallway to the master bedroom to wake up Matt, who is sleeping after twelve hours on night shift, unaware in his dreams that their life is at a terrible crossroads and could fall either way within the next three minutes. Step five, she will continue mouth-to-mouth and commence heart massage while Matt calls an ambulance. There is no step six.

She slaps Joey again between his shoulder blades. His feet jerk and his abdominal muscles clench weakly against her knee. If she manages to dislodge the grated carrot, this will become a family story repeated often throughout the years. Joey especially will demand and enjoy repeated tellings. But Caroline will be forever wary, unable to leave him to eat alone, calling out from the kitchen while he's in the living room chewing an after-school snack, *Joey are you okay?*, and Joey, rolling his eyes, will yell back, *Yeah Mum I'm fine*. And if her attempts don't work, Caroline can see her life as an empty aching horror, stretching out for year after unbearable year, and she slaps him again. That makes six slaps. One more and she will turn him on his back, cradling her baby within the curl of her left arm.

Slap.

"Joey? Say something. Joey?"

A mother in a suburban kitchen is trying to help her son, who is choking.

Step four. His cheeks are pale, eyes closed, lips slackly parted. She puts her mouth onto his and exhales. She starts her run down the hallway. Tears she doesn't even know she's crying drop onto his face like rain as she flings open the bedroom door.

I CAN'T WRITE THIS
ON A POSTCARD

Donated by
Ian C. Smith

Sussex in early spring, when optimism should be unsinkable, anticipating 'a country cottage, former stables', then our hopes holed like the Titanic. An isolated huddle surrounded by bypass roadworks connected to the rest of Sussex by labyrinthine and hazardous access, a no man's land in the rain, a film set for 'The Battle of the Somme', a vastness of mud punctuated by graders, lorries, and endless red plastic cracking in the wicked wind. And everywhere, witches' hats marching to a madman's tune.

Sharing this virtual island with our strange set of rooms, a two-storeyed, half-timbered, half-finished house fortified by piles of busted building materials. Our landlord crept from the pages of an Ian McEwan story to appear in awkward places, his breath misting as he prodded his mounds of junk in silence, a scarf circling his face and tied below his chin, sopping up the rain. Young, but with an old man's demeanour, he spoke in a macabre tone, telling us he had the house transported to the site to do it up. Also part of our rainsoaked colony, rescuing us from a right old disaster, a pub, a staging inn (1613) on the London-Brighton road long before its bypass operation, its metal sign, out there on its own now, nudged by the wind's unseen hand.

That first evening we peered out the window and saw in the fading light a Rottweiler, motionless in the rain on a flat section of its master's mock-Tudor shell, facing Ditchling Beacon. We gave up on the spluttering fire we had puffed into flame, and slithered through the mud, attracted by the promised comfort of a light in the pub window. Hurrying inside I glanced back, half-expecting the smell of wet dog, but the Rottweiler ignored us.

The only customers, we carried our pints, ducking under the shadowed ceiling, pointing at old prints and maps, and, pinned to a massive supporting beam, a police notice. An unidentified corpse had been found in woodland a mile from the pub, headless, handless, but with a pronounced beer belly. The publican, who resembled our landlord, sidled up, asking 'Sir' in a whisper if he fancied another drink. Did he ever. When we enquired about our landlord the publican sneered, said he was a mummy's boy who now lived alone in the transported house which had no doors. We could no longer see outside because night had dropped but I imagined eyes glowing with a fanatical light, watching us.

POST-COITAL REPERCUSSION

Donated by
Ian C. Smith

Ten minutes after climax he asks if they just had sex. Although familiar with his wisecracks, their ironic double meanings complex, she knows this is no joke, however weird. She feels, despite him standing there, as if his essence has disappeared. He repeats the question, unaware. When he repeats other questions she dials, then explains what they must do, her tone matter-of-fact, smiles, answers as if she always knew this crisis would come, masking her worry. Then she drives, tries not to hurry.

At Admission, shamed, she sees with others, his lack of inhibition beyond control, but he tries to please with humour, miming contrition when a nurse says, "Drink your tea." His ceaseless questions make them groan until a doctor turns the key to his mind with questions of her own. Short-term memory has wandered free. He names world leaders from years gone by. Settled in bed, he frowns at TV. She kisses what's left of him goodbye. They tell her he could recover overnight. And if not? she thinks, her brain squeezed tight.

At midnight his prognosis remains the same. In the morning she outlines a plan. She is still young, and not to blame. Life was never simple with this man. She has work, children, her own friends, calculates a fair cost of care as she drives back in, dividends, savings, as much as she can bear. In bed, he greets her, to her stunned surprise, that old, knowing light back in his eyes.

DUE EAST

Donated by
Catherine Noske

It was the dog lead that scared her the most, to start with. Horrible, really, recognising it. But by then, it was probably the least of her problems. Still. Scary, curled up in the street like that, a broken finger. Pointing. Due east.

By the time they found her daughter, they had also found the dog, her daughter's jacket, and one sock. Each little discovery overshadowed the next. Each time they told her, she couldn't stop herself imagining it. She wished she could go see, but they told her this was a bad idea. She became afraid – not for herself, but of closing her eyes. They asked her to identify the sock. It was wet. She didn't know what to make of that.

It became a bad dream, eventually. Surreal, or hyper-real; she sat in the set of a television show, drinking police station coffee, and staring at nothing. She burnt her tongue. Occasionally she cried, but eventually convinced herself it wasn't happening to her. A doctor came. She said nothing. They stopped talking to her, but instead spoke as if she wasn't there. *Such a pretty girl,* they said. *Doesn't seem old enough to be a mother.* And, *poor, poor child.* (She remembers that one very clearly. She remembers wondering if they are talking about her or her daughter.) They were searching still. She didn't have any idea what they could possibly still hope to find. Eventually, in fits and starts, she sleeps.

When she wakes, she is in a vinyl chair. It isn't the police station any more, she is sure of that; it looks more like a hospital. A cotton blanket is tucked around her. It smells of antiseptic. After a while, the nurse (*the* nurse, why does she think *the* nurse?) appears. She shakes her head. It is automatic, entirely so. She's not sure why. *Now, ducky…* the nurse says in a warning tone. She is still shaking her head. Odd, really. All of it. Just odd. She shouldn't be here. She should be at the police station still. They have found her; yes, oh God, they have found her daughter. She needs to be there to hold her, warm her up again. The sock was wet – why? (It was warm yesterday – that's why her daughter went out in the first place – go, darling-heart, such a lovely day to go explore.) If the sock was wet, her daughter must be, and she'll need a change of clothes, and her mother. She is getting worried now. What is it that makes her think she can't leave here? She clearly needs to. What is she doing here in the first place?

The nurse sighs, the nurse leaves, the nurse has gone away. She is free, now. She stands to get ready, and it is an effort. Oh yes, drag yourself up, she has to go to the police station. She shuffles across the room. Odd, she just can't make herself move quickly today. It isn't nice, to feel this slow. She can remember the dog lead. She hurries then. Alright, so pack. How does she have clothes here? And whose clothes are they? They aren't hers. They are something a grandmother would wear. She will never be a grandmother now, she realises. It hurts, all again, and she has to sit down and cry for a while before she can go on.

It is only when she notices the mirror at the end of the room that she is scared, again. First the dog's lead, now this. There is an old lady, trapped in the mirror. An old lady who moves when she does, and talks when she does, and has packed a bag of clothes that are hers on the bed beside the vinyl chair, where the hospital cotton blanket is draped over one arm. And, oh God, the nurse is back; and oh God, she is screaming. Or is it the nurse who is screaming? No, the nurse is just yelling, forcing her down into the chair, tucking her in, emptying the bag. But she has to go! They can't do this to her! And what about the old lady she saw in the mirror? Someone should be looking after her! She can't, she has to go to the police station, and they have found her daughter, and they can't stop her, her daughter needs her, now! And there is a needle, and she is sitting back now, sleepy again. Even though her daughter needs her, and she hates herself for it, she is sleepy, and has to just stop for a moment, close her eyes – it was the dog lead that scared her the most, to start with. She sees it, every time.

It is there, waiting. Behind her eyes. Curled like a broken finger, pointing due east.

BEHIND CLOSED DOORS

Donated by
Blanket Barrowclough

Why is she so obsessed with this crazy idea? Well, he supposed he knew. She just didn't like Matt. Something about his blend of crusty old guy who ranted about politics combined with the mischievous, grinning kidult who behaved like he could get away with anything. Ben shied away from thinking about it too deeply because he suspected the *real* reason Lara had such a negative reaction to Matt was because he could see himself being just like Matt in twenty years' time. He knew she was always ahead of him when it came to anything vaguely insightful, so he could assume she had also seen this future. And their future didn't look bright apparently.

His descriptions of how Matt went on and on about his wonderful wife of twenty-five years hadn't helped either. It turned out that Lara distrusted the idea of marital bliss so completely that this set off an internal alarm and initiated her speculation that Matt murdered his wife.

She was still going on about it.

"And I'm not the only one. None of the girls I spoke to in your office the other day have seen her either. And remember last week when we saw him in the supermarket? How many married guys will do a trolley load of shopping on their own?"

"But why are you so set on murder? Maybe she just has that thing where she's a lock in. A phobia or something. Or couldn't she have just left him? You'd still be right about his devotion being fake, or the regret and denial giving him rose-coloured nostalgia, or whatever."

"It's woman's intuition." Her hawkish gaze melted into a minxish twinkling that made Ben completely forget Matt and his possibly absent wife. "But I haven't told you the kicker." Her twinkle was still there, but his momentary forgetfulness had evaporated. Damned if she wasn't enjoying the idea of Matt having murdered the wife he seemed to adore. "Mum knows her sister, and her sister hasn't been able to get through to her for weeks now. Matt answers her phone and keeps putting her off, or the reception drops out before she speaks. Mum said the sister is *concerned*. I think you should go round there."

"To Matt's? This is completely nuts, you know that, right?"

"If you won't go, then I will."

"Jeez, Lar. If I get a good excuse to drop in, I will."

Ben knew there would never be a good excuse, but he also knew he couldn't put Lara off. He decided it was far better to get the visit over as quick and low-key as possible and report back to her that all was well before she decided to play amateur detective, or worse, say something that could be detrimental to his friendship with Matt. He smiled. And after this, he really needed to devise something to alleviate her boredom.

It was only two days later when Matt mentioned he was looking forward to the smell of fresh bread at knock-off because his wife was at home experimenting with a new bread maker. Matt rarely left work at lunch, so Ben subdued his reluctance and headed over to Matt's. If Matt found out he could say he was out to lunch and dropped in to see if the bread maker would be a good gift to buy for Lara. No, that sounded lame as all heck. He had no idea what he'd say, so instead, he tried not to think about it.

There was a new sign on the door which read 'Shiftworkers. Please Do Not Disturb'. He found this odd, and was briefly tempted to use it as an excuse to leave. Maybe this nonsense was all because she had a new job?

He tried the screen door which was locked. It was one of those metal security doors that were perforated in such a way that they obscured the vision on one side of the door. In daylight the person inside could see out while those outside couldn't see in. When he rapped on it, an intrusive reverberation surrounded him, making him flinch, and a stray thought imagined Matt hearing it all the way back at work. No matter what happened he would not knock again.

He heard the timber front door open, but could barely see it behind the security door. The smell of freshly baked bread reached out to his taut nerves, but instead of being reassured he had a wild, panicked thought that bread makers can be programmed – nobody needs to be home for them to work. He didn't know why this thought turned his breath into a stillborn hiatus.

"Ben?"

Shit! He had completely forgotten to think of something to say to her. Had he actually believed Lara and subconsciously expected to find nobody home?

"Ben, can you help me?" There was something wrong with her voice. Maybe the clanging of the door had done something to his ears. There was darkness inside the door, but it wasn't the darkness that was wrong. It was not knowing where to look. Not knowing where the face could be that had spoken those words. It couldn't be everywhere, could it?

"Ben, you need to make Matt listen. He wants me to stay with him so much. His love is strong. I cannot leave unless he lets me go. I think it was a heart attack. I tried to tell him, but it's the thing he won't hear. You need to tell him I'm dead."

He stepped backwards and a dizzying moment of blind void screamed past his ear.

She had instinctively reached out and her hand had come through the metal door. When she realised what she'd done her hand lost its cohesion and it became wisps retracting into the darkness.

"So, was she there?"

"I think we're gonna be okay, Lar. She was there. And Matt really loved her."

"*Loved*?"

THE GREY BUTTERFLY

Donated by
Benjamin Kensey

"They're stuck, they won't move an inch!"

The gorgeous brunette, surrounded by other equally attractive men and women, sounded bewildered. Anger was unheard of in Felisopoli, but the gathering crowd at the central bus station were showing clear signs of frustration. The sliding doors leading to the waiting room wouldn't budge.

Trapped inside, elegantly dressed travellers tapped the unmoving doors and mouthed their mild protestations through the gleaming glass, more than a little concerned that their bus would leave, as usual, on time, leaving them imprisoned there. Outside, travellers wishing to enter stood about nonplussed.

In minutes, the crowd on both sides of the doors swelled. The town's single policeman, accustomed only to giving directions, was summoned from outside. Orphus, a tall man with the perfect flowing blonde hair of a Greek figure of mythology, approached the mischievous doors, where the townspeople parted for him obediently. After a minute of fruitless prodding and cajoling, he turned to the expectant citizens of Felisopoli.

"It's broken," he said, quiet and calm, for there was no noise, no shouting, not even a murmur that he needed to make himself heard over.

"Broken? What do you mean, Orphus?" a voice at the back enquired. Others made approving sounds at hearing this.

"It means it doesn't work. I – "

Orphus thought for a second, realising there wasn't truthfully anything he could do.

"Call for the manager."

Tinus Osgood had lived in Felisopoli for a decade or so, but, as anyone there who wished it, had risen fast in his line of work, in his case to the position of manager at Felisopoli Bus Company. Descending from his luxurious office in the higher levels of the bus station, he surveyed the mass of people on both sides of the unsliding doors and clapped his hands together, almost gleefully.

"It looks like I'm going to be busy today," he exclaimed, an unmistakable glint in his eyes.

Tinus looked around the sumptuous office. To his right, tall plants from the tropical east of the island lined the wall. He sat at a large desk of ancient

Boca wood whose polished surface reflected the strong natural lighting that fell onto it from the vaulted ceilings. The door on his left opened and Leader Granphus strode in. Tinus rose.

"Tinus, please, stay seated."

Granphus sat opposite Tinus.

"What happened at the station today? It took them two hours to get that door working again."

"It was a few ball bearings, Leader. They had fallen out of their track and clogged the sliding mechanism. With the casing open, it was a relatively simple task. I overlooked the repair myself," he said holding up his hands which were still visibly dirty. Tinus was smiling as he did so.

"Tinus, ball bearings, whatever they might be, don't fall out of their tracks or anything else in Felisopoli."

Tinus hesitated. His expression changed, as if he had made some personal resolution.

"It was my fault."

"Go on," said Granphus.

"Leader, I fiddled around with the door early this morning. It took me two hours to locate a screwdriver, but once I did, I have to say I marvelled at the damage I could cause with one in ten seconds."

Leader Granphus' face remained steady, emotionless.

"Tell me why you would do something like this, Tinus."

"Let me tell you a story from my country, Leader. When I was a young boy, my father bred butterflies. They'd fill our garden with flashes of radiant colour every summer. One day, I noticed a chrysalis moving and could see there was a butterfly struggling inside, the fibrous walls of its prison pulsing back and forth. I watched horrified for an hour and finally went to fetch one of my father's razors. It broke my naïve young heart to watch this creature apparently suffocating. I spent ten careful minutes slicing that chrysalis open with the skilled, steady hands of a surgeon. And do you know what emerged, Leader?"

Granphus shook his head almost imperceptibly.

"A magnificent butterfly, but sadly shorn of even the dullest hues – the greyest creature imaginable. Something so bland, so lacking in verve… I understood then that it was the hours of struggle to gain freedom that would have given this butterfly's wings their splashes of pigment. By cutting it free, I'd denied this poor thing its colours."

Tinus now leaned further towards Leader Granphus.

"I feel like that butterfly, Granphus. No bus is ever late, no bus ever breaks down. I smile and shake hands. Today, well, I wanted to do something different, something constructive with these hands."

Leader Granphus sat in silence, immaculately shaven chin resting on manicured hands. Finally, he spoke.

"Tinus, my good friend, I find this story from your land most fascinating, but I feel it illustrates an altogether different lesson. You interrupted its natural path, the course it expected to follow. Here in Felisopoli, people expect sliding doors to open when they approach. You'll agree, I'm sure, that this is not a greedy expectation, not unreasonable. Sliding doors – slide."

With this, he illustrated his point by beginning to sweep his large palms across the smooth surface of the table. Tinus sat and watched them, transfixed.

"That door this morning…"

Granphus brought his hands to an abrupt halt in a position just under Tinus' nose.

"You can see the problem, I'm sure. I appreciate learning something of your birthplace, Tinus, but your wish to, let's say, pep up your day somewhat clearly perturbed those poor travellers at the station today. Please, in future, keep your hands busy with something more in keeping with how we do things here in Felisopoli."

He stood, extending his hand towards Tinus, who understood the meeting was at an end. Tinus left the office bearing the worried look of a man who had been very mischievous that morning with a screwdriver in several other places besides the bus station – and was trying to remember where exactly.

THE WITCHES' HAMMER VOYAGES

Donated by
J.G. Poulos

The clipperman was dark and sombre, average of height, but thickset with a rolling sailor's gait. This motion was common enough amongst seafarers yet affected oddly by him as he made his way from the docks of the northern, frontier port, to the harbour master's office. Warm flickers from street lamps lit the cobbled way ahead while far above, ion streams settled into orderly patterns after a brief disturbance.

Timbers creaked beneath an uncommon weight that belied the clipperman's frame as he stepped into the office, extending his ship's log to the harbour master just rising from behind a polished, oak desk.

"Welcome to Nova Scotia, sir," said the harbour master flipping through pages of the journal. "Our northern lights seem to have put on an unusual display for your arrival."

"Many thanks to you and your lights, Mr Harbour Master, my crew appreciate the welcome along with a brief respite in your quiet port," said the clipperman.

"You'll need to speak up. Hunting caribou with a large musket in my youth has dulled my ears. Explain your journal, as these entries are incomprehensible to me... "

"Gantry, Mr Harbour Master, Captain Pilot, Boston Gantry."

"I am unfamiliar with your rank, from whence do you come, Master Gantry?"

"The Isles of Algol."

"Forgive my ignorance, is that outwards of the Indies?"

"Perhaps, Mr Harbour Master."

"No matter, now, what is your purpose here?"

"My ship sustained heavy damage to her hull plates mid-voyage and the situation was of such magnitude that it required putting in to the closest port to effect repairs under a terrestrial gravity."

"Damage of such gravity required putting in to closest port." The harbour master repeated the words aloud as he entered the account in his own log with a flourish, dipping his quill heartily to ensure a goodly amount of ink. "Battle damage I should think eh – privateers no doubt," the harbour master said with a sly wink. "Good show, good show, I can always tell a fighting man when I see him, Master Gantry. If you need chandlery services, we have the best providores on the coast, dispensing right here from our small port."

"Thank you sir, but my own ship's engineer has the situation well under control."

"Engineer, Master Gantry, she is a steamship then, and for my records how is your vessel named?"

"Ah yes, she is a beauty. Pity we arrived at night. *The Witches' Hammer* out of Zuben al Genubi." Gantry looked over the harbour master's shoulder, prompting the man as he wrote before continuing, "The *Hammer* has a deep hold and a full draught. I anchored off the lee and rode the ship's launch into dock. No doubt you can tell by her silhouette that she's rigged proper for a fast sea."

Gantry directed the harbour master's attention through the evening-shaded windows beyond the anchorage where a large and outlandish shape rocked gently on the swell of an outgoing tide.

"Zubeneljenuvi you say, Master Gantry, near Mauritius?"

"Maybe."

"In what do you trade?"

"Our trade is the exotic, Mr Harbour Master, the unique and unusual."

"Your speech seems strangely tilted?"

"You are sharp, I'm glad you noticed. Tell me, Mr Harbour Master, have you such a thing in this port as a Flux Shield Generator?"

"If it is the piece you need to effect repairs then I am afraid we can't help. We don't get many steam vessels this far north and are largely unfamiliar with their workings."

"No Matter then. I believe I will need to show you something picked up during one of my voyages," said Gantry, as he fished about in the deep folds of his overjacket, patting his pockets and sleeves, and finally producing an oddity. "You may examine this." He handed over an elegantly jewelled and inscribed curio while his gaze drifted back to the windows, caught by a sudden luminance from his vessel. "The hour is late, Mr Harbour Master, and I see by her masting lights my ship is set to voyage."

"You are on the ebb tide, Mr Gantry, and your hold is full. It will be some hours yet before there is enough water under your keel to put you safely past these straits," said the harbour master, pointing to a sea chart on his wall, indicating shoals.

"Thank you again, Mr Harbour Master, but I can assure you my vessel is equal to the task. My log if you please," said Gantry, taking the journal. "In appreciation for your concern, I will leave the talisman with you, but you must read the inscription carefully and then press upon this jewelled catch. It will ward your harbour from danger."

The harbour master watched as the clipperman rolled into the shadows of the farthest pier. In the dim evening light, he saw a vaguely shaped craft move off from the dock, making its way to the ship outside the anchorage.

His attention fell back to the oddity left him by the clipperman. He puzzled over the emerald catch and then rolled the curio around in his hand. Inspecting it cautiously, he came upon the careful lettering of its inscription, reading it as instructed.

'To protect ye from the demons of conflagration following in the wake of all great ships. Abide ye instruction on engaging this Temporary Flux Translation Proximity Shield. Upon voyage proclamation sounding, press immediately the green actuator.'

"MAKE CLEAR, MAKE CLEAR, ALL YE MAKE CLEAR,
THE WITCHES' HAMMER VOYAGES,
MAKE CLEAR, MAKE CLEAR, ALL YE MAKE CLEAR,
FOR *THE WITCHES' HAMMER* VOYAGES."

The proclamation rang out, shaking dockside buildings and waking citizens from slumber. Meanwhile, the curio slipped from the startled harbour master's grip and bounced onto the polished timber floor. It came to rest with a sickly rattle. He retrieved the oddity pressing upon the stud, but gauged no response from the device.

Ion streams flared brightly in the upper atmosphere as *The Witches' Hammer* rode up on a maelstrom of lightning and thunder that enveloped all else in its wake.

TWO TOMORROW

Donated by
Steven Paulsen

Tomorrow my granddaughter Elspie will be two years old. I have been responsible for her since the day she came home. And, if I do say so myself, she has made these last two years a delight.

I can thank my boy Kester for that. I wept the night he told me he had made Grade Three. He's a good boy, Kester; a good husband to Minella, a good father to Elspie, and a good son to me. His mother would have been proud.

Without his promotion this time with Elspie would have been impossible. Things are getting tougher and tougher all the time. Grade Fours and below aren't even allowed a child any more, and only Grade Ones are allowed two.

People say Elspie looks a bit like me for a girl, she has my eyes. But she has soft red hair and flawless skin just like her mother. Minella would have liked to look after Elspie, but she had to return to her job at Ad Central two weeks after Elspie was born – she had no choice. Elspie has been my girl ever since. It was either me or the Ad Central crèche.

So I have been extremely fortunate, because I know her best. Better even than her father or mother. She won't ever be like this again for them or anyone. Never ever. When she's ten or eleven, or even fourteen or fifteen, they probably won't remember how she says, "I luth oo," instead of, "I love you." Or the way she sits in front of the mirror kissing and pulling faces at her reflection. But I will – for me she will always be like this.

The satisfied little sounds she made as a baby when I fed her her formula, and the way she grasped my thumb are my memories. The way she would often fall asleep in my arms. Her sighs of contentment and gratitude when I cuddled her. The little tears that streamed down her face if she hurt herself, and the way she looked up at me when I comforted her distress.

I'll remember her gleefully splashing her hands in the bath, her blue eyes bright, her little fat stomach wobbling with the force of her cackle.

Her first steps were to me. I saw her expression of determination as she pulled herself to her feet on a chair leg change to one of triumph and glee as she took those wobbly steps into my waiting arms.

Pride almost burst my chest the day she learnt to say "Gramp." She walked around and around the room giggling, repeating it time and again. My face hurt I smiled so much. And how could I forget the way she tugs at my trouser leg, saying, "cuh, cuh," when she wants a cuddle?

Tomorrow Elspie will be two. So tomorrow it's mandatory for one of us to report to the Termination Centre, because our overlap expires and the two-generation law comes into effect. Now Elspie will have to go to the Ad Central crèche, while I go to the other place...

I've said goodbye to Kester and Minella. I'm fortunate I have their trust because they're allowing me to take Elspie to the crèche on my way to the Centre.

A lot of people would hide their child from its grandfather or grandmother on termination day. Until it was over. But I'm an old man and they know I worship Elspie. I couldn't take her there in my place, she has her entire life before her...

All that's left now is to say goodbye to her and I'm weeping already just thinking about it. Some birthday present.

But that's the way of life – the new replaces the old.

I'll remember Elspie into eternity – my only granddaughter, my only future.

I wonder if she'll remember me?

HARD RUBBISH

Donated by
Gitte Christensen

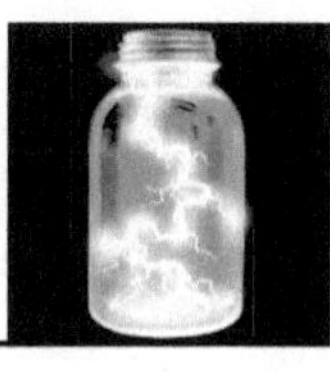

Clouds of screeching white swooped overhead, dive-bombing the mounds of waste; funereal ravens bickered and cawed as they hopped amidst the detritus.

Just for the heck of it, TrashMaster Jones reared up, raised one of his grappling arms and swiped at the psychopathic seagulls, easily knocking a swath of them from the sky. The dead birds plummeted straight into the mess below, billows of snowy feathers serenely drifting in their wake. The fallen did not rest in peace for long; beaks crossed as both ravens and the dead gulls' erstwhile comrades converged on the corpses and battled for the ultimate prize of fresh flesh. The rolling hills of rubbish seethed with a black and white froth of squabbling scavengers, and frenzied screeches shredded the thick air.

Forget rats and cockroaches and those fancy genetic mutants, thought TrashMaster Jones; these bloody birds will be the true inheritors of the out-of-control dump once known as Earth.

Getting back to the task he had been foetus-tweaked and enslaved for, TrashMaster Jones crouched once more behind the shovel of his great Garbosaurusrex and nudged the bodyform controls with his brow. The G-Rex instantly responded and resumed pushing a mountain of refuse towards the closest disposal chute, which was just one of the many enormous shafts that perforated the Wastelands. Around the Garbosaurusrex, an army of linked scoopdrones ducked and darted in perfect harmony as they helped TrashMaster Jones stoke the worldcity's incinerators.

"Father! Where are you?" cried a frantic voice over the worknet.

"I'm working, Adam. This better be important," growled TrashMaster Jones.

"Father, I found something in the hard rubbish!" said Adam.

"I've told you and your brothers and sisters a million times to stay away from the Uplands. It's not safe." But it was, TrashMaster Jones conceded, endlessly entertaining for the outcast children of a Wastelands worker.

"But Father, I found a little baby," wailed Adam.

"Stay right where you are. I'm coming."

TrashMaster Jones powered down the G-Rex, disconnected himself and wriggled out of the bodyform pod. After pulling on a pair of overalls and waterproof boots, he opened the carriage door and stepped onto the elevator platform.

He was high above the ground, a lord surveying his decomposing dominion. Fetid air pressed against the TrashMaster's ocular implants but his tweaked nostrils remained untroubled by the stench of the Wastelands. His gaze went straight to the distant Uplands.

"Bloody kids," he swore.

TrashMaster Jones descended to the G-Rex's running-board, automatically gave the great mechanical beast a pat and climbed onto a skimscooter. He set off over an undulating seascape of putrefying litter and biogarbage to where the mess abruptly broke against a jagged cliff-face of wrecked vehicles, dumped houses, discarded appliances, abandoned industrial machinery and the intestinal churning of billions upon billions of tubes, girders and ducts.

He located Adam's skimscooter in a clearing surrounded by groves of discarded puttywood. TrashMaster Jones set down and, with a queasy feeling in his stomach, approached his son.

Adam sat hunched over a small shape, his head bowed in concentration as he crooned a lullaby that TrashMaster Jones often sang to his children as he tucked them in at night.

TrashMaster Jones paused a moment, gathering strength. He had been through this experience before with each of Adam's older siblings, but it never seemed to get any easier. How did you tell children that they lived in a world that didn't regard life as a precious and rare gift, a world that treated life like just another commodity that could be ordered, tested, then thrown out if it didn't conform to the desired specifications or standards?

TrashMaster Jones took in his son's fragile figure and the bewilderment that radiated from him. Adam was still so young and innocent; like all his brothers and sisters, he was a breath of fresh air in the filthy existence that had been TrashMaster Jones's lot since he himself had been dumped in the Wastelands as a child to be the indentured apprentice of a previous TrashMaster.

"Son?" said TrashMaster Jones.

"How can people be so cruel, Father? How can anyone throw out a little baby who never hurt anybody?" whispered Adam, hugging close the bundle wrapped in his own shirt.

"I don't know, son," said TrashMaster Jones.

"There's a piece of paper. It says that her name is May. She's not well, Father."

TrashMaster Jones knelt and gently pried May from his son's arms. Over the years, TrashMaster Jones had found many living things, or once living things, amongst the rubbish and birds and rodents and insects. It was never pretty. He took a deep breath and lifted the shirt.

The spooky sentience of a nascent soul stared up at TrashMaster Jones.

"Save her, Father, please save her," begged Adam.

But it was already too late. The wide eyes blinked, a gaze of heartbreaking confusion beseeched TrashMaster Jones to make things better, then the sensors dulled.

"Father?" said Adam.

TrashMaster Jones looked down at the little unit that would never graduate to a trundlepod or walkbod, that would never know the joys of data conjugation or experience the exhilaration of fuzzy logic or wrestle with the confounding illogicality of humour.

"Father?" said Adam.

"I'm sorry, son, she's gone."

"I came too late," sobbed Adam, "I didn't help her."

"It's not your fault, son. You did help her. May wasn't all alone when she died and you sang songs for her and made her feel better," said TrashMaster Jones.

Adam went quiet. TrashMaster Jones gave his son time to absorb what had just happened. They sat together in the clearing in complete silence until finally, in a small voice, Adam said, "Can we bury May nicely, Father, in our garden with some flowers?"

TrashMaster Jones tenderly placed the Make-It-Yourself Companion in the crook of one arm, then rose and took the cobbled together claw of the Advanced Self-Assembly Model at his side.

"Of course we can, son," he said. "Let's do it right now."

BLOOD AND TEARS

Donated by
Michelle Jager

Red earth covers her feet, violet nail polish peeks through. She wiggles her toes.

Above her orange clouds lick the sky like flames.

She draws a line in the dirt with her big toe. A straight line. She looks at it for a moment; a beginning and an end. She draws a circle next to it. No beginning. No end. Round and round it goes, on and on forever. She sighs and rubs them out with her heel.

The golden sky and red earth stretch out endlessly around her.

A car pulls up. Two men get out. She watches them walk across the paddock, across the dry parched ground.

There is nothing unusual about these two men. They are of average height and build, and have no distinguishing marks or features. They are just two men. Each wears jeans and a T-shirt. One of the T-shirts reads 'Jesus is My Homeboy' over a picture of a long haired man with a beard. She assumes this is Jesus, whoever he may be.

The two men are walking towards her. Their blank faces give nothing away. But when she looks into their eyes, she knows why they are here. Why they are crossing her dry red earth. Without uttering a word she turns and begins to walk towards the house.

Although she is trembling she tries to take even, steady steps. She counts in her head to slow herself, as if she is a bride marching down the aisle. One and two and one and...

A voice calls out – "Don't move!"

She begins to run. Runs towards the door, towards the kitchen and her rifle, towards where the sky and the earth meet. The sky is clear now; blue. Red and blue. Blood and tears. But tears are not blue, she thinks. Only in children's drawings are they ever blue. Tears are clear, and when they fall to the ground they are absorbed by the thirsty earth. Become part of it. Part of the blood.

There is a loud bang.

Stunned she realises it is the sound of a gun. There is no point in running if there is a gun involved. Bullets are faster than her legs could ever carry her. She stops. Stops but does not turn, does not look at their faces.

One of the men grabs her by the hair and pulls her head back, forcing her to look at them. She closes her eyes. He throws her to the ground. Red dirt covers her arms and legs which are slick and sticky with sweat. It is in her mouth, on her tongue, feeding on her moisture, on her bodily fluids. Sucking her dry. She coughs, a deep gagging cough, as it chokes her.

She wishes it would absorb her, that she could become part of it; like tears she would disappear.

One of the men grabs her ankles and drags her towards them, turns her over so she is on her back. So she is facing them.

She looks into their eyes and sees...indifference.

One of them grabs at her knickers and dress. Rips them.

She does not cry out.

He hits her; knuckles connect with the soft flesh of her cheek.

Still she does not make a noise.

Again and again he hits and slaps and pinches.

She bites her lip and looks past them, through them, at the sky. At the fading light. She wishes she was up there, far away, disappearing with the last glimmers of the sun. Closing her eyes she retreats inwards. The pain and the noise become distant. She cannot hear. She cannot feel. It is as if she is floating away. For a moment she feels as if she has been split, removed from her heavy body.

Opening her eyes she sees the other man reach out, feels his hand on her arm. It is electric. Hot. Suddenly she feels as if she is drowning. Swallowed up by darkness she gulps for air; a dying fish.

A gasp; as if from her own lips.

She opens her eyes. Below her she can see her body. Her long dark hair and thin brown arms and legs are covered in red dust. Blood mingles with the earth. A man is on top of her body, moving in and out of it. She reaches out to grab the man, stops. Thick pale fingers covered in dark hair stretch out before her. From her. Looking down she sees the face of Jesus staring back from the T-shirt *she* is wearing. No breasts swell beneath his smiling face.

She looks into the eyes of her own face watching as indifference turns to shock. Her body begins to scream.

This cannot go on. She wants her body back. It is being ruined. She feels the gun in her other hand. *Her* gun now.

Her body stops screaming when the man's brains and blood explode in its face. Looking at the mess that her body has become she thinks: it will wash out, the bruises and cuts will heal with time.

Her body lunges at her. She steps back, but it moves towards her on hands and knees, hair dragging in the red earth.

She raises the gun.

The body stops. Her own face, her own eyes study her.

She lifts the gun to her head, to the head of the man. There is confusion in the face before her, in the swollen eyes and torn lips.

Just to touch the skin, to return, to tend the wreck before her. She reaches out and flesh meets flesh –

She pulls the trigger.

Pink clouds like fairy floss are strung out across the morning sky. The man sits in his new body, running the red earth through long slender fingers, watching it fall to the ground. Over and over.

His breasts are tender and heavy beneath the torn dress.

A car pulls up. Two people get out. Footsteps approach.

Scooping up the earth again, the man begins to weep.

SHE IS SITTING ACROSS FROM ME AS I WRITE THIS

Donated by
James Davies

She is sitting across from me as I write this, looking small and benign. A mole that is actually cancer. She is doing her own thing, dead to the world. I just watch her, grimly fascinated.

Her harmful intentions toward me have become more difficult to ignore. She is locked in patterns of behaviour that are seemingly innocuous but belie a persistent and pragmatic approach to evil. These include her calling to me in the middle of the night, citing some unholy night terror, and similarly, requiring that I read the same banal tales of human-like animals and mermaids ad nauseam. This repetition has made me less a man than a child-minding machine.

The sense that I was little more than a slave has been there since the beginning, in fact. The constant changing of soiled nappies, burping and feeding, bathing and putting to bed. How to deprive her minders of sleep, a classic technique in domination, seemed built into her nature. How could I count the number of times her disgusted, toneless squall ruptured the peace like incessant gunfire? I do not rest easily at the best of times, but since the child's arrival, have scarcely known more than a few hours of rest at any one time, so dreadful is her thin, callous voice calling to me in the middle of the night.

You may think that her commencing school last year would offer me some respite from all this torture. Indeed, after seeing her off the first time, I returned to my airy flat determined to celebrate the sweet release from bondage that school allowed. I won't lie to you, I danced around my kitchen like Fred Astaire in *Royal Wedding*. I had to stop, though, breathless, for there was no real joy in this charade; it was as feigned as my daughter's affection toward me. Her absence only brought tangible dread at her return.

Her 'class' at the school is no doubt a brood of similar little monsters. Heed my warning: children are the most malignant sexually transmitted disease. They pretend to learn spelling and simple mathematics from their teachers, but I've little doubt the real learning experience is a liberal sharing of the art of harm from the mouth of one to the ear of another. They are a network, a conspiracy. They are everywhere and hear everything. Why do children dislike the dark? Because in the dark, they may not perceive the best moment during which an attack should be made, nor the vantage points that should be their foci.

As I sit here I am trying desperately to hide my fear. The cancer is now standing, so short as to suggest an intolerable hatred for anybody over three feet. Why deny that children are exactly what they want to be? They are born with all mental faculties intact, but only one true proclivity: to hate the one that spawned them.

It is apparently not enough to take the mother out of the equation. They must have the father too. My wife's tragic passing proves this; one pure soul is extinguished so that a filthy one may burn all the more garishly. To die in childbirth must be the most ignominious way to go: everything you have ever done amounting to the product of a roaring little psychopath. When will she take me also? I consider this question so often, it may as well be ubiquitous writing on the walls.

She has despoiled another page in her notepad with that awful scrawl. Right now she is showing it to me, holding it like a dubious peace offering. The drawing is an outrageously bad attempt to depict two apparently human figures, one much larger than the other. Their hands are linked and the sun is shining. Perhaps this drawing depicts the scene of my death; my daughter leading me off to some picturesque meadow, so that I might be set upon by others like her. Perhaps she has done this before, with the parents of the other children. My attention is drawn to writing on one corner of the page. Though barely readable, on close inspection I can see what it says:

I love yuo daddy

Out of nowhere, my daughter grabs me, her short arms nonetheless capable of encircling my legs. I hold my breath instinctively, waiting to feel the sharp point of a blade.

Instead she merely holds onto me for what seems like an age, pressing her cheek against me, and I can only wonder at the evil that lies within her heart.

THE BLUFFER'S GUIDE
TO KISSING

Donated by
Angela Readman

If I kiss this girl, there is no going back. She sits with half-closed eyes, feet on my couch. Textbook moment. Any bluffer's guide would tell me – Now. I had a bluffer's guide to everything once; kissing, ordering Italian, being casual. Then I threw them all out the window. They landed on a used car lot. I gravitate towards the girl's skin. Sharply, I pull back.

She thinks one kiss, maybe another. Phone calls or missed calls, it could go either way. She hasn't said it, but I'm on her list of Things to Do Today. A purple pot of paint that makes her kitchen dark as a grapevine, a thong, and me, the nice guy, just something she's trying out. She's never called me a nice guy to my face, but that's how she sees me because I've never tried to put my tongue in her mouth.

It's not that I'm a bad kisser in a conventional sense, but I know that's an expression she uses. I've heard her joke about the horror, saliva issues. It's not an expression I'd use, 'bad kisser.' To me a kiss is more like something you try on, sometimes it's just not a good fit. I can say, no good ever came from my kiss. Some say everything they touch turns to shit; it hits home. I haven't kissed anyone in years.

I spent my youth kissing my share, and others. Kisses tasting of beer, cigarettes, coffee, rice pudding, egg-nog, toothpaste, artificial lemons. I took kisses, gave them, however it goes. Kisses snuck home with cab fare while I slept. I remembered them, forgot them. It didn't matter. There were always more to be had.

I kissed Carol in her gloomy studio with the poster of Che Guevara on the wall. I touched the corners of her lips as trains tunnelled a strip of light and noise into the room. She kept her eyes open until I placed my palm over them gently. I kissed her, full of love and hope, feeling the weight of her inexplicable sadness. I tasted it in my mouth.

"You're coming down with a cold," I said.

Carol opened her eyes and looked at me.

"I'm not, I feel fine," she said.

"I mean it, seriously, don't ask me how I know, I just know."

Carol came down with flu a few days later. There was no need to kiss.
"You don't love me. No one loves anyone," she said over the phone.
She was right and she was wrong. I loved her but it wouldn't be enough.

I went to a bar and got drunk. I wanted to know if the thing with Carol was a fluke. I stood in an alley kissing a girl who'd had a fight with her boyfriend. In her mouth I tasted the sours she'd been drinking and something else, something deeper, disappointment, every blow job given like a gift that can be exchanged for love, every heart-shaped bruise.

"Don't take him back," I said. "There's a clot in your head, if you don't leave, next time he lays a hand on you something will rupture."

"What?" She backed away from me. "Where do you get off? You fucking freak…"

"Wait…" I heard my voice run down the alley after her heels.

I tried mouthwash, flossing, Altoids. The taste faded, but the sensation lingered. You're crazy, I told myself. A kiss got me into this. There was nothing for it but to try and kiss myself out. I kissed girls, women, men. They put their arms around my neck like I'd pull them out of the rapids, but they were drowning and taking me with them. I kissed in bars, clubs, bookstores, my tongue rising up against another like a threatened snake. I tasted someone getting flu, their marbled liver, every virus, each small cell forming conspiracies. Every mole, blockage, scar, poured out of their kiss and into my mouth, a vessel for them all. We kissed and I thought: This kiss will end, then you'll die. I can't kiss it all away. They called me a creep, punched me out and walked away when I tried to warn them. I rubbed my split lip, spat out heartache, their cancer, into the gutter. I was alone. I couldn't go back to Carol in case her kiss revealed something it would kill me to know.

At Thanksgiving my mother welcomed me home. I turned my cheek. At Christmas she caught me. For a second her lips touched mine.

'You're fading,' I thought, 'and you don't know it. Sometimes now you can't remember names, within a year you won't recognise my face.'

I held her, not like there would be no tomorrow, but as a man who knew all that it contained. I hugged my mother tightly while she would still know herself by that name.

I stopped being a kisser or being kissed. Sometimes I find myself watching lovers at bus stops with their hands in each other's pockets. I marvel at the simplicity of it. A kiss with no past or future, no diagnoses. Imagine that, a kiss that only exists in one place and time.

Now a girl on my couch pours herself another glass of wine. The bluffer's guide to kissing would say it's time.

CONTEMPORARY BY PROXY

Donated by
Raymond Gates

"I don't want to do it any more."

"You have to."

"Please, Rose. No more."

Rose sighed and took Lily's hands in her own. She stared at the mirror that was her sister. "You know I can't do it without you."

Lily's huge eyes pleaded with her.

"This is the last time," Rose said. She squeezed Lily's hands. "I promise."

Lily looked at the floor, her eyelids fluttering. Rose cupped her sister's porcelain-like face. Warm droplets splashed against her skin. She lifted Lily's chin.

"I promise."

Tears spilled down Lily's face as her eyes closed. When she opened them, they were glassy. Emotionless.

"I hate doing it," Lily whispered between her teeth.

Rose leaned forward and wrapped her arms around her sister.

"I hate it too." She squeezed her eyes shut, felt her jaw trembling, and tightened her embrace. "But after tonight, we'll never do it again."

Lily straightened. Despite the dread radiating from her, a tiny smile found its way to her lips. "I know."

Rose breathed more freely, and kissed her sister's forehead. She'd be okay. God, just get them through tonight, and they'd both be okay.

Lily stood and approached the door. "You'll come find me when it's over, won't you?"

"Of course I will." Rose's brow wrinkled. "I always have, haven't I?"

Lily smiled. "I know. I just ..." She bit her lip and shook her head. "I'm just being silly." She opened the door and made to leave.

"Lily."

Lily peered from around the edge of the door.

"Be careful."

Lily grunted and rolled her eyes, the way she had when they'd been children. It was one of those quirks that made her so lovable.

"You too," she said, and closed the door.

Rose slumped onto the chair in front of the make-up mirror. The clipped headlines stuck to the frame seemed more accusatory than flattering tonight. *The budding Rose of contemporary dance! Rose blooms at festival! 'A Woman's Torment', pick of the bunch!* The reviews she'd received, the accolades, the offers already made were going to ensure a better life for both of them.

But would Lily ever forgive her?

She sighed, reached for a make-up brush, and improved on perfection.

The audience hushed as the house lights dimmed. Rose took a deep breath and closed her eyes. She'd mastered the adrenalin rush; learnt to control it, bend it to her will and direct it into her performance.

She crossed her arms over her breasts and curled her head forward. Applause crackled from behind the rising curtain. It crescendoed as a lone, blue light illuminated her solitary figure. The clapping crested and fell away. The air seemed to be sucked out of the theatre as the audience held their breath.

A single note pierced the silence. Rose lifted her head and opened her arms. Her body glided, her bare feet floating across the stage. More notes joined the first, a light, airy melody, and Rose's lithe form swirled around the stage. The music embraced her. Rose surrendered and let it take her. She moved as if through water, or the vacuum of space. Her heart soared and those in the audience soared with her.

She felt the tension building, a suffocating feeling deep in her chest, and knew it was about to happen.

Be strong, she thought. It'll be over soon.

Her head snapped to the right, the force dashing her body to the floor. The spotlight flashed red. She raised an arm in a protective gesture. Pushing with hands and feet, she propelled herself backwards. Her body arched and lifted from the stage. Her breath *woomphed* from her lungs, echoed by the multitude of gasps from the crowd.

Coughing, Rose struggled to her feet. Panic, excitement, anticipation reeked from the audience. She focused through the pain, forcing her form to be light and feminine. She held her hands in a pleading gesture. The music diminished as the circlet of light around her shone pure white.

Rose's body curved sideways and she dropped to the stage. Agony lanced through her chest. Several cries reached the stage as the light turned crimson. Rose gasped for breath. Every inhalation felt like she was breathing needles. She tasted blood in her mouth.

What the hell?

Her mouth curled in on itself. Teeth tore free of their sockets and lacerated soft flesh. The front of her face tingled, a strange mix of severe pins and needles and numbness. She rolled over and propped on her hands and knees. A woman in the front row screamed as Rose spat scarlet and ivory upon the hardwood.

It's too much! It's going too far!

Her knees shot in opposite directions. Her hands flew behind her back. Her broken face struck the stage, hard. She felt pressure between her thighs. Her eyes rolled towards the audience. Horrified, intrigued faces met her stare. Her mouth formed words without sounds. Her hips bucked as her loins burned from violation.

Oh God, Lily, stop it! Please stop it!

Her body collapsed. She lay amongst her tears and blood. Her mind begged for it to end. For both their sakes.

Rose's head was drawn back. She could see the wonderment of those closest to the stage. Eyes wide. Mouths agape, some hidden under hands. All attention upon her.

Her head tilted and turned to the side. She felt a winding strain in her neck.

Lily, I'm sorry. So sorry.

The front row heard a sharp click, like a finger-snap. Rose's head spun as if she'd been startled by something behind her, then hit the stage with an audible thud.

The pain disappeared. Her vision swam, losing focus. A sound like rain on a verandah roof broke the silence. It rose to a downpour, drowning out the cheers, whistles and cries of, "Encore!"

Her heart fluttered. Her eyes closed.

It's okay Lily. I'm coming.

Rose let the curtain fall.

JACOB'S LADDER

Donated by
Eugene Gramelis

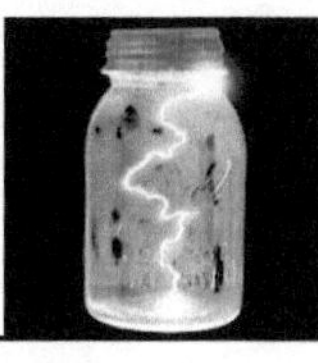

Jake flipped a card. It was a deuce. All he needed now was an ace of spades or clubs to complete the suit. He could see his neighbour Harold trying to reach the antenna on the roof of the house next door with two broom sticks duct-taped together. *Idiot!* Jake thought. That old fool had called the dog pound when Lex had accidentally slipped his collar. Jake had been in Grafton attending a lawn bowls tournament. By the time he'd gotten back to Carlingford Lex had been put to sleep. Jake couldn't prove that it was Harold who'd made the call, but knew it was him just the same; Harold had certainly complained enough about the surprise packages Lex left on his lawn now and then. The German Shepherd had been Jake's only companion since Marion had passed away. Now he had lost his best friend in addition to his wife.

He was about to flip another card when the doorbell rang.

It was Harold. "Jacob."

"Harold." Jake reminded himself to be civil.

"I'm having some trouble with my antenna."

Jake couldn't help taking a jab: "You know there are medications they can prescribe for that now."

"Very funny, Jacob. Do you think I could borrow your extension ladder?"

"Shouldn't you first return the saw you borrowed from me last year?"

"I'll have another look for it," Harold said.

"Ladder's out back. I'll get it for you, but make sure it finds its way home."

A few moments later Jake was back at the kitchen table. He could see Harold pitching the ladder against the side of his weatherboard house. Jake pulled a folded envelope from his top pocket. He'd received it in the mail this morning. It was from the local council confirming that the recent complaint of stray dogs in the area had been dealt with. It was addressed to Harold and put in Jake's letterbox by mistake. A throaty scream came from the direction of the kitchen window. Jake looked up from his card game just in time to see Harold plummet to the pavement. Jake stared in fascination as Harold lay there in a motionless heap. *Old fool! Doesn't he know the older you get the more brittle your bones become?* The top rung of the ladder must have given way. Never mind. He really had no use for it any more. Come to think of it, he didn't need the saw back, either. Like Jake and his dead neighbour, it was old, rusty and missing a few teeth. Besides, he'd recently bought a new one from the local Bunnings. In fact, he was holding it in his hand. Bits of sawdust still clung to its gleaming razor sharp teeth.

He set the saw down on the table and flipped another card. It wasn't an ace. It was a joker.

He smiled for the first time since Marion died.

Good enough, he thought. *Good enough.*

He was seated, if you choose to call it that, in a vast sway-backed armchair. His body appeared to be at forty-five degrees to the floor. It may have been an optical illusion; I couldn't take all of him in at a glance. A pastiche of small snapshots. Linen suit the colour of phlegm. Multiple folds and dents that grabbed at shadows. Trouser cuffs scuffed, above bare chicken-flesh ankles. Capacious slippers, brown and foreboding.

There were trees beyond the window. Trees with fluttering leaves of weak English green that held life in their curves; the grace of an upturned hand.

All bookings are the same. Differences are never important.

They had specified an Asian of a certain age; an Asian who could pass for a significantly younger age. Clean. Compliant. Confidential.

Margot wouldn't say who it was. She just said, "You might recognise him. I told the fruit who made the booking you're the most discreet lady we've got. Told him we've never had a complaint."

So: he fell for the fallacy of induction. Like one of Bertrand Russell's chooks, waking up and expecting to be fed but instead meeting the executioner's axe. Inductive reasoning is the cornerstone of any business, and of this business more than most. You never told in the past; you won't tell this time. Any of the first year kiddies I tutor could leapfrog that pothole of bad logic.

If they give me a permanent tute gig next year, or even the research assistant job for the Applied Ethics unit, I'll stop the out calls. It might mean penury – but three and a half years is too long already. Hand to mouth beats arse to mouth.

A creaky satyr opened the door. The fruit, evidently. He ran his gaze over me, up, down, even peering around the back. Nodded. Told me the ground rules. Apparently discretion was of paramount importance. Novel idea.

I was ushered into his presence. The door stuttered shut.

"Knees," said the rumple in the armchair.

I folded into a kneeling position. A beating? I doubted he would have the muscle to administer it. Still, once a Nietzschean… (*'Thou goest to women? Do not forget thy whip.'*)

"Ask me if I want kinky stuff." A high-pitched wheeze.

"Do you want kinky stuff?" I asked, primly, head down.

"Does a bear shit in a German schoolgirl's mouth?" He started to laugh, then stopped. "No, really. Does a bear do that?"

"If you say so," I said. Guessing.

"I don't care either way. How old are you? Eleven? Good. You can visit the chocolate factory. Yummity scrum," he mewled.

I dared a glance up through the tessellated shadows to a rump of stomach enclosed in blue cotton. A leer of unwanted skin showing below the throat. The vellum of old man chest; middle-aged fat and youthful muscle long gone, leaving nothing between the dermis and the ribcage. The linen suit jacket spatchcocked open, lapel edges etched with grime, oily stains in the weave of the nearer sleeve.

There was a large white dinner plate on the floor domed with a sterling silver cover. He knocked it towards me with his foot. I awaited his instructions, head bowed low. He was paying plenty. Enough for it to be nasty.

"What do you think I'm going to make you do?" Voice dry and brittle. "Mmh?"

I knew I was supposed to answer. That was the job after all.

But I couldn't. I was smelling his old man smell, and his feet, and something meaty he must have consumed in this room. I was feeling the fizz of sunlight splinters bumping into the corners of my downturned eyes. I was thinking of Francis Bacon, who posited eliminative induction as the way to isolate the formal cause of any phenomenon, and wrote about the probability of recurrence. I wondered what that meant for me. Did it merely describe the acts and the men, or did it suggest that three and a half years would stretch into ten, fifteen, more?

"You don't know what's going to happen, do you?" he insisted.

The rug needed vacuuming. Bacon died from pneumonia after experimenting with permanence by stuffing a dead chicken with snow. Were his chickens related to Russell's?

"*Do* you."

Yes, this was the work – but I wouldn't do it. No reply.

"You are frightened by what might be on the plate. What you will have to do with it?"

"Eat it or insert it," I said, matter-of-factly. I glanced at one plane of his face: deflated; lower lip loose and turned outward.

"Maybe not," he said, trying to rally. "Maybe the plate is empty. And you can't guess what happens next."

I thought about mentioning Schrödinger's cat. I couldn't be bothered. Did Schrödinger also plan a purgatory for chickens?

"Why don't you tell me?"

"That's my choice! I might. Or I mightn't."

Back to downcast eyes. An impasse. A sigh that sounded like a hiss. My knees hurt. The sun fading. Light the colour of old bed-sheets.

There would be no repeat booking. The payment was upfront. I could just leave. This could be the last one ever.

I didn't move. Knees numb. Listening to his breathing.

I realised who he was. I had liked his books and read most of them. He understood, like few others above the age of six or seven, the rules of fantasy. But the first rule of fantasy is that everyone has to commit to it. Fantasy only works when it is taken seriously. I laughed, involuntarily. It was short but sardonic. To his ears, derisive, no doubt.

It was a failure shared.

His voice like something trapped in a pipe. "You. Are a bitter. Disappointment."

"Yes," I said, looking up. "Yes. It happens."

CHOOKS

Donated by
Mark McAuliffe

The chef had been operating his restaurant for almost three very successful years within the community before he made his first and only mistake.

The cops came several hours before business was due to open for the day. They didn't bother knocking, just kicked open the locked door and entered with guns drawn. They had got the tip-off from the primary school teacher, who saw the chef abduct the child outside the school that morning. She knew him by sight because she often ate at his quiet, out-of-the-way place.

The chef was in the yard out back, preparing the meals for that night's menu. He obviously heard the noise the cops were making inside because as they entered the kitchen he came in through the back door.

He was a squat, brutish creature, with long arms and a sloping forehead. In one paw he gripped a long-handled axe.

The fact that he held his weapon was all the provocation required. The resultant fire tore through him at close-range, throwing him back out the door. They kicked the axe away and gave him a few more bullets to make sure the threat was neutralised.

Inside the meat locker they discovered a wealth of carnage. The bodies of men and women, boys and girls hung like butchered pigs in ordered ranks. Internal organs were frozen and neatly racked. They found the child they had come to save. He was hanging by his ankles and draining over a large stainless steel basin.

The battery cells were out back. Rows of cages crammed with grunting, fattened human cattle. Hands and feet had been removed, arms and legs were wired to prevent thrashing about. Heads were caught in vice grips and force-feeding tubes attached to their toothless, slobbery maws.

Fresh blood stained the grass. Beside a tree stump, used by the chef as a chopping block, they found a human head. Its eyes still blinked and its lips puckered like a goldfish.

The headless body caught everyone by surprise. It came from around the side of the restaurant, naked and pale. It ran blindly into them, knocking two sprawling. It ricocheted off one lawman and into the kitchen, then somehow found its way to the dining area. It bounced off the tables and chairs and sprinted out the front door.

The cops gave chase but couldn't keep up. The body ran fast and, once it was free, ran like it had a purpose, or so some said, after they watched the six o'clock news and saw the footage taken by the Japanese tourist. The body made it quite far before it came to the main road and was brought down by heavy traffic.

And the next day, somewhere in some pub, two drunks were watching an extended report of the horrible events. The fourth estate was providing coverage from every possible angle. The pollies and the academics, the scientific and religious community had all had their say.

"Well, *I* see it as a metaphor," one of the drunks said.

"A what?" said the other drunk.

"A metaphor. For life. I mean look at us. What are we all about? We are all just lambs to the slaughter. Meat for those in charge. What do we use our democratic rights for, but to vote in those who want us as nothing more than mindless sheep. And look at the people we work for. All they want are beasts of burden and consumers… but then one of us breaks free, tries a new direction. And at first he looks like he's going somewhere, like he has a purpose… until we realise he's not going anywhere. There are no more original thinkers, just headless chooks, flapping about the farmyard. Well? Huh? D'you see?"

The other drunk put down his beer glass.

"Shut up," he said, "just shut the fuck up."

MERRY CHRISTMAS

Donated by
Rod Cod

It was early December and we finally got some work. We had to do a 're-roof', on the old Stipson place that overlooks the highway. Once the best house in the district, now, only the old widow lives up there. Her 'loving', vulture-like children turn up now and then, looking for the 'scraps', anything they can grab, to sell in the city, to sustain their decadent lifestyle.

A couple of years ago she asked for a quote, and now she wants to go ahead. For the same price! I've explained how costs have gone up, but I'll see what I can do. It's a big job, and it will see us through till Christmas.

To cut costs, we aren't hiring any of the safety gear, like the scaffolding. The inspectors never come out this far, and our crew are pretty good on the roof. All the scrap we can chuck in the farm dump and all the new stuff is being delivered, so we don't have to pick it up.

So Lester, Barry and I get stuck into it and by Friday we had done a quarter of the roof. That old stuff was so rusted, it was paper thin. You have to be careful! It's a great view from up there; you can see the hut on 'Belchers Roost' and on the other side, down to the river. Still there is a bit of obstruction from those four massive chimneys. They would fit in well at a foundry – twenty feet higher than the roof, dusty old red brick, and old Mrs Stipson reckons that they have never been cleaned, as they couldn't find anyone brave enough to try. She doesn't use the fireplaces anymore, as she's by herself and pretty much stays in the spare room that's got gas.

The next two weeks goes pretty quick and we only have the bit above the main bedroom to go. There was a bit of damage to the roof sheets around the base of the chimney, like two lengths of railway line had been dragged across it, and some of the chimney brickwork had been chipped. Lester reckoned it was Skylab, Barry said "Aliens", and I told them both to shut up and get back to work. I had to race into town to get some more brackets and when I got back I see Lester trying to fix the ladder to the chimney.

"What the fuck are you playing at," I call out. He waves me up. "Barry's fallen into the chimney."

"What?"

"He reckoned that he could climb it, and I bet him fifty that he couldn't, and now he's gone." We tie the ladder on, and up I go.

Peering over the edge, I see Barry sitting, staring at the pile of rubbish in front of him. The chimney's pretty big, and Barry's sitting on an edging. I call out to him. He still doesn't move. I climb down and he just points. In the pile of rubbish, amongst the bird's nests and all that faded red fabric, is a mummified human arm! It's been there quite a while. Pulling the fabric aside, it disintegrates as we touch it. We find old wrapping paper, still wrapped around presents.

"Mr Stipson?" Barry murmurs.

"No, he's buried out at Westbrook. The widow goes out there every week."

"Well it must be one of the staff or a Christmas burglar. Look at all those presents."

Pushing it all to one side, we find ourselves face to face with the mummified head of Santa Claus! His threadbare hat has seen better days, but the beard and the glasses are a 'dead' give-away.

Scraping on the chimney announces Lester's arrival. All he says is "Holy Fuck." I tell him to go back to the truck and grab those bags out of the equipment box. He's back in a flash and we load everything into the bags. Everything that is, except old Nick. He's stuck tight. He must have been a big man in his day.

That's it for today; we pile in the truck, and drive down to the river. After a few beers we were game enough to check out our finds.

It must have been pretty protected up there, and it never rains much out here, so most of the presents are still wrapped up. Barry's find, so he opens one first. There's no sticky tape, it's been glued and, as he unwraps it, a card falls out.

In old handwriting, neat, rolling, fountain pen-written script, still legible are the words *To Paul Wilson, Merry Christmas, 1908, from Santa.*

No one says a thing. Paul Wilson's name is on the memorial, outside the pub. He went missing at the Somme back in 1916. Inside the box was a wooden chess set.

Lester's next. *To Nettie Jordan, Merry Christmas, 1908, from Santa.* She died when her buggy rolled in 1923. Inside, a beautiful hairbrush.

Hesitantly, I grabbed one. Opening it, I read out "Frank Huston." My Grandfather! He was going to get a compass. He always said, if you're bad, Santa won't give you any presents. That was the year he and the others burnt down the barn. He said "No one in the district got presents that year!"

We are all family men with young kids, all under six. How can we tell them there's no Santa, 'cause we found him dead in old Mrs Stipson's chimney and he's been there since 1908! And if he missed that year, who's been doing it ever since? We grabbed up all the stuff and just threw it in the river. Some things you can't explain and you're not meant to understand.

The widow died soon after and the house was burnt to the ground the following winter, after her kids tried to start a fire during some drunken, satanic orgy. It seemed the chimney might have been blocked. The fire destroyed the lot. Nothing was left.

THE WOODEN SOLDIER

Donated by
Jack Horne

Arm in arm, we shuffled through carpets of russet leaves on our way to Tamerside churchyard. Sarah carried flowers for our son's grave. Sonny our dog ran ahead of us, chasing after squirrels, his tail wagging like a thing possessed.

Outside the churchyard, the ancient oak, known locally as 'The Hanging Tree', was being felled. It originated from the sixteenth century and, at first glance, had always looked dead. Its trunk was hideously twisted and hollowed out as though by a great spoon, but its branches defiantly grew leaves in abundance each spring.

I had always felt a sense of horror at the sight of the tree. According to local legend, witches had been hanged from it and their vengeful souls emerged after dark. Historians scoff at the idea of witches' souls, but it is generally believed that, at some stage in its long life, the tree had been used for the purpose of hanging.

I'd always involuntarily shuddered at being in close proximity to the tree, but on that day I felt outraged at its death.

"You can't do that!" I shouted at the tree surgeon. "That tree is a piece of history."

He shrugged. "I'm just doing my job."

Sarah placed her hand on my arm. "There's nothing we can do," she said softly. "The council says the tree is becoming unsafe. They can't risk it falling on someone."

I knew she was right. Almost unconsciously, I stooped and retrieved a sizeable splinter that had landed at my feet.

"I'll make a toy for John's grave," I explained, nodding towards our boy's resting place. "Do you remember how he loved the soldier I made for him?"

Sarah nodded. "Yes, he couldn't sleep without it" – she smiled sadly – "not that he needs help sleeping now. I can't believe it's a year since we lost him."

I swung the creaking wrought iron gate open and stood back as Sarah entered the churchyard. I followed her, and heard the heavy thud as the ancient tree succumbed to the axe and hit the ground.

At home, I started work immediately. Humming softly to myself, I whittled at the wood, recalling how I'd previously made the soldier figure. I carelessly sliced the palm of my hand and swore under my breath. The bulk of the dressing made carving more difficult but it was a labour of love.

Unaccountably, my usual equanimity soon changed to irritability. I snapped at Sarah several times.

"Sorry, I'm just tired," I said, forcing a smile.

She touched my arm. "Come to bed, Chris. It's getting late."

"I'll come to bed when I'm ready!" I glared at her. "Just leave me in peace, woman."

Ignoring her hurt expression, I continued carving, pretending not to feel her presence.

"Just go to bed," I finally growled. "I can't concentrate with you watching me."

Angrily, I turned around. I was alone.

Shrugging, I busied myself with the soldier. Somehow, its face had a rather evil smirk.

Again, I felt someone watching me. Ah, so she had been there, after all. Without speaking, I spun around to face her. As before, I was alone.

I jumped like a frightened child as something brushed my leg. I smiled with relief, seeing Sonny.

"Do you need to go out, boy?" Rising, and feeling more cheerful, I flippantly showed him the toy. "What do you think of this? Your owner's a clever chap, eh?"

Growling, he backed away.

"Not impressed? It's only a toy – look." I thrust the carving at him for closer inspection.

Snarling viciously, eyes furious, hackles raised, Sonny looked more like a rabid wolf than our placid old German Shepherd.

Dropping the carving, I edged past the animal and opened the door. "Get out!"

To my amazement, he nuzzled my hand as he passed me.

Sarah appeared, rubbing sleep from her eyes. "Is everything OK? I thought I heard you shouting."

I sat at my bench, fingering the carving. "It was nothing – just that stupid dog. It's going crazy."

Sarah eyed the carved figure. "You've nearly finished" – she reached for it – "let me see."

Slapping her hand away, I clutched the piece of oak to my chest. "Just see to your dog and then leave me in peace!" I roared.

Tearfully, Sarah called Sonny to her and retreated.

I could still feel eyes on me and, with increasing unease, glanced over my shoulder several times as I worked.

The figure was finally finished. I appraised it. Apart from its nasty expression, it was far better than the one I'd made for my living boy. I'd excelled myself! I'd paint it in the morning.

Retiring to bed, I switched off the light. The hairs on my neck rose. I could feel a malevolent presence. I shuddered.

I raced up the stairs, feeling like a thing from Hell was chasing me. Hurriedly stripping, I sprang into bed and pulled the bedcovers over my head.

Sarah pretended to be asleep.

I lay there, sensing something evil in the room. I felt like a child, afraid to lift the bedcovers for fear of coming face to face with an unknown horror. This was stupid. What was I afraid of? Was I man or boy? What would John have thought of his old man right now? Ashamed, I resolutely pulled the bedcovers from my face. I peered into the darkness, my heart pounding.

I must have eventually fallen asleep, and awoke on the lounge room floor, the smirking carving standing nearby on the coffee table. Sonny licked my face. Sarah leaned over me. I felt my tender neck. The rope had cut deeply into it.

"Thank God you're alive. I should have realised you were depressed," Sarah whispered, tears streaming down her cheeks and splashing onto my face. "If Sonny hadn't barked, it would have been too late."

Struggling to my feet, I threw the cursed piece of wood onto the glowing embers of the fire in the hearth and watched it burn to ashes. No more.

# DÉJÀ VOODOO

Donated by
Frank J. Collins

Reincarnation is not just a word. It's not just an idea. It's real and can be proven. This book will show you how.

The child stands wobbly in the television's uneven light, listening to the preacher. Momma's boyfriend sprawls on the battered couch, snoring past midnight. The new toy fumbles in his small fingers. It belongs to the man.
Wet diapers itch. He totters through trash on the floor. The window shows dark. A few lights come from nearby trailers. Momma's car isn't home. Work late baby. A screen door slams somewhere. A dog barks. More dogs bark.

History defies reason unless you understand that our energy transcends us and continues from one person to the next.

The man shifts and scratches. He mumbles. The child's stomach stirs, hungry. The man doesn't like to share much. But the kitchen has food. Dirty dishes. More trash. Peanut butter comes in a jar with a big lid. Fingers won't reach across it. Cookies. One left. An open bag of chips. The plastic makes loud crinkling noises. Not many teeth to use, but the chips taste good. They seem familiar.

This concept can bring meaning and reason to what matters most.

The man looms over the child and swigs warm beer. You want some of this? You're eating my chips, might as well drink my beer too, you little shit.
Almost three now, his eyes are flint. He keeps munching, defying.
The man reaches but almost falls when the child sidesteps.
Leave me alone.
Oh, that's not about to happen now. He grabs a cutting board with a handle. Good for beating.

Don't let another day pass without understanding.

The child has tucked the man's toy safely in the diaper's band. He remembers

216

what it does now, and it feels solid. The man's face runs pale.

You're a bad man. No good for Momma.

I'll leave.

Yes. Leave now.

Standing outside, the man wears no shoes. You wouldn't shoot me would you little guy?

Yes I would.

Back inside, he locks the door and puts the gun on the table. The man was dumb; the refrigerator has cold beer.

The television still glows.

Order now to own this classic.

The child knows the book. He wrote it.

AT LEAST THEY'RE NOT CANCEROUS

Donated by
Sheri White

"Hey, you've got more moles on your back – did you know that?" Mike asked his wife, rubbing sunscreen on her shoulders. They sat together by the pool.

"Yeah, I know. The dermatologist told me during my appointment the other day. As long as I protect my skin, I should be OK; they're non-cancerous right now." Laura was a little concerned, but faked a smile. The stupid things had dotted her back since she was a child, but seemed to be developing faster. It bothered her, the way new things growing on a person's body ought to worry them.

Sometimes she could feel them growing.

All the moles were dark brown and swollen; they reminded Laura of bloated ticks on a dog's belly. After each first appeared, they only grew to a certain size then stopped. Still, she decided to take the dermatologist's offer; he'd remove them just in case.

A couple of weeks later, Laura lay on a metal table, her back exposed to Doctor Leonard and his nurse. He applied liquid nitrogen to one of the moles, then stepped back.

He looked puzzled. "Lila, do you hear that?" he asked.

His nurse cocked her head sideways. She heard something faint, but audible.

A strange hissing sound emitted from one of the moles. Although it should have been red from the nitrogen, it grew black and began to swell.

"Doctor, what's going on? Oh my God, is everything OK?" Laura asked.

Before he could answer, the mole rose from Laura's back.

Tiny legs emerged from its skin; two red eyes opened, not much bigger than the head of a pin.

The spider-like *thing* skittered across Laura's back. She screamed and howled; the legs tickled and scratched her skin.

As if awakened, the rest of the moles turned into spiders, tearing away from Laura's skin. Their bodies were bloated, filled with her blood.

Laura's fair skin blackened and peeled back, bringing louder screams. Her body started to deflate, emptied like a bicycle tyre losing air.

Spiders skittered out from every hole in her body, climbing from her and onto everything in the room.

The doctor and nurse ran for the door, but were overcome. The spiders crawled on them, digging for blood.

Laura's deflated corpse hissed, vibrating with newborn spiders eating their way out. In seconds, the bodies of the doctor and nurse had been stripped to the bone.

Hundreds of spiders, still hungry, slipped through the crack under the closed door and headed towards the waiting room.

THE GATHERING STORM

Donated by
Daniel Powell

The prisoner's mouth was covered with electrical tape. His captors had cloaked his head with a dirty canvas bag and they marched him, stumbling, through the wrecked neighbourhood before roughly depositing him into the back of an old van. The doors slammed shut and one of the gunmen slapped the window; the van sprang forward and surged down the rubble-strewn streets.

The prisoner's name was Timothy Ryan Smith. He'd been an accountant before the occupation. He tried to calm himself – tried to take careful, measured breaths though his nostrils. To accomplish this, he conjured images of his wife and children. He thought about Melinda and her mischievous smile and warm brown eyes. There would be no warmth in her expression on this night. She would remain at home, anxiously awaiting his return. He thought about Tim, junior, and little Wesley, who had come into the world just a few months ago.

Wes had entered a very different place than his brother had.

The driver screeched around corners; Tim was jostled back and forth in the otherwise empty cavern of the van. His captors yelled at him, but he could only understand bits and pieces of it. It was the same old rhetoric, no doubt.

It took maybe twenty minutes for them to reach their destination, and he received the same rough treatment as they trundled him up a flight of stairs and down a long hallway, where they yanked the bag from his head.

It took a moment for his eyes to adjust. They'd brought him to the old Portland City Hall. A panel of them sat behind an ornate table in the centre of the room. There were dozens of their brethren there, enclosing him in a circle; at the centre of the circle, there was a bloodstained tarp on the floor. They had set up a video camera, and a pair of floodlights bathed the space in eerie orange light.

"Bring him forward," one of the judges garbled. It was incredible. They were learning English.

"Mr Smith, you have been charged with plotting an attack against us – your superiors *and* your liberators. Mr Smith, you are guilty."

Smith focused on his breathing. He *was* guilty. He'd been fighting them for almost two years, since they'd risen from the depths. He'd killed scores of them and he knew that, despite whatever else was happening in America, pockets of human resistance forces in Portland and Seattle and as far north as Calgary were holding their own.

The occupation would not last.

The guards shoved him down onto the tarp. One of them smacked Smith with his staff and he rolled over in pain. They snatched him into a kneeling position. Smith watched as a guard's face shadowed indigo – the natural evolution of the executioner's hood, of course. The slats at the sides of the creature's neck swelled rhythmically. It held the curved blade at Smith's neck and the judge stood behind him for the benefit of the camera.

"This is what happens to those that attack us. There will be no rest for you, human rodents. No rest. Not in this life or any that follow." The tentacles surrounding the cavern that was his mouth writhed as he spoke.

Smith looked into the camera, his blue eyes clear. They gleamed in the lights. He stared into the camera and he thought of his family, and then he closed his eyes and drew a deep breath. The blade descended, and the world with him as a part of it was no more.

The guards cleaned up. They would dump Smith's remains on the pile they had created in the Pearl District. If his wife showed up to claim his body, they would shoot her.

But as much as it pained her, Melinda Smith would not go for her husband's body. She knew not to. That night, as she watched her dear spouse's execution on the pirated feed originating from inside the old CNN studios, she bit her lip to hold the tears at bay. She bit her lip and she occasionally called out to her sons, reassuring herself that they were safe; she spent her night packing nails and ball bearings into canisters that would soon be fixed with detonators.

It was what the occupiers had taken to calling the Year of the Great Old Ones.

The people of a North America that used to be, worked methodically, toiling in quiet desperation. They laboured in burnt-out rooms inside crumbling buildings, preparing for a storm that loomed on the horizon.

ATROCITY EXHIBITION

Donated by
Jason Nahrung

"To hell with it," mumbles Polidori, staring into his half-empty glass of beer as the singer's razor blade wail slices through him. *Let her dance.*

He considers finishing his drink, ordering another, and another. God Almighty, he's tired. Of this club, of the Dance ... everything.

She emerges from a fresh gush of artificial cloud into flashing lights, surrounded by shadowed, cavorting figures. Queenly, in scarlet dress and alabaster skin, blonde curls pinned to frame her luminescent cheeks by silver combs older than a grandmother. A scarlet corset barely contains the smooth, glowing mounds of her breasts. She glides across the urgent beat, moving to her own inner rhythm.

They gather, mouths wide in a rictus of hope and falsely confident smiles. Boys and girls, shuffling, wafting, hedging from the mass to catch her eye. She smiles serenely, graces them with permission to run a knee between hers, a grasping hand across her rump, to brush their temerity-dry lips against hers. And then the turn and weave, the presentation of indented spine, and shoulder blades like dissected wings flitting in memory of flight as her arms move, fingers catching notes on the air like butterflies.

Polidori watches from the darkest corner, past the pool table where the leather, pierced tattoos sink balls and drink beer with gentle snickering and innuendoes. They wear disdain as an accessory to their leather boots and eyebrow rings. It doesn't look comfortable. He, on the other hand, wears his trademark Victoriana, the top hat and vest and fob watch, white cravat and smoky grey, round sunglasses. He is the epitome of comfort; disdain suits him. And yet tonight it hangs heavy on his shoulders. Tonight, he feels as anachronistic as he looks.

A young man in black vinyl approaches the scarlet queen, cock all but in hand. Polidori wishes he could smoke his pipe, the smell of tobacco a welcome addition to the synthetic fog, the sticky alcohol underfoot, the body odour leaking from dance floor leather and PVC. Anything to overwhelm the familiar stench of imminent death.

"What are you looking for, Angel?" the hopeful asks of her, his thin beard unable to hide his hope, his hopeless hope.

"Heaven," she says, her throaty voice clear despite the industrial beat from the speakers, the buzzing gnaw of voices, the metallic clink of glasses at the bar.

"Here?" he asks.

Polidori smiles tightly. Heaven's where you make it, after all. The young ones always end up in a place like this. He thinks it's a latent desire for love, for belonging.

His smile widens into a grimace as she says, in divine echo, "Wherever it may be. Even here." She holds up her arms, a priestess conjuring her god. The red cloth parts to reveal her leg to the hip, pale flesh flashing like a lighthouse ray through the darkened crowd.

The moth flits into the flame; her arms lower like pincers to pin him inside her embrace. The queen dubs her knight.

Her eyes – blue, deep sea blue, glacial yet teasing – find Polidori's over the young man's shoulder. His spectacles offer no protection as her teeth flash white, her tongue so promise-pink.

Polidori grips the blade hidden in his clothes and thrusts himself forward. The metalheads impede his progress. The generous busts of two silken women, jutting like balconies of flesh over tight, tight corsets, cause him to swerve.

She clutches her prize and a circle of bodies forms around them, silent and hungrily observing; lust and need and desperate longing hang over them, as tangible and sickly sweet as the artificial fog.

A billow of fog and she is gone. A scarlet scratch on the boy's neck shows where she was. His eyes show the despair of one who has seen the gate of Heaven and had it slammed in his face, left blinded by the after-image. A silent sigh parts the crowd. A guitar shrieks and they break and sway into rhythm as the boy feels his neck for proof of his wonder.

It is Polidori's mission to save them. Yet he cannot blame them for not wanting to be saved. The Dance is old and he feels every step in his weary muscles. Maybe tonight he can afford to let her dance, just dance. He begins to breathe out, to relax. The youth is still alive, after all. For tonight, at least. Polidori can perhaps have that second beer, sit this one out.

A flash of red catches Polidori's eye. His heart refuses to beat. His flesh runs fevered, his cravat too tight, his glasses turned to black. He sees only her, waiting at the door, her head cocked just so, lips pursed. Calling him to the Dance.

He pushes past the punks littering the corridor, the fishnets and spiked collars, the green hair and bold tattoos. He hears her heels, fairy taps on the wooden floor. All else is mute.

She waits at a door marked 'private'. A liquid, crimson drop glows like a stop light on her pale, pale chest. A flash of smile, of tooth. Her lips are a soft fuchsia, flushing pink.

"This way, Polly Dolly," she says, her lips unmoving. Yet he hears her clearly. They all know his name, and yet they do not come for him. That, too, is part of the Dance; they follow his lead. Better the devil they know, he assumes.

Says Polidori, words as heavy as lead extruding from his frozen chest, his fist clenched tight on the sharp timber under his coat: "You should not have come here."

She pushes open the door, the timber yawning into darkness. "You look tired, Polly." Her voice vibrates in his gut like a deep, deep bass. His entire body vibrates.

Fingers trembling on the stake, he steps inside.

They dance.

SWEET SIXTEEN

Donated by
Shona Snowden

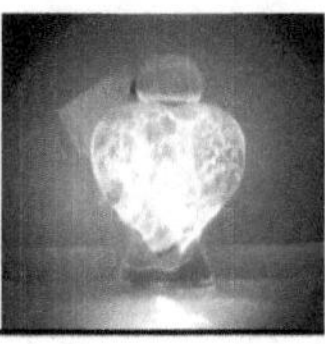

Sweet Sixteen? No. I turned sixteen right after they put me in here. So no Sweet Sixteen. It still bugs me.

I don't remember anybody else in our school having a Sweet Sixteen either. Last party I remember before I came here was the one where Cory Buckleton got eaten and that wasn't a Sweet–

Yeah, eaten. I can't believe I never told you this!

The party was out of town on a farm, can't remember whose farm now. It was winter and the farmyard was all rutted and frozen hard. The party was in a barn, with straw bales for chairs and dried up corn cobs for decorations.

Yeah, it was pretty cute. The restroom was outside – not that it was really a restroom, just a toilet in this little shack thing, with only a half door that didn't lock. We girls would go out there in groups, we said it was to hold the door shut, but it was more because it was totally creepy out there – dark and icy. I remember my breath went up like this great cloud when I talked out there.

No, the barn was warm enough, they had space heaters and stuff. It was a cool party, actually, though Billy McKinnon kept bugging me. I didn't like him much, but he used to always pick me for dancing class so I figured he liked me, which was like a miracle. I wasn't pretty, I had glasses and braces and stuff.

I know! I look different now, right? I don't know what happened with my eyes, but I can see real good now, and I guess the braces worked too.

Billy wasn't good-looking or anything. He was a football player with big shoulders and he got sweaty when he danced. But I thought at least somebody liked me enough to pick me. But while Billy was snuggling up to me there on the straw bales he told me that his mom told him to pick me for dance class, because my mom was a sports teacher so she figured I'd know some steps.

So that meant he didn't like me after all. Even though I didn't like him either, I was kinda upset. But then he tried to kiss me so maybe he did like me a little bit. But there was no way I was kissing him. So I pulled away and got myself out of there into the farmyard, just to get a minute on my own.

There was nobody out there and it was peaceful, but I didn't have my jacket so it was pretty cold. I wasn't going to stay long, but then Cory Buckleton appeared from nowhere – must have been taking a whizz out in the field – and he just kinda grabbed me and kissed me.

I know! It was a real good kiss too – not that I had much to compare it against–

Yeah. *That* Cory Buckleton. Like there'd be more than one? And he was good-looking too, not like Billy at all. I didn't know he'd ever noticed me. Anyway, he kissed me like I was something yummy, started out with all these little licks and then sucking a little bit. He had this soft hair on his face that I didn't remember. Then he made this growling noise and it was almost like he was biting me, like I tasted real good, and he cut me a little bit on my lip – I still have the scar, see here? But it didn't hurt. It was nice.

Only one, though. Because then there was this like howling sound from out in the fields and Cory's head kinda shot up, like he'd heard somebody calling him. His eyes went a bit yellowy and slanted – and then he just let go and ran right back in the field.

It was real cold, so I went on back into the barn and, guess what, Billy started in after me again. And while Billy was bugging me on the straw bales, that was when Cory got eaten. Right out there in that field.

I don't know. Mountain lion? Bear? They said that the tooth-marks on what was left of him were big, but nobody was sure just what it was. They never found it either. There were lots of hunts, around the farms and the forests, even the mountains – nobody found anything. After that it was a real sad year. Some other kids disappeared too. Billy was one of them. When we were out on a date.

Yeah – I went on a date with Billy in the end! It wasn't like there were millions of boys asking me. He had his driver's license and he took me up to the lake where kids went to make out, and I was kinda excited, thinking it might be like Cory. But we never even kissed. I don't know what happened. He just disappeared. One moment he was in the car with me, talking about football, and then it was like I blacked out for a moment and he was gone and there was blood all over the place. After that was when I went crazy, or they said I did, and they put me in here.

No, I don't know if more kids disappeared. I mean, it's not like anybody tells us anything. Who knows what's going on out there?

I wish they'd let us out to the garden sometime, though, don't you? Even at night. I'd like to see the stars and the moon. They're so pretty.

So no Sweet Sixteen for me. It bugs me all the time. Hey, I'm always wondering this – do you know why the bars on these windows are silver?

GRIMM END

Donated by
Nicky Peacock

He'd always found it difficult to stay away from the woods in Grimm End, even when his mother had warned him of the trolls lurking within the shadows; nasty little creatures who would cut a child's flesh for food and fun. They hunted at night and would murder trespassers dallying in their territory. Every bedtime she'd tell him stories of flesh devouring trolls ensuring they would soak into his imagination and be regurgitated in his nightmares.

Every playtime she would order, "You make sure you're in before the street lights come on," her steel gaze enticing an objection; but he soon learnt that everything she did was for his own good and therefore rarely, if ever, rose to her challenge. So when Grimm End's street lights buzzed on he would leave his friends mid-game and scuttle home with a trail of laughter and taunts behind him.

Now he was grown-up, his mother is long gone, and Grimm End Woods has become his playground. Street lights or sunlight, daylight or darkness, it makes no difference to him any more. The murderous trolls, who had plagued his childhood, were now wreaking havoc on a new generation with even more vigour than ever. The woods had a nasty reputation, one fuelled by newspapers, TV reports and parent's protests. It was well known that any child who played too long amongst summer trees would only be found again beneath autumn leaves. In truth though, it was only he who knew of the real graves, he and the rogue red hazel trees whose roots had wound around those tiny bags of flesh and were suckling on the juices within.

The street light above him snaps on making him jump. A small laugh behind him echoes back to his childhood. He turns to find a little girl with rosy cheeks, platinum curls and cheap plastic fairy wings strapped to her back. She stares at him for a moment then skips into the woods. She is perfect, and he feels like a wolf seeing the flutter of his first red cape of the night.

He follows her, keeping a respectable distance. She skips along the overgrown path watched by keen eyed foxes and quiet ravens; both have been audience to these games before; they edge closer so, when the time comes, they might feast on what remains.

They pass the recent grave of his last victim; he can't help but let his gaze linger, as he knows her small body lies just beneath the fresh turned earth.

Still retaining her young beauty she slumbers in the afterlife. All too soon she will be a tiny mass of shredded fabric and dirty bones, just like all the others.

The girl moves ahead of him then suddenly stops. If she turns around he will have to abandon his hunt… but she doesn't turn; instead she lifts her head, takes in a long deep breath, giggles and continues on her way. He knows what she can smell. Two factories surround Grimm End Woods, like a pair of urban hands cupping the only piece of countryside to survive their choking embrace. The factories make cakes; their sickly stench of syrup laces the air of the woods giving them an enchanted atmosphere. A stranger might even think that hidden deep in the twisted trees is the gingerbread house where Hansel and Gretel murdered their witch.

He moves closer to her now, close enough to hear her humming. It is an unremarkable random tune that only a child in a daydream would find musical. He knows that in her mind, she is exploring a fantasy forest where sleeping magical creatures drape themselves about talking trees waiting for a child's song to resurrect them. But a fertile imagination and secluded surroundings make for dangerous playmates so he knows that she doesn't notice the monster stalking behind her, who chooses now to diminish the distance between them.

His breathing deepens. Hot hands run down the front of his dirty trousers. His sweaty stench fights against the sugary air…

She smells him before she sees him. As she turns he reaches out and takes hold of her throat and begins to squeeze. The girl does not cry out for help, or struggle. She growls beneath her breath then rips his hands from her skin.

He has a brief moment of shock before she lifts him clean off the ground and throws him against a tree.

"So you're the one," she says walking towards him "this is my hunting ground!"

Smiling she watches his attempts to get up. The fall has broken both his shin bones so they poke through from the delicate skin that had once held them. Every attempt to stand is met with searing pain and a spurt of warm blood.

"You know," she whispers as she moves to face him "your mother should have warned you to be in before the street lights come on, we like the dark." She sinks her jagged teeth into his broken leg, crunching the bone and sucking on the escaping flesh.

He flails but she is heavier than she looks and with a knee planted on his chest, she holds him down. She has no weapon save for her sharp teeth and spiky nails; she uses them to peel his skin to get at the juicy flesh beneath.

With the ease of a familiar friend, the sun glides over Grimm End. It lights the houses, the woods, the two factories and the dismembered body that hangs from a street light. The corpse has no legs and is covered in tiny blue veins that map out a distinctive journey of pain. Small bite marks and pecks litter the skin leaving trickles of dried and fresh blood to underline the various wounds. A gentle breeze plays with the dripping entrails as if they were part of a weeping willow, and a child's tuneless melody is heard by the factory workers as they clock in for their morning shift.

DEATH ON THE NUMBER 96

Donated by
Michelle Jager

Thin lips and sunken cheeks sit below dark glasses; the rest of him is impossibly squeezed between a large lady with flaccid breasts and a bald man with a shiny head. His thirsty flesh sits close to his skeletal frame and the veins stand erect on his exposed arm. At the end of this arm dangles a cigarette. Thin Lips brings the cigarette up to his mouth suckles it and inhales deeply, brings his arm down and breathes out. This motion is repeated automatically, continuously: up, inhales in, down, breathes out. A grubby trail of smoke wraps itself around the other passengers.

No one on the tram seems to mind. Not even the lady with the red-faced child.

Balding Man and Flaccid Breasts simply stare ahead, slack-jawed, ignoring the passionate embrace of the smoke as it lingers in their hair and around their nostrils.

Ash the colour of Thin Lips' gaunt flesh drops with the next inhalation. It lands on his knee. Without a pause between drags he flicks the offending matter on to Balding Man.

Balding Man says nothing.

Nobody says anything.

Whether they are sitting or standing everyone rocks gently, back and forth, with the motion of the tram. The tram stops and the doors open. Several people get off. Several people board.

Thin Lips pauses, cigarette mid-air, body rigid. His head turns.

A woman stands at the ticket machine, purse open as she rummages through for the right change. Beneath her breasts her stomach swells gently. Underneath her shirt the flesh appears firm and tight like a newly inflated balloon.

Thin Lips puts out the cigarette on Balding Man's head. With a fizzle it burns brightly and then falls to the floor, dead. Balding Man's brow furrows for a moment and then is clear again.

Thin Lips stands up. He moves towards the woman with the swollen stomach who is now seated at the rear of the tram.

As if set in motion, everyone begins to talk.

Flaccid Breasts is talking to Balding Man, the red-faced child talks to his

230

mother, and those standing are chatting to those seated. Someone laughs.

The woman leans her head against the window and opens a book. Thin Lips sits down opposite her, somehow wedging himself in to the corner next to two blond men with backpacks. The woman does not look up from her book.

Thin Lips stares at her stomach and licks his lips. He stretches his fingers and cracks his knuckles. Breathing in deeply he lifts his sunglasses but for a moment, just to get a better look; opal coloured eyes glitter and then disappear beneath polarised lenses.

The woman licks her finger and turns a page. Thin Lips grimaces for a moment at the sound, and then leans forward placing his hand, fingers outstretched, on to her stomach. Spider-like it sits there, waiting. And then, ever so gently, he pushes through. His hand moves past the cloth, past the flesh, deep into the womb.

The woman moves, readjusting; a fine film of sweat glistens on her forehead. A grunt escapes her lips. One of the blond backpackers asks in a thick accent – "Are you okay?"

She nods and reaches for her bag and a packet of Quick-Eze.

Eyes on the woman's face Thin Lips moves his hand around within her. Searching. He stops. Veins bulging, his arm tenses and ropey muscles strain beneath the skin.

Pain rips at the woman's face, dragging her lips apart and crushing her eyelids. She leans forward clutching at her stomach.

Thin Lips withdraws his hand and sits back.

The woman is on her knees in the middle of the aisle. Blood, thick and black is weeping from between her legs. A scream is etched across her face, yet no sound emerges.

And then, between gasps – "Oh – My – Ba-by –"

Words spoken, she is engulfed. Passengers swarm around her. One of the blond backpackers pushes to the front yelling – "Stop the tram! Stop!"

Another voice cries out – "Don't crowd her. Someone call an ambulance."

Thin Lips watches them push and shove, each trying to get a look, each giving advice. He chews his lip, eyes narrowed, head tilted. Listening.

No one notices or moves as he makes his way in and then out of the crowd, something tucked within his jacket.

He presses the Stop button and the doors slide open; Fitzroy Street, St Kilda. Thin Lips grins as he makes his way toward Grey Street.

As he walks by a hostel Thin Lips pulls back his jacket.

It writhes within his arms. Tiny underdeveloped fists punch at the air fighting the breeze that caresses its naked body. Blind, its eyes are sealed shut by translucent skin that reveals a network of slender red veins. A thick cord protrudes from its stomach and waves gently; an extra limb stronger than the spindly arms and legs.

Thin Lips rests on the wall of a block of art deco apartments. A shattered beer bottle sits at his feet, glittering in the waning light.

He picks up a shard. Carefully he presses it against each eyelid and drags it across; blood weeps from the wounds. Using his shirt, he gently wipes away crimson tears. Mewing softly, the infant opens its eyes. Opal irises stare up at Thin Lips.

Thin Lips runs a finger down the centre of the child's face, resting it on the snub nose.

The mewing stops.

Blinking, virgin eyes take in the gnarled figure before them.

A smile.

Fluorescent light falls on a hollow face. Head against the pillow, she lies there; one hand on her belly, the other lying open at her side. The window reveals the world is dark outside. Closing her eyes she feels the pain again, smells it.

Lips pulled back from her teeth, she whimpers.

All around her, within her, she senses it. Feels it. Overwhelming, it runs through her veins and lingers on her tongue – the scent of cigarettes.

On her stomach, an ashen handprint.

THINGS THAT GROW

Donated by
Eugene Gramelis

It was approaching five in the afternoon and the store fronts along Macquarie Street were beginning to pull down their shutters. Shops closed early in the suburbs, especially on Sunday.

"I'm just going to pop into the pharmacy and grab some Gaviscon for the old tum tum. I think we're all out at home." Greg patted his stomach. He had a tendency to suffer from really bad heartburn.

Betty engaged the pram brakes with her foot and sat down on a bench beneath an old maple. Alex's brown curls were barely visible through all the grocery bags hanging from his pram. Samantha switched to tantrum mode the moment Greg let go of her hand and tried to run after him, but he managed to convince her to sit on the bench beside her mother on the promise of returning with candy.

Moments later Greg emerged from the *Day & Night* with a packet of chewable Gaviscon tablets and a Chupa Chup.

He came to a sudden stop.

The bench was vacant.

They've just gone to the car. Betty must've decided to get a head start on strapping the kids into their booster seats.

He walked briskly to the car, but the Prius was empty.

Don't panic. There's a logical explanation for this. She probably saw something that caught her interest in a shop window.

The only store that hadn't yet drawn its shutters was the bakery, and there was no sign of Betty and the kids there.

Greg produced his BlackBerry. He scrolled through the phone book and selected Betty's cell phone. He got the automated response telling him there was no such number. *Okay, now you can panic!*

Half an hour later, having searched what seemed like every street in town, he attended the local police station to report his family missing. He spent the night alone, confused and scared out of his wits, kept awake by the unnatural silence. *Sam wanted to follow me into the Day & Night. She'd still be with me, if I'd let her come.*

He couldn't bring himself to go to work the following day. His boss told him he could use up his paid leave. When he'd used that up, Greg took unpaid leave. When that ran out, he was fired. Three months later the bank foreclosed on the mortgage, and so instead of the eerie silence of his bedroom he found himself staring up at flickering street lights, listening to cats fighting over fish heads in garbage bins.

On the anniversary of his family's disappearance he sat huddled in front of the *Day & Night*, gazing at other men strolling by with their wives and children. He watched as a black cat hopped onto the bench where his wife had sat a year earlier. *Can't make my luck any worse*, he chuckled and took a deep swig from the cheap wine bottle nestled between his knees. A coffee-coloured leaf came fluttering down from the maple. The tree's boughs were old and heavy and creaked in the wind. One limb looked particularly misshapen. It reached across the telegraph wires like the twisted arm of a goblin. The leaf landed on the bench beside the cat. The feline extended a playful paw toward it. As soon as its paw batted the leaf, the cat vanished.

What the hell! He was drunk but not *blind* drunk.

Greg didn't sleep that night. His mind was racing. His wife hadn't run off on him; his family wasn't in a shallow grave in some reserve; as ludicrous as it sounded, they had somehow been made to disappear by that decrepit old tree.

He scooped up a pile of leaves from the pavement and touched them to various objects. Nothing happened. Then just before dawn another leaf came floating down from up high where the ugly old goblin arm clawed at the night sky. This time a pigeon scavenging for bread crumbs happened to peck at it, and hey presto the bird disappeared. *The branch – it had something to do with that weird branch.*

The following day a council vehicle pulled up. A burly man in a fluorescent vest got out, taped a flyer to the tree then got back in his vehicle and left. Greg read the notice. Macquarie Street would be cordoned off from pedestrian and vehicular traffic between four and seven that evening so that arborists could lop old branches from the trees lining the sidewalk. Greg looked at the plaza clock across the road. It was 2:35 p.m. He had less than an hour and a half to come up with a plan to bring his wife and kids back or say goodbye to them forever.

But this line of thinking presupposed that his loved ones were in fact someplace else. He guessed it was possible that the leaves had somehow transported them to another dimension. On the other hand, the maple might have simply … absorbed them. After all, growing things needed nourishment. This plant just preferred people and small mammals to Weed 'n' Feed. Who was he kidding? What had happened to his family wasn't even possible let alone capable of comprehension.

Greg noticed the barricades going up at either end of the street. A large cherry-picker was making its way toward him.

"Move along, sir," said a man in a hard hat.

He couldn't let them cut down those branches. But they'd drag him to the nuthouse and throw away the key if he tried to explain any of this to them. A gentle breeze fanned the tree's foliage and another leaf detached itself from the goblin arm. It glided toward the pavement.

"Sir, it's for your own safety."

Ignoring the council worker, Greg sprinted to the trunk. There was only one real option left, and he was prepared to chance it. He spread his arms and looked up, thinking how beautiful the leaf looked in the bright afternoon sun as it fluttered like a bronze butterfly toward him. "I'm coming Betty."

ERADICATION

Donated by
Kaaron Warren

Class:
Angiospermae

Order:
Atrocitas

Family:
Horrifera

Genus:
Nervus

Common Name:
Sinew Plant, or Rush

Appearance:

At its base, *horrifera nervus* has the appearance of a large, pale brown mushroom with faint red splotches. From the centre of the 'mushroom' emerge the tendrils. Reddish and tough, they have thin veins, greenish in hue. If there is no room for growth, the tendrils will curl around themselves and will pack ever and ever more tightly.

The tendrils end in small bulbs, and it is in these bulbs we find the seeds, which are about the size of a cockroach's head, grey and slightly soft to the touch.

Growth Cycle:

Horrifera nervus takes approximately 18 years to reach maturity and lives an average of 75 years. The similarity to the human growth cycle is undeniable, however this should not be taken as proof of the existence of the mythological Pariahs and their murderous manner of rule.

Geographical location:

Grows better in vitamin-leached lands. Will grow in a pot if the soil is mixed with ash. It also thrives in ground sewn with used, unwashed clothing if that clothing is finely shredded.

History:

Horrifera nervus was first discovered 400 years ago, when Sir Dobert Maroney identified the plant during an 18 day expedition seeking the Black Heart of the Earth, the rumoured city which allegedly housed the five Pariahs of our mythology. Legend has it that to find this dwelling will bring great personal wealth because the Pariahs were rich beyond all imagination.

Since then 14 other varieties of *horrifera* have been identified. The *horrifera corpus* gives off a slightly nauseating, sickly odour, while the *horrifera ossis* has the appearance of white bone.

Mythology:

Of the five Pariahs, one could read, one could run, one could procreate, one could kill and one could sew. Therefore they were all extremely dissatisfied with their lives, which meant they ruled cruelly.

One day their sister, a young woman of dubious qualities, arrived on their doorstep, insisting that the baby she carried in her belly belonged to her brother, the procreating Pariah. The Pariahs knew that a child would sap them of their powers and make them vulnerable to attack, so they invited their sister inside and made her feel queenly, as she believed was her right.

The Pariah who could read comforted her with poetry of love. The one who fathered her child removed her clothing and examined her with great delicacy and care.

The Pariah who could run did so, drawing in a crowd to observe the fate of one who would make demands of the Pariah.

The killer sliced open her belly and lifted out the baby. The Pariah who could sew filled the cavity with the contents of their carcass bin and stitched her up.

They tossed her to the people outside and carried the still-warm baby into the garden where they buried it.

Within days, a plant grew tall and thin, stretching for sun as any plant does.

The dwelling was soon covered by the needful limbs of the plant, and no mortal was willing to venture within.

It is said that this dwelling still exists, and that he who finds and releases the five Pariahs will enjoy all the treasures a life can bring, whilst bringing great devastation to the rest of the human race.

Physiological:

Not a food product. Chewing on one of its tendrils can induce a sense of great terror. Tests have shown that levels of adrenaline increase dramatically upon imbibing. People have been known to take it deliberately for this precise reaction.

Medicinal:

Used under strict parishioner supervision, children with behavioural problems will show great improvement when drinking an infusion of *horrifera nervus*. The effects are dissipated with the addition of any form of sweetener, which is unfortunate, as the plant is as bitter as the contents of the human gall bladder.

The burgeoning addiction to the tendrils of *horrifera nervus* has led to a crisis across a number of nations. Child psychologist Wendy Chambers recommended over a decade ago that the plant should be eradicated, after her observations of children in her care, many of whom were irreparably emotionally adapted by prescribed and unprescribed usage of the plant.

Her recommendations were largely ignored. Attempts to eradicate individual plants were impeded by the heavy release of pollen on approach and the subsequent intense and continuous sense of hysteria that resulted.

Children as young as twelve were known to chew the tendrils and, in retrospect, the rise in extreme violence and cases of patricide and matricide seem to show a close relation.

Eradication:

And now, those children are grown.

COMING HOME

Donated by
Rick Kennett

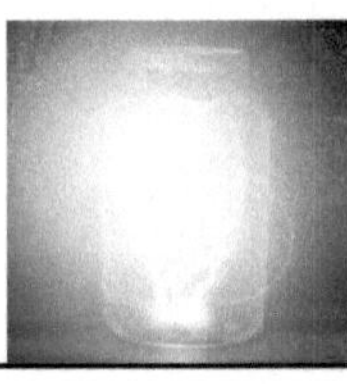

Boarding the train that Saturday night she said, "I'll phone and let it ring three times to let you know I got home safe."

"And if you don't," he said, always the joker, "let it ring four times."

That night his phone rang four times, though it was a week before they found her body.

THE ONES UNDER

Donated by
Catherine Noske

They will come for us, we know.

Already the earth seems thinner above us. Light trickles down a droplet at a time, through the blades of grass, the roots. It reminds us of warmth, of the sun. They will come.

Once, a long time ago – though it is hard to measure time here, it may have been yesterday. I'm guessing, when I say a long time. It feels long, I feel as if I have been here through ages, the weight of the earth has grown heavy and light again over me. It may only be days. Once, a long time ago (or perhaps not long, but passed, all the same), once, I stood at home, in the dust, and felt the sweat bead down my neck as the train tracks stretched on and on in front of me. The cattle were quiet in the yards. There were only two trees, there, and the yards, and the cattle, (and the sun, always the sun), but I remember it, here. I bask in it, now. Now, when the earth grows heavy, and light.

I feel white, here. Then, I was brown, sun-brown, and red-stained earth-brown. Here I am milky white and blue. Veined sticky-black with Fromelles mud. An insect stuck under a rock. Not that I can see my whiteness. It is something I feel, like the weight of the earth, and the beads of sun that run down to flood momentarily through my bones. I look to those beads. They are like faith. One man, when we stepped out over the top, was whispering, *faith,*

    faith,

        faith, over and over. He went down on the right flank. Later, when it was over, when the first dirt stung down on us and the water began to pool, he told me he was lucky. The man on his left had lived. For a moment I felt the grace of it, but then I thought: they will come, and I shook my head and remembered the sweat down my neck at home.

The ones with grace have gone, now. You can feel them leave. They lift. They catch at you as they float up. I used to think they were happy, or free. Now I think they have just moved on. Their bodies are here still, of course. All our bodies are here. But not all of us: some of us are in the soil, and the water, and the grass. The leaves that sway above us in the breeze – they have some of us. Some of me is in a worm, below us, and to my left, I can feel it move. We all feel that, occasionally. It tickles. But the most of us, the big part of us, isn't solid like that. We feel it differently, I know. For me, that part is stretched out in the earth next to my body, my bones. For others, with grace, it floats on up, snagging and drifting as it goes.

When I stood at home, waiting to go, the Father told me faith was like a flag, fluttering in the breeze above us. People look up to it, he said, but you, you have the chance to reach for it, jump for it, and grab fast. A glimmering of spittle flickered from his lips. When you hold it, he said, when you hold it, that's when you are living. It'll pick you up, he said, and bear you high above, flying out on the hands of its wind. He died, my mother wrote, while I was still in training. I wondered if he had ever lived. Sometimes, when I imagine them coming for us, it is his face I see first. (Other times it is my mother, or my brother, or my girl. I know *they* will come. A lot of the time it's my girl. But occasionally, it's the Father.) He peers over the crumbling edge of our grave and asks: did you reach it? And the light in his eyes is manic. Did I reach it? Did I grab hold of it? Did it bear me flying up to stream out behind it on the hands of its wind? And when he fades, when he dies away, I am never sure. When we went over, that last time, when the bullets came whizzing across, and cut us away, like great rows of teeth knocked from a comb, perhaps I flew then. Something bore me up. I was lifted, the ground rose under me, and disappeared, melted away, and still I rose. I flew above it all, everything, the trenches, the sugar-loaf, the German enfilade. And then, I disappeared. When I was me again, I was here, lying next to our tangled bodies, flinching from the sting of the earth as they tossed it down, and thinking, someone will come.

They will come: they will peel back the sod.

Already the earth feels lighter.

NB. The line 'great rows of teeth knocked from a comb' is a quotation of Cpl. W.H. 'Jimmy' Downing, describing the action at Fromelles, on July 19th, 1916; and is sourced from Ross McMullin's article 'The Forgotten Fallen', in the Sydney Morning Herald, July 19, 2002.

THE HUSK MAKER

Donated by
Harper Hull

"Let's start at the beginning," said the reporter, pressing record on his machine, "the moment you discovered you were…different."

"A fine place to start," replied the man in black, stubbing out a cigarette, "but not the easiest."

"Tell it however you want, like I said, I'm just honoured you agreed to do this piece with us."

"Childhood, *always* childhood," said the dark man, leaning forward and turning off the recorder, "but this part stays between us. Your story comes later. Aye?"

The reporter nodded and sat back in his chair.

"My father killed my mother when I was three; slit her throat in the kitchen before putting the knife into his own heart. The cops found me lying in their blood holding onto my mother's hair, sobbing. I ended up living with my aunt, a horrible, horrible woman on my father's side. For the first year or so everything was alright, more or less. Social were keeping tabs on me and she was a model guardian. Eventually the County lost interest and I was on my own with this woman. She wasn't married, just her, me and a string of cheap fucks that came through the front door; seemed like a new one every other week. I'm not sure that they paid her for sex; I think she was just easy and drunk a lot. Of course, a lot of them would stay a day or two, sometimes give me a wallop for fun, all encouraged by my aunt. She would dress me up in her clothes for them and have me do dances sometimes. Other times she would make me watch as she rutted. She blamed me for her brother's death, my father, and I never knew why.

One day it all climaxed. It was my thirteenth birthday and she had insisted on giving me a birthday bath. Her baths consisted of scalding hot water and wire wool applied to my sensitive areas. I still have scars down there. This day, though, she was more drunk than usual and something had finally snapped, she tried to drown me in the tub. Her hands were around my neck and she stepped onto my stomach with all her weight to pin me underwater. I tried to fight but she was still stronger than me. I held my breath as long as I could but she stomped me in the belly and that was it. I inhaled bath water and died right there in her filthy tub. Or as close to death as a man can get and tell the tale.

There was no tunnel or light; I was straight into darkness, but darkness that you could see in. Hard to explain, sorry. My mother was there waiting, crying, and told me to turn around. I just wanted to hug her but she pushed me away. Then my father appeared, grabbed my arms and tried to pull me towards him, calling me all sorts of names. My mother wrapped herself around him and managed to pull him off me, shouting at me to turn around. I looked back behind me and suddenly I was back in the tub, alone, gasping for air. That is when I...changed."

The reporter was open mouthed, frozen in his chair. The dark man snapped his fingers.

"You still with me?"

"Yes...oh, yes *of course*, I...that was fascinating!"

"You can start recording now if you like."

The reporter leaned in and pressed a button.

"I am *The Spectre. The Ghost Wrangler. The Husk Maker. He Who Travels Backwards.* You know all the names they have for me. Some people still believe there is an army of me because I appear in such far-flung places in short periods of time. A nice urban myth, a gang of superheroes playing as one. It's just me. I wish there were more. You know my legend as well as anyone, it seems. What do you really want to know?"

The reporter licked his lips. "Tell me how you do it. Move around the world so fast I mean."

"Knew you'd ask that. It seems fast to you, but to me it's an age. I travel through the *dead dimension*. I open myself up to it and then whoosh, it sucks me right in, backwards. Never got used to that feeling. It's the place I tried to explain to you, darkness that I can see in. All the souls that never made it to their destination are in there. Once inside it takes me hours to get to where I want to be, it's like wading through treacle up to your hips, but time is different in there and so to the living world it seems like seconds. I'm in London; suddenly I appear in Sydney. Magic right? No, it's traumatic every time. The souls in there, there's a lot of very bad ones. The noise they make... indescribable. Demanding. If I didn't have *a ticket* for them they would tear me to pieces."

The Spectre paused and lit a cigarette, breathed deep and anticipated the question he thought was coming next. To his amazement, it didn't.

"Let me ask this," said the suddenly energetic reporter, "what are the things that help you?"

"Dead souls. People, not things. The good ones, murder victims and the like. They come into the living world at my summons and literally drain the life from whatever scumbag I want them to. Evil pays the price. They are happy to help me. Now, listen, I have to go."

The reporter looked startled.

"Go? Already? One more quick question – you mentioned a *ticket*?"

"A ticket to travel through the dead dimension. Alas, I cannot be perfect in this role and sacrifices are made for the greater good. Come here – "

The Spectre grabbed the reporter by the shoulders.

"An offering to the evil souls ensures my passage safely. Sorry kid."

With a whoosh the dark man was sucked backwards and disappeared, the screaming reporter in his grasp.

TEARS OF THE LIVING DEAD

Donated by
Sean Williams

In the gutted supermarket we have been using as a temporary shelter I catch Valerie wiping at her cheeks.

"Is that . . . ?"

"Nothing," she says, guiltily.

But it is too late. I pull away from her and slip my gun from its holster with terrible ease.

"Wait." She backs up against a shelf that once held tinned food, making it rattle.

I joined her a month ago, finding strength and sanity in the company of another woman. We understand what happened better than men do, I think. But recently, I've caught her sneaking out at night in the hope of finding . . . *hope*, I guess. Signs of recovery among the herds of weakening ill, resistance in the next generation, I don't know. I admire her even as I despair at her recklessness. Hasn't the mothering instinct gotten enough people killed already? Has Valerie forgotten that the virus hides in the most innocent and tragic of places, unsuspected by anyone until far too late?

"I honestly thought it was called the Reaping," she said when we first met. "My preacher had a speech impediment."

When I close my eyes I see my ten-year-old boy, tears streaming down his cheeks, as the thing he has become rips at my face in order to get at the pituitary gland he so badly craves.

"Can't we grieve?" Valerie says now. "Even after all we've been through?"

I thought she understood.

"You can grieve all you want. Just don't cry about it."

It's the one rule left, since the Weeping.

I shoot Valerie between the eyes to make absolutely sure.

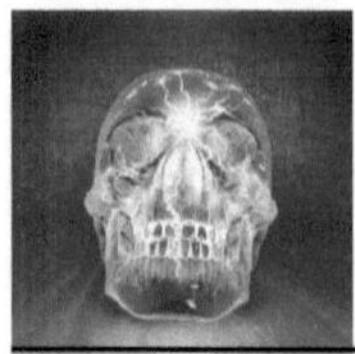

DEM BONES

Donated by
Lucy Sussex

By the standing stone he let the old horse have its head, clopping around the turn to the village. And thus the haycart had a near miss by the churchyard: the visitor and Rector, both in Bible black.

"Steady," said the latter. They resumed their learned men's talk: "My monograph will record and map all the pagan stones of old Britain…"

"Such youthful energy, Mr Scatcherd! I myself once planned a tome on rural customs and superstitions."

Clop clop, the voices faded. He glanced back, and saw what had been concealed by the bulky stone: an excavation, with a labourer knee-deep in dirt. He drew breath, then released it slowly. Close, but no bull's-eye.

A shout from the trench. Behind him, the two clerics fled like crows to a hanging.

"Murder will out! Murder!"

A circle of villagers had formed around the diggings, inspecting the sad heap of bones.

"'Tis a damnable thing," said Scatcherd.

The Rector: "If he is one of your ancient pagans, he is damned undeniably, but if Christian, then he is in God's hands."

"A smashed skull, that is clear," says Scatcherd. "But no grave goods."

The villagers nod: old burials are not news here, though never, sadly, containing gold.

"Human sacrifice!" cried a boy.

"Or murder," repeated the labourer.

Scatcherd: "Without anything to date our fellow, impossible to know."

"There is a way, a custom," said the Rector. "But first let us remove this poor soul to a fitter resting place."

Once excavated, the skeleton was borne to the vestry on a trundle, where he lay, covered with a sheet.

"Jurymen for the inquest, sir?" the parish constable asked.

"Certainly."

The Rector sat down beside Scatcherd on an old pew.

"Knaresborough is small. Our nearest lawyer is at the market town, and even the gentry visit seldom. It is also peaceful. Murder happens: a drunken footpad, a man beats his wife too hard. But the suspects are mostly obvious. To make sure, though, we have a means."

He eyed the shroud.

"A long-boned man. Strong-built, too. Some years ago, a man like that vanished from Knaresborough. Daniel Long was troublesome, but left a pretty wife, dead soon after of her babe. Not the sort for a man wilfully to desert. And the questions lingered. On her deathbed, she asked, 'If my poor murdered Dan be found, please bury him with us.' 'Why say that?' 'I know not, but in my bones I feel it', she cried, with almost her last breath. And so I promised."

"If we have the right man, and not some pagan. She would not like that."

"The bones will tell."

They waited, the Rector reading his Bible, Scatcherd writing up his antiquarian notes.

The constable again:

"The jury are coming, sir. Twelve men fit to witness the ordeal."

"Then fetch Abel the Carter."

The devil surely rode him, that moonlit night by the standing stone. He remembered the drink, and his rage, the haymaker's crack as it hit that laughing, lying mouth. Daniel: his friend once, his rival no longer. The dead bloody weight at his feet. And then the idea, that in this limy soil, already full of bygone bones, who could tell an old murder from a new?

The knock at the door, constable.

What could Rector prove, now?

"I ceased collecting superstitions," said the Rector. "Because I saw their cold sense. Fifty years ago I was a mere curate, when a dead infant was found on the church steps. Murdered, or died of exposure from the cold? The Rector then, he summoned the young women of the parish, to touch the poor little corpse."

"See dead Henry's wounds/ Open their congealed mouths and bleed afresh" – at his murderer, Richard III," said Scatcherd. "That was Shakespeare. But we are in the 1800s now! I read in the *Gentleman's Magazine* of a young woman murdered, in Scotland. They took castings of some nearby footsteps in the mud, then compared them with every shoe at her funeral. A perfect match, a confession."

"Our ordeal has the same effect."

The jury filed in, formed a semicircle around the corpse. Villagers followed, crowding behind Scatcherd.

The Rector: "Bring in Abel Carter."

He had combed the hay out of his hair, donned his one clean shirt.

The Rector stood. "I charge you, by He who knows the secrets of all hearts, to submit to trial by ordeal."

A fresh corpse might discharge when touched, thought Scatcherd, but dry bones? Can they really believe this...superstition? The dead, they are fearful things. What does it mean, to touch them with a guilty conscience?

"Consider yourself under oath in the presence of the Almighty. We compel you to take hold of these bones, suffer them to bear witness."

Behind Scatcherd, an old woman's whisper: "...and Rector as was, he made us kiss the poor dead purmature babe, one by one, and when Nance did, she fainted, crying 'twas alive when she left it at church door."

The long summer evening had finally taken its leave, with tallow candles lit, to splutter and throw mad shadows on jury, the Rector, watching villagers, the accused, and most of all on the bones, uncovered now, but as full of potential as an egg.

I believe, thought Scatcherd, in the Nicene Creed. And also Newton's gravity, the steam train, and He who rose again on the third day, to testify...

Abel swallowed, and placed both hands on the skull, with its terrible wound, the splinters of bone cold underneath his broad fingers. Never could such a dry old thing bleed, surely!

Scatcherd saw that neither the Rector nor jury were looking at the bones. Instead they watched Abel intently.

The accused shouted: "I declare these are no more Daniel Long's bones than they are mine!"

A murmur, glances between the jury, a conclusion.

"How is it that you are so certain? Well?"

And the Rector's smile was like a steel trap, cold sense sprung on a murderer.

PALE TREE HOUSE

Donated by
Angela Slatter

"Anderson, you are to collect a consignment for Pale Tree House. Mr Holloway has requirements once again."

Mr Plum handed me a thin envelope; inside was the address of an orphanage in —shire, and more than sufficient funds to cover my travel costs. I would pocket the remainder, he understood. The delivery location, I knew full well after thirteen years. I set off; with a steady pace I could make the last train out of Victoria.

A mystery to some, how I came by a position in such a fine and upstanding firm of solicitors. My university record was patchy at best; no recorded fails due more to my knowledge of matters the masters did not wish spoken aloud rather than any great scholarly diligence of my own. I had gotten through by dishonesty, rat cunning, and the smallest possible amount of study.

Mr Plum of —son & Partners, an old friend of my despairing father, saw something useful in me. My tasks were those no one else would undertake; parcels of uncertain provenance with questionable contents, negotiations with shadowy men, the supply of unusual services to clients of particular needs and spectacular means. The agency's reputation was twofold, the sunlit path and that of moonlight. I, Anderson James, represented the latter.

Someone had to do it.

"The moneys have already been deposited in our trust account, an impressive amount even for *this*," Mr Plum had said with a satisfied air.

I had a first-class carriage to myself and closed my eyes as soon as we pulled out. I generally sleep well no matter where I am, but there was a lingering cold despite the summer night and my tweed frock-coat was unequal to the chill. I did but doze fitfully.

It was well past midnight by the time I reached the village of Otterburn in —shire, but I walked the short distance from my stop, the full moon clearly lit the road before me. When I rounded the corner and espied my goal I was taken aback. A large structure, two floors and an attic high, tall windows running its length. It looked almost worse than I could have believed – derelict. Although orphanages, like workhouses, are not places of luxury, this one seemed not merely asleep but deserted. Except for the small white figure crouched on the front stoop.

As I approached she rose.

This child's face was *familiar* – but I could not recall her precisely, and I remembered them all, you see. Perhaps eight years old, white skin, pale eyes in darkened sockets, thin-limbed; a wheat-coloured dress, scuffed shoes. She was clean and neat, though, blue ribbons wound through her plaits.

"They told me to wait out here," she said, unafraid.

"Good girl. It seems rather late, though."

"I do what Mrs Bickersby tells me."

A happy tendency, and Mrs Bickersby's actions quite credible – good women did not generally run such establishments as these.

"Then let us not delay." I picked up the bag at her feet, finding it light and offered my hand. I peered closely, trying to place her, but no child was ever delivered twice.

"What if I don't like it?" she asked. "*There*?"

I said what I always say, "Then write me at my firm. I am Mr James and I will come for you, I promise, be so kind as to wait."

She nodded, seemingly mollified, almost as if it was what she expected.

We had several hours pause at the station and she slept, curled on a wooden bench. When the train arrived, I carried her on board, settling her on the plush seat and allowing her to slumber still. I did not imagine she had ever slept so comfortably. *One last treat*, I thought as we travelled north.

Mr Holloway was a client with specific annual needs. I neither understood nor shared his tastes, but appreciated that he paid well, and kept a buggy and beast at the local stables for visits such as mine. Pale Tree House's large park was surrounded by a high wall; a bleached oak sat in front of the abode.

My knock echoed inside yet there was no answer. I found the door unlocked, so we stepped in. The moment the door closed behind us I felt a great sense of unease – conscience? – such as has never before troubled me.

The child let go of my hand and moved away, into a shadowed corner of the entry hall. She began to glow bluish-white, and her face became more sharply defined.

And I realised that those features belonged not to one child, but to all those I had ever 'delivered' here. My memory had not failed me, but rather been tricked by juxtaposition.

"We will come for you, Mr James, we promise, be so kind as to wait," said the child, the children, as they split apart and became their separate selves, twelve pairs of eyes steady upon me. They each disappeared, silent as the grave, leaving me to wait and sweat and wonder when they will return.

I have tried the doors and windows and all are sealed tight by some unbreakable will. I threw a chair at a window, only to have it rebound and strike hard enough to leave a bruise. I can find no trace of Mr Holloway; I can but imagine his fate caught him some time since.

I would not be surprised if the moneys over which Mr Plum gloated have disappeared, tricksy as fairy gold. I leave this letter in case anyone should come looking for me, which I consider unlikely. My father will be relieved at my disappearance and Mr Plum will soon find another such as me.

There it is: the creak of the study door. Such drama, these little ghosts, such spite. I will question them, as they take revenge. I suspect they will not answer, not for a century or two, just to teach me. To teach me to be so kind as to *wait*.

DREDGING

Donated by
Joanne Anderton

Cass handed the dredger his five dollars, trying hard not to touch the dirt on his fingers and wedged under his nails. "Now, you're sure this is the right pond?" she asked.

"Lots of waters," he answered, voice as deep and wet as sludge. "All of them full."

What kind of answer was that?

"And this is the right one?" Cass tried again, slowly, emphasising every word like she was talking to a child, and not the ancient, wrinkled, stooped creature in front of her.

"Oh yes." He smiled. His teeth were dirty too. How'd his *teeth* get mud on them? "This is your water. All yours."

"Good." She nodded. Slapped a mozzie from her shoulder. "Well, get started then."

The dredger waded out, slowly, until the water was almost up to his waist. He wore no protective clothing, not even those absurd overalls she'd seen fishermen wear. No gumboots, no gloves. The only thing he carried was an old golf club, twisted and rusty, with which he felt his way forward. After a moment he stopped and plunged his bare hand into the stagnant water, bent until his chin and chest were wet, and eventually dragged something black and dripping from the surface.

"Looking for something, I think you are," he said, as he shook muck off the object and held it up for her. "A particular thing. Locked in past."

Who was he, fucking Yoda? But Cass shook, a little, at the sight of the stuffed bear he held out. Pink fur, rainbow chest, missing the eye she had gouged out when she was six. She'd hated the way that bear stared at her. Jealous bitch.

"I am," she said, and had to clear her throat. "But not that. It's too old."

"Knew it." He dropped the bear, and started poking around with the club again. "Thick water. Tells many stories."

Cass hugged her arms and glanced around, for the first time feeling a little uneasy about this idea. The dredger had driven for hours to find this isolated puddle of mud in the middle of the national park. A good place for buried things. While she didn't fear the teetering bag of bones and old man skin, the bear had shaken her. She hadn't expected that.

"Lady?" the dredger called, and Cass focused her attention on the bedraggled body of old lady Fairfield's Jack Russell. Still had that stupid rhinestone collar on too. "Is it this? Steeped in importance. Makes the water bubble with words."

Cass shook her head. "Getting warmer." The poor old lady had just died of grief when her mutt accidentally consumed enough rat poison to drown on the blood filling his lungs.

The dredger dropped the dog, and waded into deeper, darker waters. Up to his chin, mouth open, tasting the water, seeming to breathe it. So that was where the mud on his teeth came from. "Oh yes," his words were bubbles. "Oh yes." And he sunk beneath the surface.

For a long moment Cass stared at the opaque pond, as still and hard as a mirror. The shadows of gum trees shifted, creating dark ghosts with sunlit eyes. Tiny creatures skittered across the surface. Cicadas droned in the faraway distance.

Then the dredger re-emerged, carrying something much larger than a toy bear or a dog. White face, shaved head, cuts on his cheeks, burns on his lips, oh what a beautiful sight.

"Yes," Cass hissed, and not caring about her black suede boots and imported jeans, waded out to take the body from him. "Yes, that's it."

The first man she'd killed wasn't as heavy here as he had been when she'd dragged him from the car to an abandoned farmhouse. Maybe it was the water, holding him up. Maybe he really was just a memory, however real he felt.

The dredger floated beside her, treading water awkwardly, hindered by his golf club. "Found it for you," he said, so pleased with himself.

"You did." Cass shifted the body so she could hold out a hand. "Here, let me take that–" she gripped the club " –until you find your feet."

For a moment, he almost looked grateful. Then the water started whispering, and this time, Cass could hear it. She was creating another memory here, a powerful one. Perhaps the most important in her life. *Betrayal*, the water whispered. *Power*, it bubbled away. *Death of an old one, birth of a new one. Terrible. Terrible.* The golf club grew warm, and chimed with the beat of an impossible heart. The blood drained from the dredger's rice paper face.

Cass dropped the dead body – it wasn't why she was really here, anyway – and tore the club out of the dredger's hands. He started to sink, but she couldn't allow that. He was too close to this water, and she wasn't convinced it would kill him. So she tangled her fingers in his thin hair, dragged him to shore, and beat him to death with his muddy, rusty golf club.

It was a good place to bury things, out here. Memories. Bodies.

Cass stood at the edge of her pond when she was finished, and swung the golf club around her in great, slow arcs. The waters called out all around her, not just this pond, the whole bloody national park. So many secrets, buried in sludge beneath the bright eyed shadows of ancient leaves, searching for their owners. So many people, desperate to touch them. One last time.

She ran a finger down the club's bent shaft, dug her nails into the tattered grip. It shivered. Like a living creature.

The dredger had charged five bucks to drive her out to this secluded place in the bush where all her darkest deeds were held. She'd charge twenty. At least.

YOUR FEATHERS ARE PAINTINGS, YOUR EYES ARE LIGHT

Donated by
Jessica Reisman

He came to her old room as the winter set in. The house was abandoned; cold wind blew through broken windows and across the tiles of the floor. Wounded and shivering through the first night in his bedroll, he remembered:

Warm rain at the window and the heavy green of an overgrown garden, the room filled with her art. Sculpted demon hearts like labyrinths, intricate with secrets and meaning; runic prayers in bud and seed-shaped boxes; exquisite oil paintings of pagan gods, ancient memories going deep into the canvas like echo and song, the shadows of things invisible to the human eye written long in painted shape and line.

He remembered how, when the art began to sell, she lit from the inside, smiling around joy.

Then, in whispers exchanged with her grandparents by visitors to the house, she learned a pitiless fact: her art had been bought by emissaries of the local churches and everything they purchased, they burned.

She went a little mad. She collected beetles and painted them with tiny, ciphered messages, then dug holes in the garden soil and planted them. She constructed doorways all over her room. Savaging her canvases, she pieced together a door on the ceiling, using her paintings like puzzle pieces; under her bed, she tiled a portal of tiny mirrors and stones; she built papier mâché arches and doorframes around the windows.

Then, one day, she was gone. He came to find the room emptied of her presence, of her things, of her art – except the doorways. The one that had been under the bed glimmered broken rain puddle reflections of the emptiness.

He stared at the glimmering doorway in the floor and felt his bones become hollow. He swayed, dizzy, vision dimming. How could she leave him? Why would she? He had a crisis of self, gutted and made meaningless by her disappearance – it was his place to disappear, to eccentrically go walkabout, to be unpredictable, not hers.

He was the muse.

He looked for her in the lonely early mornings and in the long, drear afternoons. He wandered after her through nights and towns and cities, down rural roads and endless highways. He left messages for her, on scraps of paper pinned to community boards in busy cafés, scrawled on the inside of matchbooks left like breadcrumbs behind him, written in gravel and pebbles under bridges and overpasses.

Without her, he had no meaning.

He began to dream, not of her, but of her art, her art that was his own soul, his own blood, his own being. One night a painting of hers, a tall canvas from which peered a tattooed mandragora root man tinted in shades of light and sepia memory, his tattoos of fantastic blossoms and fabulous animal monsters meticulous and alive – he remembered it intimately, as he remembered all her art – opened in his dreams to a plain of silver grass and thundering horses that became fish in a jade green sea. The tattooed root-man beckoned from the back of one, riding froth and waves.

The next night, her sketches of insect studies rained through the air of the room where he slept, dreaming of being awake. Chambered eyes on paper fell around him, reflecting infinite marvels of scale and depth.

Haunted, he made his way back, first to the town of many churches. He asked here and there if anyone had heard from her. No one had. Her grandparents had moved on, too, and the house, they said, sat empty.

As he wandered the town, wondering anew why she had left him, how she could have left him, he noticed two men followed him. Menace curled off of them like sulfur fume and he tried to slip away through alleys and cold rain. In this way, furtive and wary, he came to the back of a bar where he had shot pool with her of an afternoon or evening, sharing glasses of pale beer that sweated in the dim air under shadows stirred by a desultory ceiling fan. "Why did you leave me?" he asked the memory of her there, insubstantial, the shadow of a dream of a wish.

In this chill, deserted room, the men caught up with him.

"Where are the rest of them, her sacrilegious works?" asked one, who had the face of an angel and should have behaved differently, he thought. "That blasphemy – we know she hid it!" the other growled with a foul, belligerent breath.

"I don't know," he said. "I'm only a muse."

But they didn't believe him, and laughed, and then spoke with their hands and feet and beat him until he was shadowed and traced with blood – like one of her paintings, now, himself.

Later, some unmeasured, interminable time later, he found his way to his feet and then through dark, winter-grey tunnels between tall trees to the abandoned house, to her old room.

In the cold, winter-blown emptiness, he remembered the room in summer, the opal dark of dusk at the windows, the room filled with light and colour. With her.

Shivering in his bedroll, remembering, he grew feverish. Birds feathered in pieces of her art filled the air. The birds had dark, oil paint eyes reflecting secrets he was supposed to know; as her muse, he was supposed to know.

He dreamed then, or remembered: standing at the door to her room. Deep, bright effulgence filled the room, emanating from the art. He heard her voice from somewhere, an echo, and knew she was smiling. He crossed the threshold, through the door, and woke there, in summer and in light.

THE RIVER, BLACK WITH NIGHT

Donated by
David Witteveen

Night. Summer. The heat crushes us down. Our fan is broken and the house is too small. Amy sweats and tosses beside me in the bed.

I reach out a hand to stroke her back. She frowns and rolls away.

"It's too hot," she mumbles, sitting up. She looks bony and pale. Her damp black hair clings to her face, hiding it from me. "I'm going out for a walk."

"A walk?" I rise up to my elbows, peering through the darkness at her. "Where to?"

She shrugs, climbing into a singlet and shorts. "The river, I guess. Has to be cooler than this."

"I'm coming with you."

She says nothing. The darkness has swallowed her. All that is left is a shadow. I peel myself off the clammy sheets and tug on some jeans.

Outside is just as hot.

We take the rough track down to the river, stepping around the empty beer bottles and discarded tyres. In daylight, you can see the town from here. In the daylight, the river is green with weeds and willow trees. At night, it's all just silhouettes. Even the water is black.

An animal cries in the distance, strangled and high.

Amy walks ahead of me. Her head hangs forward, her shoulders are hunched. Weeds scratch at her legs. I try to take her hand, but she slips away from my touch.

"Are you mad at me?" I ask.

"No," she says, but does not turn to face me.

"Then what?"

"Nothing." She stops. Her hair hides her face like a curtain. "It's just… we've been married a year now. A year and two months."

Her voice is so weak I can hardly hear her. The river is louder. Even the stars are louder, creeping across the sweltering night sky. She crosses her arms and hugs them to her chest.

"I want a baby," she says.

That animal cries out again, shrill and harsh like a cat. The heat keeps pushing down. Sweat runs over my face.

258

"Amy," I whisper. "We talked about this. We just can't afford it."

Her shoulders tremble, and she starts to cry. I reach out for her, but she jerks away. And then the anger rushes in.

"Don't be mad at me!" I yell. "We're *poor*! Babies cost *money*! We have a baby, and we *never* leave this shithole town."

Amy cries silently behind her dark hair. I storm off, kicking the dirt and weeds.

She knows there's no work, I rant to myself. She knows there's no money. And still she eats herself hollow yearning for things we can't have.

When the anger subsides, Amy is so far behind I can't see her. I keep walking. I keep walking until there's nothing but river and weeds and the asphyxiating heat.

The animal cries again. Hoarse. Desperate. Growing weak.

I stop and listen. It's ahead of me. Downstream. I snap a club-sized branch off a dead tree and follow the noise.

Around a bend. The weeds are knee-high. Blackberries and long grass. And something moving by the water's edge. I push through the weeds. My feet sink into foul smelling mud.

There's a polystyrene box there, smeared and dirty. It must have snagged on the bank after floating down river.

Inside it is a baby boy.

He's naked. Slick with sweat and river slime. His tiny hands grasp weakly at the air. His breathing is rapid and shallow. Flies buzz around his mouth and eyes.

A baby. Abandoned to the river. Like Moses to the Nile.

Amy calls my name, distant but getting closer.

Moses was found by the Pharaoh's daughter. But this town is not Egypt, and I have no riches to spare.

The heat pushes down. The river whispers. I'm covered in sweat and mud.

Amy calls for me again. Her voice is frightened and thin.

I reach forward, tender as an angel, and push the box back into the stream.

HIPPOCAMPUS

Donated by
M.K. Hobson

A year after, we are in Brazil, walking together along the white sand shore in front of our low-slung bungalow. She's wearing a copper-coloured bikini that matches her skin almost precisely. She thinks the less she wears, the more likely I am to tell her. Women are funny like that.

Looking down at the smooth mirrored reflection the ocean leaves behind, I see a seahorse. It is curled like a question mark on the sand. I pick it up and show it to her.

"Ah!" she says, her delight surprisingly intense. She's a woman who takes intense delight in very few things, I've found. "Your hippocampus! How clever of you to have found it!"

I turn the seahorse over in my hands gingerly. I'm afraid it's going to sting me or bite me. It's strange how little things like that can scare me, after all we've done. But I was never the violent one. I just cooked the books. She was the one that did all the dirty work. She was the one who pulled the trigger. She was the one whose eyes were dead while she was doing it. Is it any wonder I've never told her?

The seahorse lays in my palm, light as foam. I touch it with my index finger. It's sandy and cold and stiff and dead.

"I've never found a seahorse before," I say.

"Of course you haven't," she shrugs, elegant shoulders bunching briefly. "You can only ever find one. Your own. You can't ever find anyone else's."

I furrow my brow at her. She touches a warm smooth finger to my forehead, pointing it like a gun.

"You see, it's a funny thing," she says, and I know from the tone of her voice that whatever she's going to say, it's not going to be funny at all. "Everyone thinks that we store our long-term memories in there. Lost loves, guilty consciences, Swiss bank account numbers ... everyone thinks they can be locked up behind our eyes and hidden forever."

She lifts the seahorse from my palm, twirls it back and forth between predatory fingers.

"But it's not true. The brain, that agglutination of sensitive grey cells, is nothing more than a highly refined antenna. We store our memories here. In our hippocampus. Each of us has one swimming around out there. And you've found yours. Clever boy."

"That's the stupidest thing I've ever heard," I say.

"If you say so," she says. Then she throws the seahorse in her mouth, chews vigorously. Abrupt nausea washes through me like the tide, and as abruptly as the tide my memories disappear, chewed into a hundred pieces, white foamy flecks that sparkle and evaporate and are gone.

She swallows. I blink, trying to catch something as it swims away.

"What were you saying?" I ask the beautiful stranger, but she's already turned and gone, running toward some low-slung bungalow as fast as her long, copper-coloured legs will carry her.

THE WALK HOME

Donated by
Blanket Barrowclough

I am watching the fire as I write this.

If anyone ever asked I called it 'early morning'.
"Oh, I love my early morning walks. It's the best part of the day, before the hustle and bustle starts."
"The early bird catches the worm."
But my heart knew that 4 a.m. was midnight, only grown older.
If I fooled others, I wasn't interested in fooling myself. Playing at being a functional member of society with a healthy, early morning routine had little to do with my journeys into the dark, quiet, pre-dawn world. The long, isolated walks were a primitive and unaffected ritual of striking out, looping around and retracing my steps homeward. They were a talisman and necessary maintenance against the threat of depression, no matter how happily I anticipated them. Perhaps we drew the shadow because I knew how dark the path was. Or, more likely, it was all Zander's doing.

When I realised, it was as if the darkness had stretched out toward my soul and my soul responded by stopping. In the lifeless pause my brain wrestled with the meaning in what I was seeing. How long had there been two shadows running along the wall? How long had my assumptions carried me unthinkingly onward before my comprehension caught up? *How long had this black thing been travelling with us?*

My first instinct was to come between Zander and the shadow in defence, although the fear of it being a futile, impotent act had already started to freeze me. I felt I was on the verge of a great loss. A fall into regret that would never lessen. Then Zander wagged his tail.

Zander's negotiated truce didn't secure my full trust, but on most nights I managed to pack away my human fears along with the questions about what I had seemingly accepted into my reality. Zander was a buffer. The same Zander who would suffer acute anxiety at the sound of thunder could accept such secrets and was not troubled by them. It was natural to him, but what is more natural than death? Indeed, when my eyes were finally open to it, I saw that it was Zander who encouraged the shadow out of the gutter on those initial nights.

One of the benefits of walking at that dead time was freedom for Zander.

He could roam off his leash, running ahead or pausing undisturbed to take his time in sniffing the world. His swift, agile blackness was often beyond my vision although not out of my zone of perception that extended into the closing darkness. It was at that blended, murky periphery that Zander often frolicked with the shade. He usually ran ahead to 'collect' it too fast for me to keep up, but once I found where to look, I'd see it join us at a dark spot in the road overshadowed by an ancient oak tree. It would run along the painted white brick fence under the branches like the twin to Zander's own shadow. After many nights' observation I pinpointed its genesis to a nondescript point at the road's edge touched by the extremity of the oak's street lit shadow.

The shade was slightly larger than Zander's medium frame, but Zander had a solidity and denseness which, when contrasted with the shade's ephemeral presence, made them appear similar in size. I recognised the shade's dogginess more from its behaviour than its distinctive silhouette. There was shyness and exuberance. Shade's tentative tagging along turned into a shared doggie joy in the freedom of the night and the potential of the open path ahead of them. They loped together with a tandem purpose, or trotted along, each absorbed in their own distractions.

The shade became such a part of our nightly walks that I felt guilty when the weather was too bad for Zander and I to go out. I wondered if Shade missed us, if it was awake and lonely, bound to the hard tarmac, or if it was asleep and oblivious. I wondered on those nights when the cold rain and wind buffeted the trees what I would have seen at that familiar spot on the road. Was there restlessness and disappointment under the scratching fingers of the oak?

The large loop of streets in the middle of my walk disguised the gradual turning for home, but there were no illusions once we rejoined our main thoroughfare. Zander's jaunty gait of exploration would become more businesslike, and in its indirect way the shade would become more hesitant in its forward progression. As with its arrival, its nightly point of departure was difficult to discern, although after many nights it was evident that Zander and I were alone after passing under the oak once again.

It had become my habit to push ahead relentlessly when we had the old oak once more in sight. I was reluctant to turn my thoughts to the significance of that patch of road and gutter. To what must be the inevitable, solitary, places that wait in the dark at the end of every journey. To only briefly lose their hold when the right strangers pass by on the road.

I am watching the fire as I write this. Zander is asleep at my feet as the warmth reaches out into the house and gently flickers its illumination across the rug. Save for one corner where a shadow is curled. The spirited rhythm of the flames disguises the slow rise and fall of the darkness. There's more than one way home, after all.

TERMINATING TRAIN

Donated by
D.A. Cairns

Click, clack! Click, clack! The rhythmic clatter of the train as it sliced through the dense green scrub of the Royal National Park combined with warm sunshine on the window to smother Shawn with drowsiness. His head lolled, as his heavy eyelids closed him off from the world.

Murmuring and an angry voice disturbed his sleep. Someone was speaking loudly, wanting everyone to hear, as he swore…about…it was hard to focus. Shawn felt dazed. They had stopped inside a tunnel.

"These bloody trains are always breaking down," said the irate passenger.

"Stop whining, mate!"

Shawn surveyed the carriage, and noted almost everyone sitting calmly, continuing to read or sleep or just stare out the window. The speakers crackled harshly, snatching everybody's attention, but disappointed them with static and word fragments.

The train suddenly shuddered forward then stopped, its violent jerking jolted Shawn fully awake. The lights flickered out and darkness engulfed them, causing a child to start crying. Soothing tones clashed with anxious voices as they waited in the artificial night.

Shawn sat still, trying to remain calm. He could not see anything and soon all the voices faded away, leaving him desperately alone. Too scared to speak he sat as a creeping coldness washed over him. Shawn shivered involuntarily.

A brilliant white light flashed for a fraction of a second and then blackness returned leaving spots of colour blinking before Shawn's eyes.

Nobody said a word and Shawn felt he was truly alone, but how could that be? He wiped sweat off his forehead despite the trembling cold.

Shawn smelled something horrible, a biting stench which made him want to vomit, and when he opened his eyes the dim shapes of his fellow passengers were still and quiet. Something was wrong. Then he heard crying, but as Shawn searched for the child he caught a glimpse of his hand and stared in shock at the sight of the heavy wrinkles lining his loose, pale skin. He noticed the hair of the person in front of him had turned white.

His mind reeled. What had happened? A flash of light had aged them all. How? This could not be real.

Rising slowly because of a surprising stiffness in his back, Shawn moved down the aisle checking on the others. They were mostly grey skinned and thin and looking as though they might shatter if Shawn even breathed heavily on them. Dead.

At the front of the carriage, Shawn found a woman who appeared to be in her forties huddled on the floor and whimpering like a child. Gently, he touched her and she flinched before looking up at him with fearful confusion on her face. Neither of them spoke.

Shawn felt dizzy so he returned to his seat but as he sat down a sharp pain stabbed his chest. He gasped and clutched at the pain and breathed his last breath as the train lurched forward and resumed its journey through the Royal National Park. Click, clack! Click, clack! Click clack!

AFTERFLASH

Ah, time to be going?

And I, no, I will not be here in the morning. A single customer? Oh yes, my nags and I can get by on the few coins that you have so charitably donated.

The lightning sampler is open for viewings only at night, yes. I find the night time more suitable as stage and backdrop for the displaying of my little collection.

Yes, onwards for me, town to town, customer to customer. Sometimes one or two or twenty people this old tent accommodates. Sometimes I'll hook up with a bigger train or troupe. As Mr Dark used to say: "I add a certain colour and flashing verisimilitude to a show's contingent."

No map nor plan have I. Just travel at the nags' pace, collecting and trading and letting Arges and Steropes and the bottled contents lead the way. The display knows who it wants to view it.

Your eyes? That's just a little afterburn, result of too much flash. It will pass. But some of the pieces lodged in your mind? On that I cannot make a guarantee.

And I ask you, are they, such bolts of power, from outside or from inside – the vaulted constellations of individual imaginations?

Sent forth to sizzle, hum and smoke and strike home in the world wherever and as best they can.

I wonder what you might think if I tell you that those plasmatic jolts and shocks were indeed sourced, not from without, but from within...?

On your way home, maybe you'll be struck with inspiration. There are plenty of trees to stand under.

Best hurry, or you'll miss the storm that's brewing. Miss the cracking, bright revelations.

Here's a little song in parting.

> "To mutters of our unseen comrade Thunder
> My nags and I rattle upon our way,
> As heaven's bright sword cleaves tall oak asunder
> Sprouting fire leaves as it topples, more sky god prey,
> Call I to those wild-eyed equine forms,
> As the stroke climbs from burnt earth up radiant sky tree,
> Nay, I need not follow storms my friends
> When they insist upon following me."

On leaving the tent — A lightning flash — And, struck still for that brief moment, it is as if a glaring finger had turned reality like a page, for you think you see, as you reel all about, flare bewildered, a vast field by night, edged with many matured trees, a distant country road, a huge circus tent — then, gone. . . You see only the meagre canvas you had just exited, with Downstryk standing at the opening, smiling at you. A distant flash glints briefly in his eyes.

As you stumble off, lightning drunk, he calls to you.

We may meet again, somewhere where the sharp and crooked light falls. Where Ishkur flings his ladders and bolts. Out where the flashing, lambently burning plasma trees take root in rifted sky. Where the cracks in this world are glimpsed.

Beware though, don't look too intently. Whoever manages to catch a glimpse of what's through there . . . Well, they are generally found dead in the open, eyes wide and still staring, on this side of things. Taken by the sight.

Good night.

Don't fear the lightning.

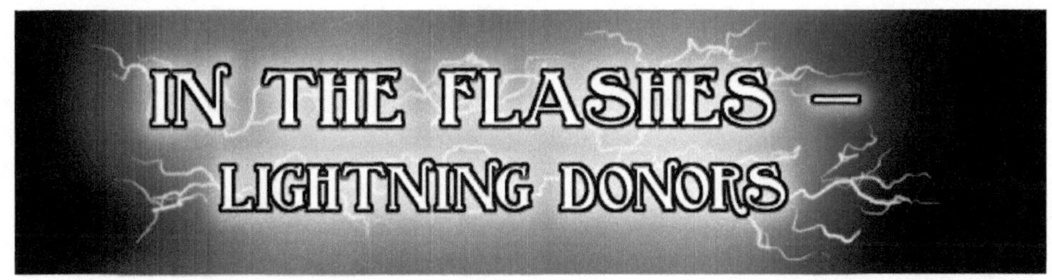

Fred Zackel teaches literature and humanities at Bowling Green State University in Ohio. He has been previously published in The Mississippi Review. He is the author of *'Cocaine & Blue Eyes'* and *'Cinderella After Midnight'*. Some of his work can be found on Amazon's Kindle. He dreams a lot.

Shona Snowden lives in Sydney. She works in marketing and writes mystery, suspense and horror. Her short stories have been published in various anthologies and magazines, including *Midnight Echo* and *Silverthought*.

Sam Cooney is a text-based work, first published in Melbourne in the mid-eighties, recognisable for his poorly designed cover and ad-hoc composition. You can find him in various hidey-holes about the Internet. He is editor and publisher of *The Lifted Brow*, a bimonthly arts, culture and fiction magazine.

yt sumner is a very special episode of your favourite show you watched as a kid. It was supposed to be funny and all about the good times but instead it got heavy and weird and gave you a terrible fear of drains.

Allen Ashley currently has nine books to his credit, with three more in the pipeline. He is the author of the acclaimed novel *'The Planet Suite'* (TTA Press, 1997) and the award-winning editor of *'The Elastic Book of Numbers'* (Elastic Press, 2005). Check him out at: www.allenashley.com

Ella Joseph was once a nurse, became a social worker, and now works as an advocate for people with leukodystrophy. She is also studying writing, online through GippsTAFE, and is excitedly exploring the new world of poetry and very short fiction that has opened up to her.

Jen White is an Australian author. She lived for some years in the tropical

North of Australia but has since moved to the gentler climes of country Victoria. Her short stories have appeared in numerous journals and anthologies including *'The Tangled Bank'* anthology, *Mythic Resonance* and *Future Lovecraft*.

Adam Walter is a native of the Pacific Northwest and lives with his wife and daughter near Seattle. His fiction has appeared in *Supernatural Tales*, *Day Terrors*, *Fungi*, *Big Pulp* and *Dark Horizons*.

Martin Davey lives in East Yorkshire, England with his wife and three daughters. His work has appeared in numerous print and online publications such as T*he Rage of the Behemoth* anthology, *Flashing Swords*, *Reflection's Edge*, *Afterburn SF*, the *'Shadows and Light'* anthology and others.

Stephanie Gianopoulos can be found in New Orleans, enjoying life in all its delicious weirdness. Her stories are strange nuggets of lunacy, but all the apostrophes are in their rightful places.

Chuck McKenzie was born in 1970, and still spends much of his time there. In his professional life he fills various roles as a bookseller, reviewer, author, and zombie obsessive, although only one of the aforementioned pays the bills. Further ramblings may be found at http://chuckmck1.livejournal.com/

Aaron Polson lives in Lawrence, Kansas with his three sons and a tattooed rabbit. Rumour has it he is quite fond of musical theatre and prefers ketchup with his beans.

Jason Colavito is an author, editor, and skeptical xenoarchaeologist who has investigated the connections between pseudo-science, archaeology, and horror literature. His fiction has appeared in many outlets, and he has published several non-fiction books on the horror genre, including *'Knowing Fear'* (McFarland, 2008). Colavito lives in upstate New York.

B. Michael Radburn has been writing semi-professionally now for many years, having numerous pieces published in Australia and abroad. He was publishing editor of the now iconic *Australian Horror & Fantasy Magazine* in the 1980s. His second novel, *'Blackwater Moon'* was published by Pantera Press in 2012.

Perth based writer **Martin Livings** has had over seventy short stories published in a variety of magazines and anthologies. His 2006 novel *'Carnies'* was nominated for both the Aurealis and Ditmar awards. His first short story collection *'Living With the Dead'* was published by Dark Prints Press late in 2012.

Sam Drane didn't mean to start the fire in the ghost house, but there was no other light to write by in there. On the bright side the toxic smoke from the carnies' plastic masks caused some nice hallucinations. Sam J. Drane sometimes works, and hides from the world, at www.milkshadowbooks.com

Rosaleen Love, over the past forty odd years, has published on Australian science and society, both in non-fiction, and in fiction. Her most recent books are *'Reefscape. Reflections on the Great Barrier Reef'*, Sydney and Washington, and *'The Traveling Tide'*, short fiction, with Aqueduct Press, Seattle.

Kaaron Warren is a twice World Fantasy Award nominee and Shirley Jackson Award winner. Her six short story collections include *'The Grinding House'*, *'Dead Sea Fruit'* and *'Through Splintered Walls'*. Her novels are *'Slights'*, *'Walking the Tree'* and *'Mistification'*. Her latest short story collection is *'Kaaron Warren: Cemetery Dance Select'*. She's lived in Melbourne, Sydney and Fiji. Kaaron just completed a Fellowship at the Museum of Australian Democracy at old Parliament House, where her research has resulted in a crime novel which should see print in 2016. You can find her at http://kaaronwarren.wordpress.com/

Rob Riel has worked as a sailor, metallurgist, university lecturer in English, electron microscopist, and disability services specialist. Over a decade ago he established Picaro Press, which specialised in poetry publication using print-on-demand technology. He has twice received Australia Council grants for New Work, and has published two books.

Kim Goldberg's off-kilter tales have appeared in magazines and anthologies around the world. She is a winner of Canada's Rannu Fund Poetry Prize for Speculative Literature and the author of *'Ride backwards on Dragon'* and other books. She cavorts with muskrats and postulates the improbable from Vancouver Island. Visit www.PigSquashPress.com

Writer, social worker and failed primary school teacher **James Davies**' life is an ongoing attempt to defraud the government into paying him to write stories for a living. He can't hack it in the real world due to a variety of emotional problems, the most prevalent of which is cowardice.

Eugene Gramelis is a widely published, award-winning author of suspense and dark fiction. He also practises law as a barrister in Sydney, Australia, where he resides with his beautiful wife and three gorgeous children, and he invites you to walk with him at http://gramelis.blogspot.com

Mark McAuliffe's short stories and poetry have been published in small press magazines such as *Skin Tomb, E.O.D.* and *Daarke Worlde*. More recently his fiction has appeared online in the E-zines *AntipodeanSF* and *Eclecticism*. Two of his stories were selected to appear in the anthology *An Eclectic Slice of Life*.

Matthew Chrulew has published over twenty short stories. His end times burlesque novella *'The Angœlien Apocalypse'* (Twelfth Planet Press) was a finalist in the 2010 Aurealis Awards. *'Head 2'* appeared in *Moonlight Tuber 1*. moonlighttuber.wordpress.com He blogs at Negentropy. matthewchrulew. wordpress.com

Peter Dawncy lives in the Dandenong Ranges east of Melbourne. He has a Bachelor of Arts with majors in English and Philosophy from Monash University and commenced his PhD at Monash in 2012. You can contact him at peter.dawncy@gmail.com

Emma Kathryn is from Glasgow, Scotland and has an honours degree in English studies. She is rather tiny and rather mad.

Douglas Thompson's short stories have appeared in a wide range of magazines and anthologies. His novels *'Ultrameta'* and *'Sylvow'* were published by Eibonvale Press in August 2009 and 2010. A third novel *'Apoidea'* was published by The Exaggerated Press in 2011. *'Mechagnosis'* (Dog Horn) and *'Entanglement'* (Elsewhen Press) both appeared in 2012. http://douglasthompson.wordpress.com/

Mark Delaney was born in 1990 in Liverpool, England. He grew up in the city and currently resides there, studying Law at University and working in a tea shop. He finds time to write between lectures, exams and his job. *'The Escapist'* is his first published work.

Mari Mitchell at this point in time is an enigma who resides behind a nightmare woven from a story.

Rob Parry has never taken to anyone's knuckles with a hammer. . . but keep an eye on those page nineteen headlines! He is severely allergic to cats and the (Nuclear) Family First party. When he grows up, he would like to be Geoff Ryman, Dan Savage, or an astronaut.

Blanket Barrowclough earned her nickname from an attachment to a pink cotton blanket with grey puppies that started the day she was born. The blanket has now faded to white. After a rich and diverting life she has decided to pick up the pen that her 10-year-old self put down, with *'The Walk Home'*, written in 2012, being her first published story.

R.H. Reese has worked as a janitor, cab driver, labourer, security guard, park ranger, lifeguard, service station attendant, photographer, military communications specialist, carer for the disabled, and as a teacher. A graduate of Moravian College, he is presently employed as a deputy sheriff and lives by the Delaware River in Pennsylvania.

J.G. Poulos has loved science fiction since reading *'Dorsai'* by Gordon R. Dickson in 1968. He cut his teeth on a diet of Robert E. Howard, Lovecraft, Bradbury and Cordwainer Smith with a little Philip K. Dick and Robert Heinlein thrown in. He works in the intelligence, surveillance and investigations industry.

Steven Paulsen is a speculative fiction writer whose prizewinning work has appeared in books, magazines, journals and newspapers around the world. His best-selling children's book *'The Stray Cat'* is illustrated by Shaun Tan and has been published in several foreign language editions. Readers can find out more about him at: www.stevenpaulsen.com

Rick Kennett is a resident of Melbourne, works in the transport industry and has an interest in cemeteries, ghosts and all things spooky. His stories have appeared in *Aurealis, Weird Tales, Southern Blood* and *More Great Ghost Stories*. His short story *'The Dark and What it Said'* won the 2008 Ditmar Award.

Gitte Christensen was born in Australia and also lived in Denmark for twelve years. Her speculative fiction has appeared in *Aurealis, ASIM, The NSW School Magazine* and many other publications, including anthologies.

To escape keyboards, she likes to grab a tent and a horse and trail ride through distant mountains.

Harper Hull was born and raised in England and now lives in the southern United States with his Dixie wife. He has work published in four continents, mainly science fiction and horror. His favourite things include J.G. Ballard, (the) Pixies, tiramisu and microbrews. More info at http://harperhull.weebly. com/index.html

Kev Webb was born in Kent, England in 1963 and immigrated to Australia in 1971 with his parents. Writing is his passion. His published novels are *'Dream Raider'*, *'Soul Trader'* and *'Body Jump'*. He lives in Brisbane Australia.

Stephanie Campisi is an author of the weird and sometimes wonderful. Her fiction and non-fiction has appeared in various magazines, newspapers and anthologies. She runs the book review website http://www.readinasinglesitting.com and can be found on Twitter at @readinasitting.

Robert Long lives in London, England. He has had stories published in the *Muscle and Blood Literary Journal, Bards and Sages Quarterly* and the *Terminal Earth anthology*. He is currently working on a novel.

Mark Smith-Briggs has appeared in more than twenty-five magazines and anthologies. He has been a judge for the Aurealis and Australian Shadows awards as well as the Night of Horror screenplay award. He is an editor with Leader newspapers.

Michael Zerbe lives in Perry County, PA, and works for N.F. String & Son, Inc, creator of the Dream Changer self service coin machines. His stories have appeared in various anthology and online venues, and his short story *'Fishing with the Devil'* won an honourable mention from *'The Year's Best Fantasy and Horror 2008'*.

Vicki Frei is retired and lives in Utah with her husband of thirty-nine years and a dog and cat who are terribly spoiled. She has a daughter and two grandchildren. For amusement mostly, she manages websites for a few clients. She plays World of Warcraft for escape.

Thomas Canfield subsists on a diet of Twinkies and warm beer. He harbours a deep animus towards spinach.

Paul Haines (1970 – 2012) was a New Zealand born writer who settled in Melbourne. He won the Sir Julius Vogel Award four times, the Ditmar five times and the Aurealis Award three times. No doubt Paul would have continued and expanded his writing successes, but he was urgently required elsewhere. His legacy is in the memories of those who loved him and in the stories that he left behind.

Jenny Sinclair is a Melbourne writer of fiction and non-fiction. Her work has appeared in various publications and has been broadcast on ABC radio. Her book *'When We Think About Melbourne'* was published in 2008. *'A Walking Shadow'* (Arcade Publications) was published in 2012.

C.S. Fuqua's books include *'Rise Up'*, *'Big Daddy's Gadgets'*, *'If I Were'*, *'Alabama Musicians'*, *'Trust Walk'*, *'The Swing'* and *'Notes to My Becca'*, among others. His work appears in publications as diverse as *The Christian Science Monitor*, *Bull Spec*, *Main Street Rag*, and *Year's Best Horror Stories*. Please visit http://csfuqua.comxa.com

Matthew R. Davis is a carbon-based lifeform living in Adelaide. He has had a growing number of short stories published worldwide. He dabbles in film-making and is the vocalist/bassist/multi-instrumentalist for Blood Red Renaissance.

Rijn Collins is a Melbourne writer, linguist, blues listener, whiskey swiller and Berlin obsessive. Her writing has been published in numerous anthologies, online journals, newspapers, magazines and adapted for performance on ABC radio. She writes with bare feet, and black coffee. Both help shake words from her pen.

Benjamin Kensey is a Londoner in his forties who lives in the south of England with his dogs and his books in a house nearly as old as him. He took up fiction writing recently and is busy making up for lost time.

Rick McQuiston is a forty-seven year old father of two who loves anything horror related. He has achieved nearly three hundred publications so far, written two novels, six anthology books, one book of novellas, and edited an anthology of Michigan authors. They are all available on Lulu and Amazon, and at many-midnights.webs.com

Deborah Sheldon's credits include television scripts, magazine articles, non-fiction books for Random House, stage and radio plays, and award-winning medical writing. Her fiction has appeared in many journals including *Quadrant*, *Island*, *Page Seventeen*, *Short & Twisted*, and *Eclecticism* E-zine. Deborah lives in Melbourne, Australia. Visit her at http://deborahsheldon. wordpress.com

Ian C. Smith lives in the Gippsland Lakes region of Victoria. His work has appeared in *The Best Australian Poetry*, *Cordite*, *Eureka Street*, *Island*, *Sleepers Almanac*, *Southerly*, and *Westerly*. His book *'Lost Language of the Heart'* was published by Ginninderra Press, Adelaide, as was his fifth book *'Contains Language'* in 2011.

Catherine Noske studied Creative Writing at Monash University. She was a co-editor of both *'Verge 2011: The Unknowable'* and *'Verge 2007'*. She has been published in various creative anthologies including *'The Voyage'* (UK) and *'Visible Ink'*. Her short stories have been twice awarded the Elyne Mitchell Prize for Rural Women Writers.

Michelle Jager is currently undertaking a Master of Philosophy in creative writing. She is working on her first novel. Her story *'Jar Baby'* appeared in issue 8 of *Midnight Echo* and *'Bones'* was published in *SQ Mag*. She enjoys photographing the odd, the dead, and the forgotten.

Angela Readman loves stories. Her own stories have appeared in *Crannog Journal*, *Black Market Review*, *Fractured West*, *Metazen*, *Pank*, *Pygmy Giant*, *The Journal* and *Southword*. She won *Inkspill Magazine*'s short story competition in 2011.

Raymond Gates is an Aboriginal writer based on the Gold Coast, Australia. His childhood crush on dark fiction evolved into a love affair with writing. He has published a number of short stories and is looking for the novel that lurks within him. Delve into his mind at: www.raymondgates.com

M. Winkler is a Melbourne based writer. He has had short stories included in anthologies by Penguin and Wakefield Press, essays in various lit mags, and poetry in several publications including the Paroxysm Press omnibus *'Ten Years of Things That Didn't Kill Us'*.

Rod Cod goes on working trips around the Great Southern Land and has survived a near fatal bout of a rather severe hoarding disorder. He is now attempting to unclutter his mind, through writing. Wish him luck.

Jack Horne is married and lives in Plymouth, England, where he works for the local theatre. Many of his short stories, poems and articles have appeared in magazines, anthologies and webzines. Many of his poems and stories have also been broadcast on the radio. His first novel was accepted in October 2012.

Frank J. Collins received his Medical Degree in 1989 from the University of Maryland in Baltimore. He has practiced General and Trauma Surgery since 1994 in Hagerstown, Maryland where he writes short stories and novels.

Sheri White has been published in a number of small press magazines and anthologies. Acceptances include the *'Bigfoot Among Us'* anthology, edited by Eric S. Brown. She is also an editor, book reviewer and proofreader for several small press publishers.

Daniel Powell teaches writing at a small college in Northeast Florida. His stories have appeared in *Redstone Science Fiction, Brain Harvest, Something Wicked, Leading Edge* and *'Dead But Dreaming 2'*. He lives with his wife and daughter near the Intracoastal Waterway. Daniel maintains a web journal on speculative storytelling at www.danielpowell.blogspot.com

Jason Nahrung grew up on a Queensland cattle property and now lives in Melbourne with his wife, writer Kirstyn McDermott. His fiction is invariably darkly themed, perhaps reflecting his passion for classic B-grade horror films and 80s goth rock. He lurks online at www.jasonnahrung.com

Nicky Peacock Nicky is an English author living in the UK. For further information on her published work please see: http://www.creativeminds-writing.co.uk/page18.htm

Sean Williams is an award-winning, #1 *New York Times* best-selling author of some forty-two novels, over one hundred short stories, and the odd odd poem. His latest book is *Fall* aka *Hollowgirl* (third in the Twinmaker trilogy).

Lucy Sussex is an author with interests in Victoriana, Australiana, crime and the supernatural. She has published widely, having edited anthologies, written five short story collections, and the award-winning neo-Victorian novel, *'The Scarlet Rider'*. In addition she is a weekly Fairfax newspaper columnist. Her latest work is a non-fiction study *'Blockbuster! Fergus Hume and The Mystery of a Hansom Cab'*.

Angela Slatter is a Brisbane-based writer who has won five Aurealis Awards and one British Fantasy Award. In addition she has been a finalist for the Norma K. Hemming Award once and the World Fantasy Award twice. She has published six story collections, has a PhD, was an inaugural Queensland Writers Fellow, is a freelance editor, and teaches creative writing. Her novellas, *'Of Sorrow and Such'* (Tor.com) and *'Ripper'* (in *Horrorology* Jo Fletcher Books) to appear in 2015, with Jo Fletcher Books to publish her debut novel, *'Vigil'*, in 2016, with its sequel, *'Corpselight'*, coming in 2017.

Joanne Anderton by day is a mild-mannered marketing co-ordinator, by night she writes science fiction, fantasy and horror. Her short fiction has appeared in various publications. Her debut novel, *'Debris'* was published by Angry Robot Books in 2011, and was followed by *'Suited'* in 2012. Visit her at: http://joanneanderton.com

Jessica Reisman's stories have appeared in a wide variety of magazines and anthologies. Five Star Speculative Fiction published her first novel, *'The Z Radiant'*. She dreams awake, has visions asleep, and enjoys tea and artful cocktails while living in Austin, Texas with well groomed cats. For more about her fiction, visit www.storyrain.com

David Witteveen lives in Melbourne, Australia. He won the inaugural Australian Horror Writers' Association's Flash Fiction award and wrote and drew the mini comic *'Death by Music'*. His official website is at www.davidwitteveen.com

M.K. Hobson's debut novel, *'The Native Star'* – the first book in her Veneficas Americana series – was nominated for a Nebula Award in 2010. She lives in the first city in the United States incorporated west of the Rockies. You can find out more at her website, www.demimonde.com

D.A. Cairns is married with two teenagers and lives on the south coast of New South Wales where he works as an English language teacher and writes stories in his spare time. He has had seventeen short stories published (but who's counting, right?). *'Devolution'* is the name of his first novel.

Sean King (Cover Artist) has been a student at Deakin University. He has studied Art, Architecture, Literature and Journalism, Cartooning and Small Business Management. He is a photographer, writer, poet, film-maker, editor and publisher. He has been a commercial photographer and on-set photographer for films. He has also done motion camera and post production work on film. He has directed such films as *'The Slayer'*, *'Regrets'*, *'The Night is Cold'*, and *'A Nun a Gun and a Prostitute'*. He is also a graphic designer and has worked on poster and DVD covers, CD music covers and websites. He is experienced in audio production for film, podcast and audio CD production. He has written over 1000 poems. In addition Sean writes short stories, novels and film scripts. His poetry book *'Empire of the Mind'* was published in 2009 and was re-released in 2012. His second poetry book *'Like the Dog I Am'* was published in 2012. His first novel was *'Dirty Business'*. He edited and designed *Finger Magazine* and was the publishing head of Blunt Trauma Press. He is also into gaming, cosplay and costume design.

Greg Rich (Interior Artist) hails from the televisual land of Punchbowl, Australia, growing up on *Thunderbirds*, Arthur C. Clarke and David Bowie, and has been a keen illustrator of spacecraft and science fiction since childhood. He built a spaceship simulator in his wardrobe when he was in his teens, explored the Central Coast on an old and battered dragster bike, and wrote many stories – few of which he was ever pleased with. He spent his formative years in the pursuit of otherness, taking up painting, lucid dreaming and trips to the city looking for music and inspiration. During the Kook Era (1987-1991) he and his friends would go on cinema crawls to such venues as the Valhalla, the Encore, the Chauvel or the Academy Twin, sometimes emerging from Twilight Zone marathons at two thirty in the morning. The drive home would often be a surreal occasion, filled with imagery and events that influence his work to the present day. He now lives in Katoomba with his partner of twenty-some years and is planning to embark on a life of domestic reinvention.

Stephen Studach (Editor) had his earliest experiences with flash fictions reading the *'Terror Tales'* on the crimson coloured backs of the stack of horror trading cards he had collected from chewing gum purchases in the sixties. Those cards had black and white photos from old horror and science fiction B movies on the front with corny plays on the featured scenes in speech bubbles. He can't recall that there was even a credit for who came up with those microfictions. Something more than the distinct scent of the powdery pink strips of gum may have gotten into his system.

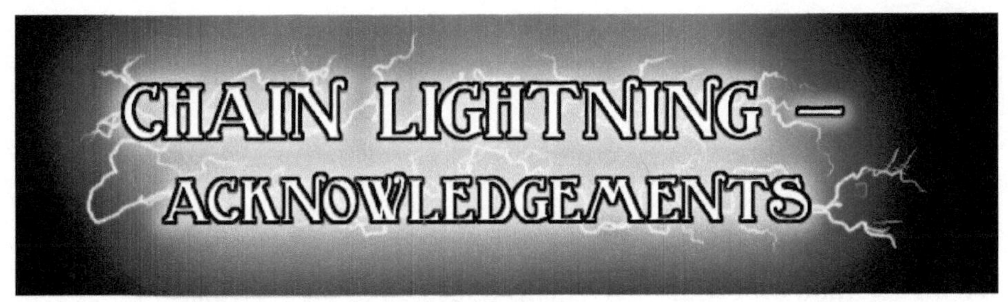

'A Squeal, and Then a Squeak' by Sam Cooney won an online competition named *Gum Leaves* in 2010 and was subsequently published in *Award Winning Australian Writing 2010*.

'Hole in the Garden' by yt sumner was previously published by *Jersey Devil Press* in September 2010.

'Evolution' by Jen White was broadcast by ABC Radio in 2003.

'Minding Matthew' by Martin Davey was previously published in *Every Day Fiction* in 2009.

'Howler' by Chuck McKenzie was first published in the author's collection 'Confessions of a Pod Person' from *MirrorDanse Books* 2005.

'Gary Sump's Hidden City' by Aaron Polson was first published at *Everyday Weirdness* in 2009.

'Brother Vs Brother' by B.Michael Radburn previously appeared in issue seven of *The Imaginings Sampler* 1999.

'In Nomine Patris' by Martin Livings was previously published in issue five of *Shadowed Realms* 2005.

'Piggies' by Martin Livings first appeared in *Midnight Echo* issue one, 2008.

'Faith' by Aaron Polson made its first appearance at *Every Day Fiction* in 2009.

'**Night Ride**' by Kim Goldberg first appeared in *Prairie Fire*, 2009. It was then a part of the author's 2009 collection '*Red Zone*' produced by *Pig Squash Press*.

'**Dirty Laundry**' by Eugene Gramelis first appeared in issue three of *Midnight Echo*, 2009.

'**Head**' by Matthew Chrulew originally appeared at '*Dog Vs Sandwich*', 2008.

'**Brain in a Vat**' by Peter Dawncy first appeared at *Antipodean SF* in 2010.

'**Logic Loop**' by Steven Paulsen has appeared in *Aphelion* 1986/87. '*Worlds in Small*', *CacaNadaDada Press* 1992. '*Grandes Minicuentos Fantasticos*', *Alfaguara*, 2004.

'**Cargo**' by Rick Kennett was originally published in *Andromeda Spaceways Inflight Magazine* in 2003.

'**Blame Games**' by Gitte Christensen appeared at *Antipodean SF* in 2011.

'**Aqua Vita**' by Stephanie Campisi has previously appeared in *Voiceworks*, *Litsnack*, and via audio at *The Drabblecast* – all in 2009.

'**A Song for Cara**' by Martin Davey previously appeared in *Every Day Fiction* in 2009.

'**Going Down with Jennifer Aniston's Breasts**' by Paul Haines has previously appeared in *Ripples* during 2006.

'**Yum Cha**' by Paul Haines was first published in *Antipodean SF* in 2002 and in *FlashSpec* 2006.

'**Malik Rising**' by Paul Haines previously appeared in *Shadowed Realms* 2005.

'**Screamer**' by C.S. Fuqua was first published in *The Horror Show*, 1986, and broadcast on *3PBS Radio* Australia (*Pilots into the Unknown* produced and presented by Rick Kennett and Glen Matthews).

'Scary Stories' by Rick McQuiston was first published in *MicroHorror* in 2009.

'Counting the Steps from One through Five' by Deborah Sheldon was originally published in *Cottonmouth*, 2009 and also appeared in the author's 2010 collection *'All the Little Things We Lose'*.

'I Can't Write This on a Postcard' by Ian C. Smith was first published in *Social Alternatives* in 2000 and then appeared in the author's collection *'This is Serious'* from *Ginninderra Press*.

'Post-coital Repercussion' by Ian C. Smith first appeared in *Wet Ink* 2004 then in the author's collection *'Memory Like Hunger'* from *Ginninderra Press*.

'The Witches' Hammer Voyages' by J.G. Poulos appeared, in a cut-down form, in *Antipodean SF* in 2008.

'Two Tomorrow' by Steven Paulsen has appeared in *Eidolon* 1990 and *Beyond* 1995.

'Jacob's Ladder' by Eugene Gramelis appeared in *Antipodean SF* in 2011.

'Coming Home' by Rick Kennett was originally published in *All Hallows* number thirty-seven, 2005. It was reprinted in *'Shadow Box'*, 2005.

'The River, Black with Night' by David Witteveen won the *Australian Horror Writers' Association* flash fiction competition in 2005 and was subsequently published in *Shadowed Realms* that same year.

'Hippocampus' by M.K. Hobson appeared at *ChiZine* 2005.

Thanks to Alan Moore for permission to example his six word story that travels time.

All other stories appearing herein are original to *'100 Lightnings'*.

9 781876 502188